Legends

A Joint Task Force 13 Anthology

Three Ravens Publishing
Chickamauga, GA USA

Credits:

Cover art by: J.F. Posthumus

Edited by: Philip K. Booker & William Joseph Roberts

Legends: A Joint Task Force 13 Anthology
by William Joseph Roberts /Three Ravens Publishing –
1st edition, 2022

Trade Paperback ISBN: 978-1-951768-53-9

Contents

Acknowledgements

Without the help of a number of people, and the team that is Three Ravens, this collection would have been even harder to put together than it was. With the major life events going on here at Raven Central, this collection was unfortunately delayed.

Without the help of Jenny Wren, Philip Booker, and of course our beloved Word Witch, Meg, this collection may have been in the stack for month longer.

A Cold Day in Hell
By: Michael Morton

Hell isn't hot. It's cold.

It's a cold that drives needles into your nose when you inhale. A cold that then burns its way down your throat and makes your chest ache. You get so cold, that your mind is numb to anything resembling thought. It makes you want to lie down and go to sleep so you can dream of being warm again. Only when you wake up, you're still cold.

North Korea in December is that cold. The ground is frozen hard like concrete or it's slimy mud that sticks to boots and wheels like glue. The mountains loom over you like stern, unforgiving gods, sending the winds as punishment. It howls down to sting your cheeks with ice crystals, forcing you to squint and shield your eyes.

Our company was dug into the hillside overlooking the main supply route. We huddled in our foxholes, scanning the countryside for the Chinese. They'd come out of the night nine days ago, just after Thanksgiving, swarming the positions of the 1st Marine Division and damned near wiped us out. Things settled down when we got our feet under us, and they realized we were here in force. The perimeter was holding, and we got word that we were pulling out, headed for the harbor at Hamhung, and out of here.

We had stacked the bodies of the Chinese from the last attack around our foxholes. It provided some protection from incoming fire but mostly served as a windbreak. That goddamned wind sliced your face with every gust, leaving the skin dry and chapped. It found its way into your clothes, chilling the last vestige you thought was warm. The cold kept the smell of the dead bodies to a minimum, but we were past caring. Our own smells were bad enough.

Just after dawn, we heard them blow their whistles, signaling the next attack. Trumpets followed, playing their own damned version of 'Charge'. I looked left and right at what remained of my squad, sitting in their foxholes with weapons at the ready. The company was in a horseshoe-shaped ring around the top of this god-forsaken hill that had no proper name, just a number on the map.

The roar of voices reached our ears, and hundreds of Chinese stormed the hill. Mortar rounds began landing in our positions, sending earth and debris up in a fountain. Sometimes the fountain was accompanied by a scream.

The platoon on the right side of the horseshoe, opposite us opened up. The sounds of our rifle and machine-gun fire became mixed with that of the Chinese weapons until it became an unholy din. Still, we saw nothing in front of us. A thin mist was rising as the sun heated the ground.

"Sarge? When they gonna come?"

"Shut it, Williams. Be glad they ain't here yet. You get a few more seconds to live." PFC Williams was the squad's biggest worrier. That he was still alive was, in part, due to his worrying.

Another man spoke up. "I see somethin'. Bout a hunner'd yards out, on the ground."

"Where, Leckie?"

Lance Corporal Bob Leckie gave a short chop of his hand. "Thataways. Yep. Think they're trying to sneak up on us all quiet-like under the cover of battle."

"Right. Everyone, watch your sectors. Tell the squads on either side of you." I turned to the man next to me, Private Loudin. "Message to the LT. Infiltrators trying our lines. Expect a general attack soon."

He nodded, his young face pale under the thin fuzz of a day's growth of beard. But Loudin was still alive, too, meaning he'd learned something. He slithered out of the foxhole, belly-crawled a few yards, and then ran back towards the rear.

"Leckie, hell, anyone, you get a clear shot, take it. Ain't no point in letting them get closer than they are."

Leckie banged out a shot almost immediately, and a scream of pain followed from down below. Whistles followed the scream, and then the yells as mustard-yellow uniforms sprouted from the ground out of the mist.

"Open fire!" I followed my own command, aiming and firing at the mass of bodies.

The squad, and then the entire platoon opened up. The Chinese were less than a hundred yards away, firing from the hip with their Russian-made submachine guns as they charged.

Grenades flew from the back of their formation, most of which landed short. But a few found targets and rifles on our side went silent. Bullets were flying past, making that *wheet* sound like an angry wasp. One hit the ground in front of me, spraying my face with a shower of dirt and frost. Here and there, a man was hit. When your head and shoulders are the only things sticking out of a hole in the ground, you rarely survived a hit.

Fifty yards now.

The BARs were taking a terrible toll on them. Our platoon had taken at least fifteen casualties since the Chinese counterattack, but we kept the BARs fully manned. It was the only way, short of artillery and close air support, to stop a charge.

Thirty yards now.

Amazingly, the Chinese ranks were thinning, with gaps in several places where we'd taken enough of a chunk that they couldn't fill the holes. Our own grenades went out now, landing short, so the Chinese walked into the explosions.

And then it was over.

A few Chinese at the back of their formation made it back down the hill alive, but not many. Bodies writhed on the ground in front of us, whimpering and moaning.

I scanned the battlefield as I reloaded, ejecting and catching the partially spent magazine, then inserting a fresh one. "Weapons and ammo check! Walters, casualty report."

The squad busied itself with redistributing ammunition and checking their weapons. My assistant squad leader, Corporal John Walters walked over. "One dead, Sarge. Private Tammany. Took one right through the eye. A couple of guys got zinged by some grenade shrapnel, but that's it. We got off lucky."

I nodded. We certainly had. "Okay, Hatzl, Givens, with me. Let's check the bodies for any papers and see if we have some that might live long enough for the intel boys to question them. Walters, cover us and make the report back to the LT."

Checking the dead and dying is a rotten task and I didn't send the same guys out each time. It takes a certain amount of detachment to go through a dead man's pockets. I'd done it enough I could roll a body over to search it for any papers and ignore the fixed and staring eyes.

"Sarge! Come take a look at this!" PFC Hatzl stood a few yards away, rifle pointed at the ground.

I levered myself up and walked over. It looked like another dead Chinaman in that quilted uniform they wore. But the face was all wrong. Deformed by the impact of two bullet holes, one square in the nose and the other through one eye, it had never been human in the first place. Teeth like those of a shark showed in the gaping mouth, which itself was too large to be human. It held a pistol in one hand, but the talons that tipped the fingers, a part of me wondered why it needed one.

"Fuck, Sarge. That thing ain't human!" Hatzl's voice was shaky, and the barrel of his rifle trembled.

I put one hand on his weapon and gently pushed it to point at the ground. "Easy, Hatzl. Whatever it is, it's dead. Don't go popping off a round and hurt one of us. Did you find any live ones that we can take back to HQ?"

He swallowed heavily, eyes not leaving the body on the ground. "Uh, no, Sarge. Most was too bad hit. Ain't nothing on them, either."

"Okay. Let's get back to our positions." He nodded and started to turn but stopped when I cleared my throat. "And Hatzl. Don't go spreading scuttlebutt about this. We got enough to worry about without you making up stories about boogeymen."

Later that morning, the lieutenant had me take a working party back to the rear areas for more ammunition. We were also able to bring back a surprise for everyone.

"Hey, Sarge! Whatcha got?"

I stopped at the first set of foxholes and set the jerrycan I was hauling on a rock. "Hot coffee, boys. Get your canteen cups out."

The men took turns leaving their positions to fill their cups. Nobody got a lot, maybe half a canteen cup, but it was a welcome warmth and comfort.

As they sipped on the now-lukewarm coffee, I scanned the surroundings. The weather was nice and clear for now, but I'd grown up in the mountains of Montana. Things could change in less than an hour's time.

"Sarge, hear any scuttlebutt about when we're pulling out?"

I winked at the older man. "Sure thing, Leckie. Back at the mess tent. That means hot chow for dinner tonight. Last of it for a while, too."

Leckie perked up at that. He was an old hand from the island-hopping campaign in the Pacific against the Japanese. "We pulling out? Scuttlebutt's true?"

"Seems to be. Word will come down at dinner, I think. And First Sergeant Mays put out the call for anyone who needs new gear. Says anything we can't carry out gets destroyed, so the Chinese can't use it."

"Man, I can't wait to get my ass out of here. Gimme a soggy jungle any day. And these Chinese ain't no joke, either. Make a banzai charge look like a buncha kindergartners running around on the playground."

I straightened. "Get me a list of who needs what. No, even better. Take care of it yourself, Leckie. You know what we need, officially and unofficially."

He grinned and laid a finger alongside his nose. "Sure thing, Sarge."

I watched the mountains to the north. The clouds were building up there. It reminded me of the Rockies in winter when that Arctic racetrack was in full swing. "Walters. Get everyone working on overhead cover and a warming tent. Storms's coming in."

The winds were picking up as evening came on. I could taste the snow in the air, even if nothing had fallen yet. Bad enough fighting in subzero temperatures, but to do it in wind and snow was going to be even less fun.

The captain came up just before dark and gathered all the platoon leaders and sergeants. "Fifth Regiment is holding the line while Seventh is going to clear the road out of here. Means we gotta hold off the Chinese until everyone can get on the road. Ammo's coming up now. We ain't bringing it back with us, so use it all up or destroy it. Come first light, if the weather holds, we'll have close air support. We've beat everything they've thrown at us so far, so let's keep that streak going. Semper Fi, Marines!"

There were cases of ammunition being stockpiled at the command post, and we made sure every man had all he could hold, plus several grenades. The LT walked the line, checking our lanes of fire and sighting in target reference points for the artillery. We had been surprised before, but now we were ready for them. And we had a mission.

Hatzl came to see me not too much later. He'd been jumpy all day, and I guess I couldn't blame him. When you have nothing to do but stand around and watch for Chinese, it gives you time to think. Me, I'd been working on resupply, position planning, target reference points, and a dozen other things and hadn't had time to think about what we saw.

"Sarge, you got a minute."

"Sure thing. What's on your mind?"

He leaned in close so he could whisper. "I know you said don't spread any gossip. And I didn't. Only Ramirez kept poking at me, bout what was bugging me. So, I took him out to show him the body."

I sighed. "Dammit, Hatzl. Why'd you have to do that? Now it'll be all over the company before dawn."

"No, it won't, Sarge. That's the thing. We got down there and the body was gone! Plenty of blood on the ground around, but we saw boot prints walking away from where it was laying. Ramirez thinks I'm funning him, but you saw it too. You saw how bad it'd been hit. Ain't no way a man is getting up and walking away from that!" His breathing came faster and faster, and his eyes were wide.

I put a hand on his shoulder and squeezed. It wasn't easy through the thick winter clothing, but I got his attention. "Hatzl. Hatzl! Lock it down, man."

Once I felt sure he was calmer, I moved my hand and laid an arm around his shoulder. "Look. We saw something out there; I'll grant you that. But who knows what we saw? Maybe some of those wounds were small? Maybe he wore something under his uniform? Who knows? Thing is, he was hit just like everyone else, and here's the kicker, he bled like everyone else. He isn't shrugging off them bullets, so you can shoot him, and he'll go down. Just make sure if he comes back that we shoot him a lot, okay?"

Hatzl's eyes grew a bit guarded. "If he comes back?"

Shit. Wrong thing to say, but I couldn't take it back. "If. Not saying he will. But if he does, you know what to do. Just shoot him a lot and he'll go down and stay down. Just like anyone else."

The other man's face relaxed slightly, and he nodded unconsciously. "Okay. Yeah. I can do that. We gots lots of ammo. I can shoot him a lot."

"Carry on, then. Show him a marine knows how to handle this only one way, and that's with superior firepower."

The storm hit before midnight. Flurries at first, with the wind whipping into your eyes and nose. The clouds hid the moon, making the night as dark as coal. The mortars were ready to fire illumination flares when things got interesting.

For now, we sat in our foxholes, listening for any sign of movement beyond the moaning of the wind through the mountains.

It would come and go, making you dread the noise and the cold that came with it. When the wind wasn't blowing, you could feel your body heat rise and warm you. Then the wind would come through and rob you of that, kicking in the eerie howls to boot.

Then I heard something new. A moan that sounded when the wind died down. It was lower than the wind's keening, and longer. It had a feeling to it, like a hunger that could never be filled.

Others heard it, too. Mutters came from the other fighting positions. I thought about speaking out. But I couldn't move. Couldn't speak. A deep chill settled over me, like ice had been poured over my soul. One by one, the others felt it as well. The mutters and curses quieted, and you could feel the fear rising. We could all recognize that. It was the fear we'd felt every day since the Chinese counterattack began, only before we'd been able to keep it under control. Squashed away inside a box deep inside ourselves, where it couldn't hurt us.

Only now that moan had opened the box. Fear rushed out of us, a miasma that surrounded our whole unit. Men sobbed openly. There were cries for wives, for mothers. And above all, the fear of dying, where you think, *"Dear God, not here. Not like this! Not so far from home!"*

The winds picked up, smelling of snow. The flurries intensified, and we didn't care. Men were crawling down into their holes, to curl up in a ball and cry. A shot sounded from somewhere nearby, a single pistol round. Snow began to pile up on those prone figures, and the wind whipped it in front of us like swirling dervishes. It revealed and concealed the terrain, teasing with glimpses of what could be motion and what could be imagination.

The Chinese attack came in the middle of that. Whistles blew, horns sounded, and human throats took up the cry.

But still, we were frozen by our fear.

All except Hatzl. He stood up in his foxhole, screaming, "Die, you bastards!" firing his Garand. Shots banged out rapid-fire, emptying the clip in seconds. Reloading as quickly as the bulky gloves would allow, screaming all the time, Hatzl saved us all.

I found myself moving, standing up, and opening fire with my Thompson. It didn't have the range, but I didn't care. I needed to empty myself of this fear and with every round downrange, the fear ebbed. More and more marines were following suit, firing as rapidly as they could at the advancing horde.

Someone got the mortars online, and illumination rounds began popping overhead. The enemy was only yards away now, sub guns firing in long bursts at our positions. Marines went down by the handful, those that were too caught up in erasing their fear to take cover once again.

One of our machine guns opened up from a flank, long sweeping bursts that scythed mustard-yellow uniforms. Some popped back up after the fire had swept by, unharmed, and continued their charge.

Two of them charged right at my position. My fear was nearly gone now, and I was more in control. I opened fire in short bursts, butt to my shoulder and cheek to the stock. The closer one took my first shots full in the chest, the heavy .45 caliber bullets punching through his quilted uniform with ease and knocking his feet out from under him. The second one took a round through the shoulder, which spun him around and dropped him, causing the rest of the burst to miss. His weapon bounced across the frozen earth, away from him.

I shifted my gaze to further down the hill. The Chinese were still coming, but now that I could think and see clearly, I realized there weren't very many of them. The vast numbers I'd imagined faded, replaced by the reality of only a few dozen attackers. Even now, we were cutting down the last of them in front of our positions. The firing died away as targets disappeared, with calls of 'Cease fire' echoing up and down the lines.

There were calls for medics and ammunition, and I got out of my foxhole to begin coordinating our efforts. That's when I heard the wounded man in front of my hole. He wasn't crying out or screaming, like most of the other wounded. He was laughing.

I approached him cautiously, weapon at the ready. It was a weak, thready laugh, but it continued as I approached. His eyes found me in the dying light of the flares, and he smiled. Blood smears covered his mouth and as he laughed, blood sprayed across his chest.

Kneeling next to him, I frowned. "What's so funny, bud? Hit your head?"

He only smiled. It was a joyous smile, one of relief and gladness. He mouthed a word and coughed with a spray of blood. Spitting weakly, he said the word again, breath rattling in his throat.

"Zìyóu."

Then he died, a smile on his face.

I found Hatzl later, standing over one of the Chinese bodies. The mortars were only firing an illumination flare every few minutes now, and the dim light hid things in shadows. You couldn't tell what the face had looked like before the bullets had chewed it apart, but the clawed hands were untouched. Its uniform was soaked with blood, which looked black in the faint white light from above.

Hatzl smiled, a grim thing. He held his Garand loosely in his hands, bolt back. I gently touched him on the shoulder. "Hatzl, reload. And get some more ammunition. Your bandolier is about empty."

"You was right, Sarge." His voice came across low and raspy.

"Right about what?"

"Shoot 'em enough and they stay down. Musta hit him five, six times as he charged. Then when he went down, I put another clip into him. Bastard ain't gonna move now."

I tugged on his arm. "Okay, Hatzl. You did it, just like you were trained. Superior firepower wins every time. Now let's get back to the line and get you ammo'd up. No telling when the Chinese will be back."

"Yeah. Yeah, they'll be back. But not this guy."

We trudged slowly back up the hill, Hatzl chuckling under his breath at his own private joke.

The next morning, they told us that 7th Marines were still clearing the road. They needed one more day to make it safe to get the evacuation going. All we had to do was hold our positions for one more day.

We got hot chow for breakfast and lunch, as the mess kitchens used up their stocks. We actually had breakfast twice, potatoes and ham and powdered eggs each time. But it was hot, so we didn't care. Coffee too, as much as you wanted. I hoped this wasn't the last meal of the condemned, though.

Hatzl ate mechanically, as if the food held no joy for him. Military food never tasted great, but it was hot and filling. You lived for hot food in your belly and hot coffee warming you on the way down. But Hatzl ate like he was stoking a furnace, shoveling it in to feed a fire that burned inside him. His eyes stared into the distance, and he didn't take part in the small talk around him.

Walters saw where I was looking and sighed. "Hatzl's had it, Sarge. If he makes it out of here, they'll Section 8 him for sure. Something broke in him last night."

I wondered if something broke in me, too. "Yeah. Yeah, you're probably right. Keep an eye on him, in case he breaks down before we're out of here."

We expected another Chinese attack during the day, but our air support foiled that. We saw the Corsairs firing rockets into the hills beyond our position, wheeling like a giant roman candles in the sky. There was a continuous rumble echoing off the mountains from the explosions, and every so often we saw a secondary where they caught an ammo cache. The sight cheered everyone, and when the show was over, we settled back into our foxholes. We could hold one more day.

The wind and snow picked up again in the evening, with less wind but more snow. You could still see a couple hundred yards, plenty to catch them if they tried to sneak up. The wind was intermittent and light, a contrast to last night. It made things almost bearable, even if the snow settled on you like a soft blanket.

The bodies on the hillside were soon covered with white. The horror of war was blanketed away by nature, as if it wanted to hide the sight of man's cruelty from the whole universe. Nothing moved and the only sounds were quiet whispers and the creak of leather as someone shifted position.

We heard it again. That low moan that sounded like the wind but wasn't. This time, men were ready. People started moaning back at it. There were low moans, aping the sound. There were hooting moans, like monkeys crying back at a predator that was beneath them in the trees. There were the obligatory sex-filled moans, with encouragement and offers to help him finish.

I let it go for a few minutes. They needed the release and after last night, needed to feel back in control. Finally, I gave a sharp whistle and called, "Awright, that's enough. Lock it down!"

The moaning died away, replaced with general laughter and catcalls. Men settled back into their positions, comfortable that the fear was back in the box. They were back in control of themselves.

"Sarge, something's moving out there!"

I peered out into the gathering darkness. Through the falling snow, I thought I could see a dim figure walking. There was only the one, though. No, wait. Another, several yards away. Walking towards us with a slow, steady gait. They were about a hundred yards away, walking in a calm, unhurried fashion.

"Leckie! Take one of them down. Rest of you, hold fire!"

Seconds passed, and we all waited. Then a shot banged out. We could all see the one he hit stagger a step, and then keep walking. Leckie fired again, and again, and again. Each time, the figure paused when it was hit, and then kept walking. After about a dozen hits, it toppled in mid-step. But another one appeared out of the darkness, walking with that same steady gait. Leckie was reloading as quick as he could, but when it got to the closest concentration of snow-covered bodies, it stopped.

Leckie started firing again, but the figure raised its hands, palms up. The low moan from before began, only this time we heard it from multiple directions. Each figure walking towards us, almost a dozen, had halted next to a clump of Chinese bodies. They were all standing there, hands raised, their moan building in the air around them.

I saw twin points of blue light appear in the face of the one closest to me. They blazed like twin stars, and the hate in them slammed into me like a physical blow. I knew, deep inside, that this creature wanted me dead, and it wanted my soul. My guts turned to ice, and I could feel my bladder let go.

Snowy bodies began to move from where they lay, sitting up. With a complete lack of grace, they pushed themselves to their feet. Each cluster now stood around the blue-eyed figures, motionless. No one on our side fired or made a sound. This was completely beyond anything we'd seen before or had trained to fight. Bodies don't get back up after they've been dead most of a day.

I tried to give the order to fire, but my mouth was suddenly dry. The cold air burned my nostrils as I inhaled, a shaky breath that gave me air, but I still couldn't make a sound. More of the Chinese bodies sat up. Those standing began to lurch in our direction, halting steps that kicked up snow in a spray.

I felt warmth on my legs. I looked down at the growing stain on my crotch.

No. Not like this. Dear God, not like this.

"No," I croaked, a barely audible sound.

"No." I could put emphasis on this one.

"No!" I shouted.

Multiple voices sounded throughout the falling darkness. Some were soft, as if in prayer. Others were full of defiance. Maybe one or two were in denial.

"Open fire!" I gave the command and started firing myself. Aiming at the closest staggering body, I fired in a steady, controlled manner. The cold settled into me, wiping away the fear from before. All I could feel was the recoil of my

Thompson against my shoulder and the heat rising from the breach with each shot.

The thing shuddered with each hit but didn't stop walking. The bolt slammed back and stayed there. I ejected the magazine and reloaded without taking my eyes off the thing. With calm deliberation, I pulled another magazine from the pouch at my waist, inserted it, and raised it to fire. Moving closer and closer, it moaned again in a tone full of pain and desire in equal measures. It moved faster, like it knew my weapon was empty.

The thing was only ten yards away as I raised my rifle back to my shoulder and fired. My first shot took the thing in the head, and it collapsed like a puppet with its strings cut.

I could hear more weapons fire up and down the line as others shook off their fear. But as they saw that the dead Chinese wouldn't go down after a few shots, some threw down their rifles and ran. This infected others, who followed suit. The firing line collapsed.

As men streamed to the rear, I could see Hatzl standing in his fighting position, banging away at the approaching forms. He reloaded with unhurried motions, even as they swarmed over his position. I saw him disappear under a mass of bodies, firing as he went.

The moans from the blue-eyed monsters intensified, becoming even more hungry. The wind whipped the snow around us, dropping visibility to only a few yards. I could hear the firing dropping off to my left and right. To my left, Leckie struggled to reload, fumbling with the clip until one of the dead Chinese reached him. It latched both hands around his throat and bore down on him, pushing him to the ground as it strangled the life from him.

I got up out of my foxhole and walked backwards, firing as I went. I could only see vague outlines in the swirling snow, but the center of mass is easy to fire at. I saw others in my unit swarmed over by the Chinese, those men whose fear was so great it paralyzed them.

Further back, I could hear shouting, followed by two pistol shots. The shouted words came to me clearly through the chaos.

"Marines, stand your ground! The next man I see running won't get a warning shot!"

Lieutenant Doherty. God bless him, he was trying to rally the boys. I wished him luck.

I watched as marines gathered around him. There were maybe a dozen, but I would bet at least that many had already run off. Maybe we could still stop this thing from falling apart.

The air next to the LT became a mini-tornado, spinning in place and pulling in the snow around it. Seconds later, one of those blue-eyed monsters stepped out of that mess like it was a door. It grabbed Doherty, both clawed hands and its eyes blazed like floodlights.

I raised my rifle to fire, but I couldn't get a clear shot. The LT was between us, which allowed me a full view of what happened. Within seconds, the poor guy's skin turned blue and then white. A layer of frost climbed up from the ground over his body, covering him completely. He stopped moving, mouth frozen, literally, in an open-mouthed scream that never came out.

The monster stepped back; its work done. This gave me a clear shot, and I put one square between its glowing blue eyes. It staggered, the moan turning to a ragged, deep howl. I fired twice more, hitting it in the neck and its open mouth. The thing fell backwards into the snow like a fallen tree, sending up a cloud of snow.

The whole thing sent the men scattering away from the scene, most with weapons forgotten in their hands. They moved even faster when a bright blue light rose from the creature's mouth and drifted up into the storm.

After that, it was every man for himself. Like a dam breaking, men ran for the supposed safety of the rear areas. What they thought they'd find there, I don't know. Those rear area boys, the cooks, clerks, and supply guys were even less well-armed than the infantry.

I reached the frozen statue of the lieutenant and paused. This seemed like as good a place as any to die. At his feet was the radio, dropped by the operator so he could move faster. The handpiece crackled a few times, and I could hear a voice coming through.

Picking it up, I listened numbly to the voice while watching the advancing figures. They continued their staggering gait, untroubled by the incoming fire. The snow alternately concealed and revealed their shapes. Already some were past my position.

I returned my attention to the radio. The words kept repeating.

"Any forward station. Can you provide coordinates?"

Pressing the transmit button, I made my mouth work. "Charlie Baker Seven to calling station. Call for fire, over."

"Charlie Baker Seven, your position is reported overrun. Do you have targets?"

"Calling station, Charlie Baker Seven affirmative. Target is personnel in the open. Coordinates are my position."

"Charlie Baker Seven, do you require an Excalibur mission?"

"Interrogative. What is Excalibur?"

"Charlie Baker Seven, were the targets dead before now? Are they moving again?"

I looked at the handset in disbelief. How the hell did they know? "Calling station, affirmative. I say again, fire mission on my position."

"Charlie Baker Seven, good copy. On the way. Take cover."

I dragged the radio with me to a nearby foxhole and hunkered down. I'd never been this close to an artillery barrage. And why would it even matter? They were going to obliterate this area real soon. There wasn't any hope of surviving but then, I was already resigned to dying. Better our own guns than those things.

Seconds later, I heard the whistle of incoming rounds. They landed long, where the Chinese had been before. I keyed the handset. "Drop one hundred and fire for effect."

"Charlie Baker Seven, roger. On the way."

The dead bodies continued to stagger past my position. None paid me any attention. With dogged determination, they lurched along, heading for our rear area. Spaced here and there among them were the monsters who'd animated them. None paid any attention to the whistle of incoming fire.

Dirt fountained high where the rounds impacted, tossing bodies to the ground. The malignant sounds of shrapnel whizzed by from the airbursts above me. I bent over in the foxhole and covered my neck with my hands. It would be sheer luck that something would hit me, but it could happen.

The ground shook and jumped under me. Thunder assailed my ears, making them ring. Still, the bombardment went on and on. I realized I was screaming along with the shelling, although whether it was in fear or in joy, I didn't know.

Finally, it ceased. Whether it had been minutes or seconds, I couldn't say. I raised my head above the lip of the hole and looked around. The smell of fresh-turned earth filled my nose, competing with the smells of war; smoke, cordite, and blood. The snow flurries had almost stopped, and the wind had died away around me.

Too still. Like something about to happen.

I looked back to the Chinese lines. There, the snow swirled, moving with a purpose instead of being blown by the wind. A shape was forming in the snow, long and sinuous, moving with the wind and yet displacing the snow. A head appeared, sprouting horrific deer-like antlers but with angles and spikes instead of the curves of a normal beast. The mouth opened and out came that horrific moan. The winds billowed and flowed along with it.

The handset lay forgotten in my hand as the icy wind blew past and sent a chill through me. My cheeks grew numb in the face of that wind and seeped through my clothes. I shivered so hard that I almost dropped the handset.

"Charlie Baker Seven, is the threat neutralized?"

I raised a shaking hand, my eyes never leaving the monstrous shape only a few dozen yards away. It was becoming more solid by the second, and I could see its feet touch the ground now and again. The moan came again, deep and hungry.

"F-f-fire m-mission, my po-position. Single target in the open. I don't know what it is."

"Charlie Baker Seven, on the way. Keep your eyes closed."

Right. Close my eyes when this thing was coming for me. I could see the eyes clearly enough now to recognize the hunger in them. The same hunger that we'd been hearing in the wind. Not a hunger for flesh, but your soul. You looked into those eyes and knew, for a certainty, that it would devour our soul and you would never know heaven.

But I was already in hell. I closed my eyes and crouched back in my fighting position. My whole body shook, from fear and from cold as I heard the wind build over me. The moan was continuous now, and if I'd had anything left in my bladder, I would have pissed myself.

Then I heard the incoming whistle of artillery. I squeezed my eyes shut as the rounds went off. It wasn't the deep boom of a high-explosive round but a softer crack, and the world grew bright. I could see the brightness through my tightly closed eyes as more of the rounds went off. There was a hissing noise and the smell of smoke. More acrid than regular smoke. I'd smelled it before in the aftermath of an attack. White phosphorus.

I wondered if I was going to die this time and realized I didn't care. This is hell. Things couldn't get worse. If I died, I wouldn't be cold anymore.

The rounds stopped exploding, and I raised my head. The world was bright all around, and I cautiously opened my eyes. The ground was burning in patches, the white phosphorus giving off white smoke.

Several yards away, the deer-headed thing slid its wounded body across the ground as dozens of burns scarred its flanks. White phosphorus will burn until it goes out. Water won't put it out. A man who gets it on him will suffer horribly from the burns it inflicts and will keep burning as his comrades try without success to put out the fire and stop him from screaming. Usually, only a bullet will end the screaming.

The creature wasn't screaming. I could see great plumes of steaming breath rising, its body quivered and shook as its flesh burned. The smell was like the sweet smoke you got from burning incense. A welcome change to the burnt pork smell of a burned man.

It wasn't horrific anymore. It was dying. I could see it get slower and slower, its breath coming more and more shallow. Finally, it collapsed, head on the ground. The body burned, and smoke congealed around it instead of flowing up into the sky.

Seconds later, it gave an agonized moan, no longer full of hunger but of pain and despair. The moan died away to a whisper and then to nothing.

The smoke dissipated, leaving behind blackened earth where it had died, and two massive antlers.

I sat there as the winds died completely, leaving me warmer than I'd been in days. It felt like heaven.

I don't know how much later they found me. I didn't even see them arrive. Marines were flowing past me to take up our old fighting positions. Three of them stopped in front of me, two officers and a corpsman. While the latter started checking me over, the other looked over the battlefield. They were both pretty senior, a major, and a lieutenant colonel, but I just didn't have it in me to stand from my sitting position on the edge of my foxhole.

The major gently removed the handset from my grip and set it aside while the lieutenant colonel crouched down so he could look me in the eye. "Sergeant Polinsky. I'm Lieutenant Colonel Torres. Can you answer some questions?"

I nodded. Questions were fine. Just don't ask me to move yet.

"Sergeant. Did we get them all with the artillery strike? Especially whatever was controlling them?"

I nodded.

"That's good. Now, the corpsman's going to make sure you're okay to move. Then we're taking you back to division headquarters. I'll ask you some more questions once you have some hot chow and rest. But I think you'll do just fine for us."

My mouth moved of its own accord. "Who's 'us'?"

He stood and smiled. "Sergeant Jerome Polinsky, welcome to Task Force Thirteen. You walked the line between heaven and hell and came out the other side intact. You'll do just fine in Thirteen, Sergeant Polinsky. Just fine."

Michael Gants

A Snake in the Grass
By: Michael Gants

The rain finally slacked off, giving a small amount of relief to the marching column of marines. At the head of the group, Corporal Prescott swung his bolo, clearing a wider path through the vegetation-choked game trail. The knife's nearly foot-long, heavy leaf-shaped blade crashed through the wet stalks. Water and foul-smelling sap splashed into his face and mouth. He cursed, using the back of a sweat-stained sleeve to wipe the muck out of his eyes.

"This is ridiculous," the thickly muscled man complained. "The last thing we need to be doing is trailing after some fairy tale creature when the rest of the battalion is fighting their way through the hills, trying to roust the Spaniards from Santiago and that fort up on San Juan Hill."

Sergeant Rogers, the platoon's leader, snorted. "Hunting fairy tale creatures is kind of what we do now. Didn't you listen to the captain's briefing about us being shifted from the battalion to

Section 13? Or were you still too drunk from carousing that night? Happened right after the fight we had down in Louisiana, as I remember."

"I was there. Even remember it through my headache," Prescott growled. He continued swinging the knife as he spoke. The other men in the column chuckled at the statement.

"Well, that pretty well laid out what we're doing from now on. Before that lecture, we fought the Spanish or Cubies or pirates or whoever we were told to point our guns at. That's what we're trained to do as marines. Follow orders and kill people. Unfortunately, ever since that blasted walking alligator-thing in Louisiana, or whatever the captain ended up calling it, attacked us, we've been hunting down things my memaw used to talk about around the fire at night. This big snake probably ain't no different." Rogers winced internally as he listened to himself talk. The tall, thin man's Arkansas Ozark twang grated on his own ears. He hated to think of what others thought of it. Since joining the Marine Corps at seventeen to get away from the family farm, he'd worked on leaving both behind, but the stress of this hunt was bringing it to the forefront.

"What 'xactly are we huntin' this time, Sarge?" asked Private Moleson. The West Virginian had only completed the sixth grade. He could sound a little slow because of his speech, but the group's combination cook, teamster, and all-around scavenger was an intelligent and well-liked lad. He marched at the back of the column, slightly behind everybody else, occasionally tugging Bartholomew's lead to keep the mule walking. Getting the animal through the hilly jungles of Cuba was proving to be tougher than marching without him would have been. The mule pulled back on the leather, trying once again to see if he could slip free and nibble at the green plants around the trail. Moleson tightened his grip and kept pressure on the strap. He glanced back and frowned at the reluctant animal. "Stop that, ya sorry excuse fer meandering glue."

The only reason they'd brought Bartholomew along was the light field piece he was pulling. The cannon was an unusual specimen of artillery in multiple respects, from its weight to its ammunition. However, the oddest thing about the gun was the marines, even Section 13, didn't have any assigned to them.

Earlier, when Rogers was assembling the column for the march, Moleson had unexpectedly arrived with the mule and gun. Rogers had pulled the private aside and questioned where he'd gotten his hands on the artillery piece. Moleson, according to his own words, had "borrowed the weapon from Colonel Roosevelt's cavalry regiment." The answer threw up warning flags in Rogers's mind, leading to an internal struggle. On one hand, there was a strong argument that the Army unit would need the weapon in the upcoming encounter. On the other hand, when it came to killing fey and fairie, Section 13 had learned the hard way that more and larger guns were the preferable method of dealing damage. The dynamite gun was absolutely the largest weapon they had any chance of moving with them on the hike.

He'd decided he'd rather risk the lives of the calvary in a battle with the Spaniards than his own men's against things from dark campfire tales. The need to give his men the best fighting chance possible won out over the prohibition against stealing. As he could truthfully say, no one was accusing Private Moleson of stealing the gun, and as Bartholomew was assigned to the marines, he decided not to pursue the question any deeper.

"Locals call it Magüi. Some sort of magical giant snake or legless lizard or something," Rogers said, ignoring Moleson's continuing argument with the mule. He slapped a mosquito that landed on his neck. The insect's tiny body burst under the blow. There was now a black stain on his hand. No red. The nasty bug hadn't bitten him yet. He was thankful for that. He'd seen enough people with malaria to avoid getting it if he could. That's why he required all his men to keep their uniform sleeves rolled down, even in the heat of Cuba. "All I really know is the locals claim it's been around forever. They're of the mindset if it kills the occasional cow, that's okay. Apparently, they believe the reason the river doesn't dry up during the hot season is because of this thing. From what else I could gather, over the last twenty years, it's killed five or six people and regularly eats cows, and no one seemed to be bothered by those facts."

"That changed yesterday. One of the Army's infantry officer boys was reported missing from muster. When the white arms asked around, they found he'd been spending the evening with a local. A shapely one from the description. They tracked down the house the woman lived in, and she said this thing took him when he stepped out to empty his bladder. Anyway, the white arms reported back to their command, and then the captain got informed."

"And they believed her? Thing just stole him away?" asked Randell, the other corporal.

Rogers nodded his head. "Yes, they believed her. No reason not to. Weren't any Spanish around and since most of his uniform and underthings were still in her house, it was clear he hadn't up and deserted. The white arms weren't sure what happened, though. When they questioned her, she was apparently pretty upset and speaking broken English."

"He probably hadn't paid her yet," murmured one private, loud enough to be heard all the way up the line. Rogers declined to ask who said it, especially since it was, more than likely, correct.

"Cubies may be okay with people getting taken by the monster, but Uncle Sam isn't." Rogers waved his free hand at the thick foliage pressing in on both sides of the trail. "We aren't going to let some fairy beastie go around killing Americans. Which is what brings us to this—"

Rogers abruptly stopped talking when Prescott halted and crouched. The scout slipped the bolo into the sheath on his belt and unslung his rifle. The men behind followed without any order, each marine readying their rifle, swinging their guns outward and to the side, covering all points on the trail. Moleson dropped Bartholomew's lead and pulled out the shotgun he preferred, turning around to cover the back trail. The night was silent except for the faint call of night birds and the buzz of insects. Rogers waited a moment before stepping up and tapping Prescott on the shoulder.

"What'cha got?" he whispered.

Prescott jutted his chin down the trail, to where it curved to the left. "Something big's moving ahead. Caught a bit of sound."

Rogers turned his head and gestured, pointing at the curve. The men shifted their guns until all the barrels pointed up the trail. He raised his own pistol, cocking the hammer, ready to drop it down and shoot as soon as an enemy appeared. Rain started up again, the plop-plop of the water dripping from the broad leaves masking many other night sounds. Only a faint glow from the cloud-shrouded moon gave light, making it impossible to see very far through the thick foliage. Ahead, Rogers now heard something moving through the underbrush. He tensed, ready for action.

A black shape exploded outward, grunting and shrieking. Without thinking, Rogers slashed his pistol down. As soon as the gun came level with his shoulder, he sighted past the end of the barrel and pulled the trigger. The explosive noise of his first shot merged with his men's overwhelming barrage. The creature continued its forward charge, mud flying from beneath it as it raced toward the men. Rogers rode his gun's recoil, thankful for the weapon's double action as he brought the revolver back down and fired again.

The muzzle flashes painted a series of unseen still pictures, the bright light partially blinding the mer's night-ready eyes. There wasn't time to identify what was attacking them. Rogers fired once more before the creature slid to a halt in front of Prescott.

"Hold fire," he ordered calmly, all trace of his accent gone.

It was impossible to see the mounded shape clearly in the near-darkness. He blinked and shook his head, trying to banish both the white spots from his eyes and the ringing of the gunfire from his ears. "Be ready. I'm getting some light." Keeping the pistol pointed at the unmoving shape, he used his left hand to fish out his lighter from the front breast pocket of his uniform blouse. He snapped open the hinged cover and rolled his thumb. A yellow-white light bathed the area. Two or three feet in front of Corporal Prescott lay the bullet-ridden remains of a brown-haired bush hog. The beast's mouth was open, revealing razor-sharp teeth and a pair of four-inch-long tusks gleaming in the flickering light. Its pinkish tongue lolled out and deep red blood pooled beneath its body, seeping slowly into the rich jungle loam.

"Damn, t'wernt the snake thingy," Moleson said in a frustrated tone. Bartholomew snorted in response and returned to browsing on the thin grass poking up at the edge of the trail.

"You say that like it's a bad thing," Private Givens commented.

"Well, if it t'were the beast, we'd be head'n back ta the barracks ta sleep till t'morras battle. 'Stead we gotta keep goin' now." He pointed his Winchester at the hog. "Cain't even stay long 'nough ta get good meat outta him."

"No, we aren't staying here." Rogers stood and holstered the gun. As he extinguished his lighter, he gestured for the column to follow suit. "That Magüi's still out there and, unlike this fellow, it's still alive. Means we've got a job to do. Prescott, lead on."

The scout stepped around the bloody corpse, unsheathing and swinging his blade as necessary. The rest of the marines followed. Moleson looked down at the bullet-ridden body and frowned. "Prob'ly tougher than shoe leather anyways."

Rogers called a halt as the column entered a small clearing. The clouds had finally begun thinning, and the waning moon hung low on the horizon. The marines shrugged off their heavy packs and set about rigging tents. Moleson beat a stake into the ground and picketed Bartholomew to it, then unhooked the dynamite gun from the mule's harness. Four of the men helped him push the almost thousand-pound weapon to the edge of the jungle for the night. Once they'd set camp, Rogers assigned a guard schedule and climbed under the canvas of his small tent. He slipped his hat over his eyes and fell asleep before the guard had completed his first round.

The next morning, when the guard woke him, Rogers's first sense was the smell of coffee and beans. He climbed out of the tent and checked over the area. The sun was nothing more than a silvery sheen of light along the top of the trees on the horizon. Moleson tended a small fire, cooking a simple breakfast for the platoon. The guard continued around, rousing the rest of the men. Most of them had probably gotten four or five hours of sleep. Not enough to be restful, but enough to keep them in the fight. Rogers watched them ready themselves for the march, breaking camp, grabbing a bite, and shaking themselves into fighting order. As soon as his Second was up and moving, Rogers motioned Prescott over and they huddled next to the fire, each holding a tin plate of beans. He gestured to the other end of the clearing. A small river cut off easy progress to the west.

"I figure we'll follow the bank until we find where the snake's gone to ground. From the description, I figure it'll be a good-sized hole or living up in a favorite tree."

Prescott nodded. "It ain't leaving much of a trail, that's for sure. Rain last night won't help none either. Anything it left behind has probably been filled in or covered by now."

Rogers thought about that and watched a freckled-faced marine take his canteen to the river, then turned back to Prescott. "Any idea on which way is the best then?" he asked through a forkful of beans.

Prescott shrugged. "Nope. Don't know enough about the critter to make a guess."

Someone screamed, a high frightened tone. Rogers whipped around, trying to see what was happening. He glimpsed something exploding out of the water, grabbing the freckled man's bandolier in its enormous jaws and dragging the struggling marine into the water.

Frantically, Moleson and another private raced forward, attempting to grab their companion before he disappeared. The river's waters frothed as the two reached the muddy edge. A hand flailed out and there was a flash of blue and green iridescent scales. They watched in horror as both the hand and the creature sank beneath the churning water.

"Get back," Rogers shouted. "We'll lose both of you if you go in there!"

Moleson had stopped running and was struggling to get his gear off in preparation to go after the marine. "Cain't just leave him, Sarge," he shouted back, but paused in what he was doing.

He unlimbered his shotgun and fired at the heaving mass. The pellets impacted the river's surface, raising small waterspouts to the right of the disturbance.

The other private slapped the shotgun's barrel upward as Moleson triggered another round, sending the pellets harmlessly into the air. "Dammit, you'll kill George if you keep shooting at him like that." By the time the two returned their eyes to the spot, the waters were returning to normal, with only widening ripples and wavelets splashing ashore gave evidence of the struggle.

The other marines had their rifles out, scanning the river for any sign of either Private Williams or whatever had grabbed him. A blue cap bobbed to the surface, floating on the now gentle waves.

"All of you, get back and form a skirmish line," Rogers ordered. The men, including Moleson, set themselves up, all standing several yards from the river's bank. They stood with their rifles pointed at the water, waiting for the beast to return. Rogers stepped forward and lowered his rifle into the river, catching hold of the hat's brim with the bayonet. He lifted it out and stepped away from the bank, never turning his back to the falsely safe appearing water. Once he was a sufficient distance away, he slipped the hat off the end of his gun and looked it over. There was a hole torn in one side, large enough for him to push three of his fingers through easily, and a faint trace of red around the ragged fabric.

After almost fifteen minutes of no motion, Rogers waved the men's guns down.

He pointed to two of the remaining privates. "McHenry and Givens, keep watch. The rest of you, get the camp cleared and ready to march. I don't think that thing's going to come back right away. Probably taking Private Williams somewhere else to eat him."

"Saints and angels keep him," said one of the men, crossing himself as he looked out over the blue-green water.

Rogers pulled Prescott to the side. "We need to find where this snake is keeping itself," Rogers said as the men quickly broke camp the rest of the way and packed their backpacks. "I didn't even think it'd be in the water."

"Me neither," said Prescott. "I expected it was like a huge rat or garden snake. Wrap up its food, squeeze it, and swallow it right there. Didn't think it'd swim like a moccasin. Seemed too big to do that. I was wrong 'bout that."

"We both were. Don't take it all on yourself. 'Nuff blame to go around for all of us. Question now is, which way did it go?" Rogers looked out over the now placid river. "Can't really track it if it swims."

"If it's like the moccasins back home, it'll have a nest near a pool of still water. Won't mind swimming in the current, but it prefers to live out of the water and get in somewhere where it ain't gonna get swept away during a rainstorm. Figure we find a calm part of the river and start there." Prescott shrugged. "Best idea I got anyways."

Rogers watched as Moleson bent over and checked Bartholomew's harness, properly hooked the dynamite gun up for the march, and thought for a few moments. He didn't have a better idea, and Prescott was the best scout in this group. It would be foolish to disregard his suggestion. "We'll do that. Looked like it can come a fair bit out of the water to strike, so my plan is to keep us all in the tree line along the river. Should make it harder for it to pluck one of us up that way."

The group finished the camp breakdown and marched out. Prescott took the lead position again. He found another game trail, this one less defined than yesterday's but still usable. He hacked at a broad-leafed plant, cutting a wider opening. The marines trooped through, heads swiveling to the left and right as they marched, listening for and trying to spot anything which might attack them. Bartholomew balked at the entrance to the jungle. It took Moleson and two more privates to get the mule moving. The beast snorted and softly whinnied as he walked.

Getting Bartholomew moving proved only part of the problem. The undergrowth here was thicker than before, especially along the river's edge where sunlight was plentiful. Because of the shrubs and vegetation, Moleson often needed time to direct the animal off the path and deeper into the jungle. Maneuvering the gun through the additional trees was difficult and slow. These detours, while necessary, meant the unit's most powerful weapon was often too far away and had too many obstacles between it and where the target was likely to appear. On top of the distance, the heavy gun's wheels often sank into the rich, wet loam.

As they continued the march, Rogers considered stopping and leaving the gun behind. There would be time to retrieve the towed piece on their return journey. He weighed the options of doing so carefully. Having gotten a glimpse of the size of the creature and how powerful it seemed to be, he hesitated. Not having the extra firepower ready if they needed it would be worse than their current troubles moving the gun. He directed an additional private to help Moleson, and the group forged onward.

Three hours later, Prescott signaled for a halt. The marines stopped in their tracks and crouched, quietly bringing their rifles to bear. Rogers moved forward at a wave from Prescott.

"Got another bend up there, Sarge. I caught a look at a sandbar through a break in the trees. Water's been getting narrower too. See how wide the banks are getting? I'll bet this river is a seasonal one and the waters, they're drying up. Add all those things together and it suggests the current slows pretty good here. Might even be getting near the river's head. Good place for a moccasin to make its nest. Ain't seen evidence of much flooding here either. No piles of deadwood or river debris, not like the last spot we stopped at." Prescott gestured between the boles of two trees. "I'd say we have a chance of this beastie being up that way, where the mud is flattened. Kind of looks like something big and curved pushed over it."

"I agree," Rogers said as he looked over the impression. "I'll have Moleson get the gun moved up here and positioned before we go sidling up that way. He can't fire it effectively from where it is right now." He gestured to one of his men. "Givens, I want you to move out to the right. Find a clear-ish spot and hunker down. If this beast is making its home here, I want to make sure we aren't caught by surprise 'cause it isn't where we think it is." The private nodded and slipped quietly through the undergrowth, disappearing behind the bushes and plants within moments.

A Snake in the Grass

Moleson and McHenry prodded and goaded Bartholomew around as close as they could to the bank. Then they unhooked the gun and pushed it until the barrel faced the opposite bank with a clear field of fire. Once in position, they removed the two smaller wheels and stowed them. Each of the men threaded a rope through the larger wheels, attaching the free ends to the carriage's tongue to prevent the gun from rolling back when fired. Moleson checked the gun's elevation and went about verifying the pneumatic compressors' smokeless powder chamber was clean and ready.

Rogers directed the other men to form a firing line along the bank with the cannon in their middle. As the men shifted their positions, he returned to Prescott. "I'm thinking we're going to need some sort of bait to bring this thing to us. You're the most familiar with these kinds of snakes."

Prescott scoffed slightly. "Wouldn't term myself familiar. I've seen water moccasins, even shot one once that dropped into my punt while I was fishing. Never tried to call one out before though, certainly not one that ain't even natural. All the regular ones I've dealt with eat rats and opossums."

"An animal then?"

"Maybe," said Prescott and scratched under his hat. "Ain't sure what kind, though. Mean that thing grabbed Williams, so whatever we use needs to be man-sized or bigger."

"I won't put any of us in that kind of danger," Rogers said and glanced about. His eyes fell on Bartholomew, and he hmm'd under his breath. Prescott followed his gaze.

"Oh… That won't make Moleson happy."

"I'd rather deal with Moleson being snippy than risking one of the men," Rogers said. The sharp report of a rifle caused him to stop talking and jerk his head to the right toward where private Givens had gone. "That wasn't one of ours."

"Too loud and deep. Sounded like a Spanish Mauser," said Prescott.

A second shot followed the first, then another. The crack of a marine's Springfield 1892 responded. More shots from the Mausers echoed down the river.

"Damn. There's more than one. Sounds like Givens found some non-monster trouble." Rogers whistled and swung his arm around beside his head, then pointed a knife hand where the shot sounds were coming from. Moleson and another man hooked up the dynamite gun hurriedly. For once, Bartholomew gave them no trouble.

The men began moving at a near run through the jungle, rifles sweeping the area ahead of them. The group made little noise, aware of the need for both speed and stealth. Rogers signaled a halt when he noted pale wisps of gun smoke drifting on the wind. Another signal and the marines spread out in a loose skirmish line. Rogers pulled a pair of binoculars from the leather case on his belt and lifted them. Blurry patches of green and brown danced crazily across his view until he steadied and focused the lenses. Another shot sounded and he twisted, searching for the origination point. A soldier in a whitish straw hat and pale blue uniform sighted down his rifle, scanning for a target. The Spaniard stood on one side of a roughly constructed wooden palisade stretching across the river.

"Looks like the reason the river is drying up is the Spanish have built a dam," Rogers said, continuing to search for additional soldiers with the glasses.

"They manage to fully stop up the water and our boys and the Cubies will have to pull out. No way to live around here without this river. Dry enough down there during this time of year as it is," agreed Prescott.

Rogers nodded without moving the binoculars. "Means we're going to need to break the dam, take out the Spanish, and find the snake. Rough part is none of those conditions are more important than the others."

"Spanish are here and so's the dam. Ain't seen the snake since breakfast. I say we open the dam, take out the Spaniards, and then get back to hunting for the monster."

"That's the plan I'm leaning toward." Rogers lowered the binoculars. "Moleson," he called out softly, "Get the piece shifted and aimed at the center of the dam. I want to start this off by blowing holes in it."

There was no reply as Moleson immediately got to work. Rogers dropped the binoculars to hang and lifted his rifle to his shoulder. He called out to each side. "On my shot."

Three rounds from the marines hit the Spanish soldier on the edge of the dam. He fell backward, clutching at the wounds in his chest and screaming in pain. A wild set of shots from beyond the dam savaged the tree line where Rogers and his men were positioned, though none of the bullets hit anyone.

"There's 'bout eleven or twelve of them from that return, I'd say," remarked Prescott, keeping his eye down the barrel of his rifle.

"Even odds. Guess we need to be better shots to make sure things go our way," Rogers replied. He took a quick sweep of the other men's positions. "Anyone seen Givens yet?" he called out softly.

There were no replies.

"Keep an eye out. Right flank, move forward, keeping cover. See if you can get a clear view of the Spanish."

Three men crouched and quickly adjusted their positions, moving closer to the dam. One man dropped to a knee and fired his rifle three times, cycling the bolt as quickly as he could. Another cry of pain answered his shots. Bullets tattered the vegetation around the marine. The private nearly dropped his rifle as a lead bullet tore through his bicep. His companions fired in the direction the shot had come from, but there was no indication their bullets had any effect.

Rogers looked over his shoulder. The dynamite gun now pointed toward the dam and where he thought the Spanish had taken cover. Moleson was still sighting the weapon in. They needed to keep the other side occupied for a few more minutes to give the crew time to finish prepping the artillery piece. The fire from both sides had changed from fusillades to single shots as each group fired only when they thought they had a target. Prescott tapped Rogers on the arm.

"What?" Rogers asked in annoyance.

"I think I could get myself across the river, maybe get a better angle on them," Prescott said.

"If I stay below the dam, they won't see me, and I can sneak up behind."

Rogers shook his head. "No. Too dangerous. We aren't to the 'take foolish risks' point yet." He glanced back and smiled. "Besides, Moleson's got the gun ready."

Moleson added the smokeless powder to the compression chamber and slid one of the thin-finned projectiles into the breach, then shut and locked both doors. He took a final sighting and yanked the firing cord. The gun let out a soft whoomph, and Rogers watched a black object streak across the sky. It impacted the river behind the dam a second later. The round exploded and a huge geyser of white water jetted skyward. Surprised shouts and cries came from the enemy positions. Rogers had heard enough cursing to get the general gist of what the Spanish were saying.

"They didn't expect that," he said. Moleson hurriedly adjusted his aim point and reloaded the cannon. The second round bounced when it hit the tree trunks making up the barricade and exploded harmlessly in the air.

Three soldiers popped up out of the trees across the river, firing at Moleson and the gun. He ducked behind the cannon, trying to use it as a shield. One bullet sparked off the barrel.

"*Sheet!*" he cried out. "They hit wrong and this thing's outta commission."

Several of the men making up the left flank shifted their aim and began shooting at the Spanish. One of the blue-uniformed soldiers dropped and the other two took cover behind trees. Rogers wasn't certain if the man who had fallen was wounded, dead, or just trying to get to ground. The battle was now split into two major sections, with the right flank pinning the men behind the dam and Rogers's left flank caught in a fight to protect the dynamite gun.

"Keep those bastards down," Rogers yelled. "Moleson, get out there and get that dam blown apart." He aimed at another blue uniform and fired, then ejected the casing and shot again. The flash of blue disappeared behind a thick tree trunk.

Moleson kept crouched down and worked furiously to prime and reload the gun. He ignored the splatter of mud as another bullet hit the ground to his right. He grabbed the firing cord, then ducked back around the gun. Several men, both on the far side of the river and near the dam, stepped out and fired a series of shots. Bullets impacted the trees behind him and the ground around the artillery carriage.

He pulled the cord, and the shell impacted the makeshift structure. When it struck, the round rebounded backward off the wood, leaving no mark, and detonated ineffectively. Suddenly, the dam's logs exploded outward, the force sending whole trunks flying. Moleson looked up in time to see the head of a massive snake push through the ragged gap. It was almost impossible to believe what he was seeing. Two massive horns, the color of white-water rapids, curved out from the side of the beast's head. Its body was covered in scales, a mixture of blues and greens, shifting from lightest on top to darkest along the creature's belly. He even noted a rippling pattern on the monster mimicking sunlight striking waves in a pond.

The Magüi reared up above the roiling waters, its body nearly twice as thick as the tree boles it scattered without effort. In a lightning-quick strike, the Magüi lunged forward and snatched up one of the Spanish soldiers, its wide mouth gaping open to envelop the doomed soldier. The man's scream of terror cut off abruptly when the beast's jaws closed down and swallowed him whole. Silence reigned for less than a second.

The Spanish soldiers' reaction speed impressed Rogers. Even as the Magüi turned to grab another of their companions, well-aimed rifle fire peppered the creature. *"Es la Madre de Aguas!"* he heard a soldier yell. *"Lo debemos derribar!"*

Though he spoke no Spanish, the overall meaning of what the enemy was screaming out was clear to Rogers. "Marines, aim for the head. Fire at will," he commanded. Raising his rifle he fired at the nightmare creature as fast as he could jack the bolt. The trigger clicked on an empty chamber, and he grabbed a handful of rounds from the canvas bag on his waist, rapidly feeding them into the gun's rotary magazine. Rogers assessed the situation while he mechanically performed the actions. The initial barrage of coordinated gunfire had once again changed to the uneven sounds of individual shooting. He saw a bright splash of water when Prescott's carefully aimed shot hit just behind the creature's horn. There was no other sign of the impact, no blood, or even a tremor from the beast. The Magüi seemed to ignore the gunshots. It struck again and dragged another of the Spanish soldiers into the water with its body. The blue-uniformed man had only one arm free and was ineffectually beating at the coils pinning his body. He grunted and coughed up blood as the muscles of the Magüi's massive body smoothly constricted, the sound of breaking bones plainly audible during a lull in shots. One detached part of Rogers's mind noted beads of water continuing to fall from the long body and splashing into the river, even though the creature's upper section had now been out long enough for everything to have run off already.

"I don't think this is working," Prescott commented calmly as he refilled his Krag's magazine. "We're gonna need something bigger to pierce that hide."

"Agreed," Rogers said. "On the brighter side, looks like it's focusing on the Spanish instead of us. Keep trying. I'm going to see if Moleson can't get an effective shot with the cannon." He patted Prescott on the shoulder and moved quickly back from the firing line in a crouched run.

The scrappy private barely glanced up from his shotgun when Rogers arrived. "Sarge, I don't think we's doin' much good. This critter's ignorin' every message I send his way. Kinda reminds me of that woman I tried to interest at the tavern in Baton Rouge."

"I think this one might be better looking," retorted Rogers.

Moleson grinned as he shot again. "Probably true. I 'member talkin' to her, not 'xactly what she looked like."

"Well, as far as messages go, let's send something a little more impressive. Think you can hit that thing with a shell?" Rogers tapped the wheel of the dynamite gun while he spoke.

"It's a little off. Nowhere near's good as regular cannon," Moleson temporized.

"That a yes or a no?" asked Rogers.

"It's a maybe. Can't guarantee nuthin' with it. I'll do my best though," Molson said, and slung his gun back over his shoulder. He quickly primed and loaded the dynamite gun again., slipping the explosive shell carefully into the breach and closing the door. Then he stood behind the cannon, gauging the sight picture and aim point. "Need to come a few degrees left," Moleson said.

Rogers grabbed the adjustment staff attached to the carriage tongue and pushed. The gun pivoted slowly, the locked wheels pushing up thin furrows in the black mud.

"Hold," Moleson called out and Rogers stopped pushing. "Tha's 'bout right." He stepped away from the cannon's back. Rogers covered the ear closest to the gun and leaned slightly away. Moleson did the same, giving the trigger cord a quick tug. Even this close, the cannon made less noise than Rogers expected, more of a whoosh of air than the explosive thump he'd experienced around most artillery pieces.

The shot flew true; the fins causing the round to spin in the air and stabilize the flight. When it hit the Magüi, the explosives inside the shell blew up, sending shrapnel into the air. The impact rocked the creature's head to the side and drew its attention to the cannon and the two marines standing nearby.

"That didn't have as much effect as I'd hoped," said Rogers as he unlimbered his rifle and began firing again. The rounds pinged off the hide. "Damn thing's completely bulletproof. Shoot it again."

"Down ta only two rounds left, Sarge," Moleson complained while he began the loading process.

"Grab more from the mule."

"Cain't for two reasons. One, the blamed beast done run off, and two, I already grabbed all of 'em when we set up. Two's all that's left."

Rogers cursed under his breath. "Then we'd better make the next shots count." He said the last in a higher pitch and with a little of his accent showing.

Diving to the side to avoid the beast's strike, Roger rolled in the wet mud along the river's edge, coating his uniform in the thick black muck. The creature's mouth snapped shut where his torso had been moments earlier. Coming to a stop, Roger levered himself up on one knee and drove his bayonet at the Magüi with all his strength. The heavy blade splashed water when it struck the thick scales and skittered along until it struck the left horn and bounced upward.

The massive snake jerked its head back from the attack. Crystal water flew from the creature. Its frustrated hiss sounded loud and angry. The beast coiled, drawing its body into a tight curve, and prepared to strike again. Rogers heard the loud swish of the pneumatic launcher firing. He didn't see where the round landed, only heard the dull crump of the explosion somewhere past the snake.

"Tarnation!" cried Moleson. "Didn't arm in time. He's too close ta hit effectively."

Rogers didn't say anything, he was too involved in avoiding the Magüi's bite to reply. Moleson would need to figure out what to do without his input. The creature seemed to need some distance to strike, so Rogers ran close to it, jammed his rifle under its jawline, and pulled the trigger. The resultant discharge blew the gun from his stinging hands and sent the Magüi's head snapping upward. Rogers landed on his hands and knees. He looked over and saw a trickle of blood from where the bullet had struck. Whatever damage he had done was not enough to kill the beast, though.

Several hundred pounds of monster snake slammed down, trying to catch Rogers under its body. He dove toward the jungle, getting out of the way as the creature's trunk hit the ground. The impact knocked both him and Moleson prone. Rogers heard a crack and looked back. One of the dynamite gun's trunnions had snapped off and the cannon now hung limply in the carriage, the narrow gape of its bore pointed at the edge of the river.

Moleson fired two blasts from his shotgun before the monster slid back into the water. Everything grew silent except for the moans of the wounded and the tick of cooling metal. Rogers could hardly hear his own breathing over the ringing in his ears. The air was thick with the haze of gun smoke and the acrid bite of sulfur fumes.

"Can you see it?" Rogers called out, scanning the water's rippling surface. The sun created twinkling spots of bright blinding light, making it impossible to see into the river's depths.

"Nope, cain't see anything," said Moleson, leaning over the broken gun and peering at the river.

"I'll get a bit higher," said Prescott. He slung his rifle and began climbing a tree at the edge of the jungle. Thankfully, the lowest branches were easily within reach of the big man and made for fast movement. He used one hand to shade his eyes and looked down. "River's churned up something fierce. Can't see much but muddy water."

Upriver, the few remaining Spanish soldiers slowly stepped out from cover. They pointed their guns at the water, ready to engage the creature if or when it returned. One soldier, an officer judging from the amount of gold braid flashing bright in the sun, waved a bare-bladed saber over his head.

"Truce. I suggest a truce. No fighting between us," he shouted in thickly accented English.

Rogers wasted no time and raised his hand over his head, ensuring his own marine's rifles were pointed down at the ground or river's surface. "Agreed. No fighting each other. Kill the snake."

The officer nodded and lowered his sword. He turned to his men and began speaking. Rogers could hear the words somewhat, though it was muffled by both distance and the ringing in his ears. "We're at truce with them, at least till we kill this thing," he said loudly. "Anyone found Givens yet?"

"I did Sarge," said one of the men, keeping his rifle pointed toward the river as he spoke. "He didn't make it. Bullet got him right through the heart."

"Damn. Get his body, we'll carry it back. Not until we're done here, though," he added when the private turned to go back to the body.

"Watch out," shouted Prescott, bringing his rifle to his shoulder.

The Magüi burst out of the river, its head aimed toward the Spanish side. The officer shouted orders and waved his sword while retreating from the shoreline. One soldier fired, then stepped closer and fired another well-aimed bullet. The snake didn't flinch. It bore down, causing the man to backpedal. Even as he scrambled away, the snake struck out.

A Snake in the Grass

The man didn't have time to scream before the massive jaws closed on his head. Blood spurted from the wound and the now headless body crumpled, bright red arterial spray pumping into the river. Rogers watched as the Magüi's swallowed. The horrid action gave him a flash of insight. He scrambled back to his feet and ran to Moleson, holding out a hand.

"Give me the round," Rogers shouted.

"What? The gun's broked. Cain't fire it off," he complained as he fished the last shell from the pouch at his side.

"Won't need to." Rogers stuffed the round between his belt and trousers, making sure the flight fins held it fast. He scooped up his rifle and aimed carefully. His shot struck the Magüi's horn.

Incised, the giant snake twisted around to glare balefully at him.

"Come on, you overgrown lump of salesman fodder." He fired again, this time his round hitting just over the right eye. Water splashed away at the impact.

The Magüi hissed loudly and slithered across the river, leaving a long vee wake behind itself. Rogers dropped his rifle and pulled the shell out with his left hand. He continued to shout and wave his right hand to hold the creature's attention.

"That's right. Come over here and eat me."

"Sarge, what're you doing?" cried Prescott, firing at the Magüi as rapidly as he could. The whine of ricochets sounded like angry hornets.

"Killing this thing," Rogers answered calmly, all trace of his accent once more gone.

The Magüi reared back, its mouth gaping. Rogers could see the rows of sharp thin teeth, all pointing backward, which filled the mouth and the muscles at the throat opening, already pulsing with the motion of swallowing. He stood his ground, the finned shell held tightly in his hand. As soon as the Magüi struck, Rogers shook his hand and leaped sideways. Inside the thin metal skin of the cannon round, a steel cone flew out of its nest, striking the flint igniter and raising sparks. The sparks lit the fast-acting fuse and burned upward to the nitrocellulose gelatin mixture. "Enjoy your time in Hell," Rogers said as the Magüi bit down on his left arm, severing it cleanly at the elbow. Thrown off balance by the strike, Rogers fell sideways, rolling to keep his wounded arm out of the mud. The last clear memory he had was the explosion ripping the Magüi's head apart, and the decapitated body falling back into the river, disappearing beneath the waters in a massive splash.

Rogers blinked, looking up at the clouds. He leaned back against something lumpy and felt a rope tied around his chest. Rogers raised his left arm, staring momentarily at the stump and the brown and red bandages which enclosed the end. The world swayed left and right in a rocking motion. At first, he wondered if he was on a ship or boat, then sniffed. The earthy smell of mule filled his nostrils. "See you found Bartholomew," he rasped.

The rocking stopped, and Prescott came into view. "You're awake. Wasn't certain when that'd happen."

"Yes, I am. I take it we killed it?" Rogers asked.

"Yep. That bomb did the trick. Thing's head was in about a hundred pieces when the body slipped away. Captain'll have to take our word on it, though. None of the men nor the Spanish wanted to risk trying to find the remains." Prescott shrugged. "Can't blame 'em. Who knows what else was in the waters? Besides, the Spanish and us came to an agreement. Both groups left the river and headed opposite ways after recovering bodies. Guess the fight had run out for both of us."

"That can happen," Rogers agreed. "How many?"

Prescott frowned. "Five total, so a good portion of our number. Only one to the beast, rest during the firefight. Got them draped and tied on the cannon."

"Brought that back too?"

"Moleson argued we couldn't just leave it there for the Spanish to get. Plus, he figured someone in the Army could figure out who took it. This way, he thinks we might get it back and blame the damage on the Spanish." Prescott grinned. "He's gonna make a fine officer someday with the way he thinks."

Rogers laughed, coughed, and winced. "The cost was higher than I'd like."

"Cost of war always is. My granddads fought in the War Between the States, on opposite sides even. I remember one of them saying he wished someone else could have figured out a better way to do things." Prescott shrugged. "Sometimes there ain't."

"No, there isn't," agreed Rogers. "Sometimes the only thing to do is kill the snake in the grass, no matter what the consequences are."

Call Sign Doc
By: Magda Jones

"*Dumkopf!*" I shouted. "That nachtkrapp's beak will snip that finger off if you don't get it out of that cage."

The offending guard shifted his grip on the cage as his companion waited. They cautiously turned towards the lab door. The cool air of an April morning breezed in as another guard held the door open for them. They trudged the laden cage to the truck waiting just outside.

The evacuation to Mauthausen due to encroaching Allied forces had everyone on edge. Guards snapped at the Jewish prisoners, who were packing the lab equipment. The specimens paced in their enclosures. The Nazi scientist, Herr Muller, gathered the recorded data and left, entrusting me, a mere kapo prisoner, to coordinate the move of the lab. It was a responsibility I didn't want in a job I never asked for.

I looked around the room, mentally checking off the last specimen to be transported. The kobold cage required three or four strong men to carry. The bars had to be extra thick to keep the beast's claws from tearing them apart. Although the kobold was snoozing soundly, it would still be difficult to get it on the truck.

Four nachzehrer guards stopped in front of me, awaiting direction. Their heinous deaths in the Dachau concentration camp had transformed them into mindless ghouls. Ironically, they were now loyal servants to their former tormentors. I directed them to carry the kobold cage to the idling Opel Blitz. The stout vehicle should be able to get the entire load safely to Mauthausen. Each guard grabbed a corner of the cage and schlepped it out the door. With one last glance around the now bare tables, I followed. With surprising precision, they hefted the mass carefully onto the truck bed. I climbed in behind it. Two of them secured the cage, while the other two closed the tailgate and tarp. When they finished, we were off.

Five hours later, the German scientist complained about how long it had taken us to get to Mauthausen. "Mayr, you should have been here two hours ago."

"The heavy load on the truck and the hilly terrain reduced our speed. When we arrived at the camp, the gate guards did not know we were arriving and wouldn't let us in. It took them several minutes of frantic discussion to figure out where we should be and then several more to give us directions to the farmhouse," I explained.

"Pitiful excuses." He slapped me across the face, knocking me to the ground. "Now get the lab set up. We need to resume our experiments as quickly as possible."

We immediately began unloading the cargo, starting with the kobold cage. The nachzehrers simply lifted the cage and carried it to the first floor of the abandoned home we were housed in. The lab would occupy the open space on the lower level while the scientist would reside upstairs. They allotted me a cot in the corner of the lab.

Several Jewish prisoners arrived to help unload. They were so frail that it took them twice as long to hobble back and forth. My undead guards continued to help, making the unloading go faster. By the time the sun set, I was feeding the creatures and contemplating the new lab arrangement. I pushed one end of the rectangular table to the wall by the cabinets to provide more walking space. Shortly after, I collapsed on my cot and passed out.

The next morning, Herr Muller conducted an inventory to make sure all the experiments arrived unscathed. Three gruesome elven creatures called alps hissed as we passed their cages. They had learned not to like people in the Nazi uniform. Two raven nachtkrapp flapped their wings as much as the cage would allow and backed away from the scientist. The kobold flinched when Herr Muller prodded it. It opened its black eyes, hissed weakly, and slowly rolled its lanky brown striped body over.

"What is wrong with this creature, Mayr?" he asked.

"I had to sedate it, so the cage could be transported. It should recover over the course of the day." I replied.

"That will delay our findings. Herr Bauer will be furious."

"If I had left it untreated, it would have attacked the guards as they carried the crate. It would have taken even longer to get it here."

"Well, rouse it with another drug and proceed with the scheduled experiments. We must get our results as quickly as possible." Herr Muller turned on his heel and strode out of the room.

After giving the kobold a stimulant, I checked the daily schedule and gathered the necessary tools. There were multiple tests required for the day. None of the beasts cooperated, but could not get far enough away to escape, either. Their squawks and chitters seemed to repeat the same phrase. I am trapped.

So am I. I thought. *So am I.*

Two days passed and the lab work fell back into its normal pattern. Though the creatures didn't like being poked and prodded, they responded more favorably when I spoke to them kindly and fed them well. As I sat rewriting my notes for the day, I noticed a shadow wiggling in the corner created by the table and the kitchen cabinet I had tucked it next to. A young man peered up at me from the dark shadows. Startled, I pushed my chair back.

"Sprichst du Englisch?' he whispered. *'Parles-tu Anglais?"*

"Yes, I speak English, French, and German. And a few more as well. Stop kibitzing and pick a language."

The man blinked up at me, stunned by my stern words.

"Who are you, and how did you get in here?" I tried again.

"Private First Class Smith, but most people call me Hollywood. I snuck in here to hide while you were feeding the gremlin."

"The what?"

"The gremlin over in the far corner."

"You mean the *kobold*?"

"I've never heard it called that before, sir. Madame Chevrolet called them *Pouques*. My crew and I thought gremlin was easier."

Though the guards were used to me talking to myself while compiling notes, talking to the floor might seem suspicious. I looked around the dim room and out the uncovered windows. The night guards were circling a nearby tree, searching the ground beneath it. The younger guard started towards the house.

I rubbed my forehead as if in thought while I asked, "Did you hide under the tree, Herr Smith?"

"Yes, sir. How did you know?"

"The guards must have found a trace you left behind. One is coming this way. Stay hidden. I will get rid of him." I pulled back up to the table and continued my notes.

The guard walked in. "Have you seen anyone about tonight?"

I finished a word and glanced up at the guard. "No, I have been recording my findings for the day. Is something wrong?" I replied quietly.

"There's evidence of someone hiding behind the tree in the side yard. I need to search the lab."

"Was your mother a demented ostrich?" I whispered fiercely as I stood. "If someone was in here besides me, the animals would be making noise. Do you really want to bumble around down here searching for a shadow and wake the officer sleeping upstairs? Herr Muller will tear you apart faster than that kobold in the corner." I pointed my pencil at the cage for emphasis and glared at him until he backed away, looking down. "Now get back to your duties and leave me in peace."

As he left the building, I rearranged my chair and returned to my notes. He peaked in each window, searching all he could see, then stalked off. He and the second guard spoke for a minute and headed off in opposite directions. When they were out of sight, I spoke to Herr Smith again.

"He's gone."

"Thank goodness. It's cramped down here."

"You should stay down there for now, in case they come back."

"Good idea. Thanks, Mr.…uh… You didn't tell me your name."

"It's Mayr, Herbert Mayr." I paused. "How did you know it was safe to speak to me? That I wouldn't turn you in?"

"Considering how you spoke to the creatures and how they reacted to you, I guessed you would be sympathetic. I guessed right."

"How do you know about the kobolds?" I asked.

"My squad eliminated a nest of them near Cristot, France. Nasty little creatures were holed up in a cave. It took us a whole lot of firepower to knock them down."

"That sounds right. The one in that cage was the sole survivor of a nest near Dora-Mittelbau. They were wreaking havoc in an underground bomb facility. It was exhausted when I got there. I sedated it with metal scraps dipped in chloroform."

Herr Smith squirmed for a minute, rearranging his limbs. "What are the other creatures called?"

I stood and walked to the far end of the room, peering into the kobold cage. Herr Smith crept to the end of the table, watching my progress through the room. I continued my round, stopped at the nachtkrapp cage, and half turned towards my makeshift desk. As I spoke to Herr Smith, it appeared I was speaking to the raven-like creatures.

"These are nachtkrapp. I retrieved them from Natzweiler-Struthof in 1942. The beasts are normally nocturnal, but the Jewish miners were such easy pickings that the nachtkrapp started swooping in and picking them out of the lines marching back to camp at dusk. The guards knocked these two out and took them back to camp as trophies. I was sent to collect them after the birds destroyed their quarters. It was an *interesting* introduction to the supernatural."

I continued my rounds to the three smaller cages lined up on the kitchen counter. Their inhabitants were balled up tightly to conserve warmth. "These demons are called alps."

"Demons?" Herr Smith gulped.

"Not really," I replied. "They are more like your elf. They give their victims nightmares that cause sleep paralysis. While the sleeper is immobilized, the alps suck their blood. These creatures got spoiled, sucking blood out of the full breasts of new mothers raped by the guards in Ravensbrueck. The breast milk added a flavor they preferred. When the forced sterilizations reduced their food source, the alps started attacking the guards. These three were captured, and I brought them to Dachau."

I finished my survey of the room and returned to my chair. Picking up my pencil, I broached the real subject. "I doubt you came for mythology lessons, Herr Smith. Why are you here?"

"I am scouting for the US forces, trying to gather intel on Mauthausen. I followed the trail from Dachau. I saw your light outside the camp proper and came to see what was over here."

"US forces? Are you coming to free the prisoners?"

"That's the general idea."

I paused for a moment, considering my options. "If I help you, could you get me to America? I have a cousin there. The rest of my family is gone, thanks to the lousy Germans."

"We would certainly try. Why are you helping the Germans if you dislike them so much?"

"I had no choice. I used to work with my cousin as a research assistant. When he took a job in New York, I had to stay behind. My family needed me to support them. I worked for Fritz Dressel until the Reichstag fire. The Nazis took me to Dachau shortly after. One of the scientists there recognized me and pulled me into the lab. It was work for him or die."

Herr Smith rubbed a hand down his face. "That's a rough position to be in. Let's work on getting you out of it. Tell me everything you can about the camp."

For the next few hours, I told Herr Smith everything I could remember about Mauthausen as I finished my notes. I frequently worked late into the night, so it did not surprise the guards to see me awake. I told him about the daily routine and what times things occurred, like meals, guard shift changes, and lights out. He took copious notes in a pocket notebook. As my throat got hoarse, I remembered the nachzehrers.

"There's one more thing, Herr Smith. Four of Herr Muller's guards are nachzehrers."

"What's a nachzehrer?" he asked.

"Nachzehrers are the revived corpses of people who died under terrible circumstances. They are stronger than normal humans, especially after they eat."

"What do they eat?"

"People."

"Well damn. They must be feasting on the gas chamber victims."

"It *is* a convenient arrangement for the Nazis. The plentiful food also keeps them loyal."

He shook briefly, as if he felt a chill. "How will we know which ones are Nachzehrer?"

"They can't die by normal means. You must put a coin in their mouths to paralyze them and sever their heads."

"Ain't that swell," he sighed. "LT's gonna love that. Speaking of LT, I am going to have to report back soon. Is it safe for me to come out?"

I got up and strolled around the room, looking at the animals and checking out the windows. When I returned to the worktable, I saw his boots sticking out. "It's safe, but you can't linger too long."

Herr Smith crawled out from under the table and stretched his limbs. He held out his hand. "Thank you, sir, for all the information. Expect us soon."

I shook his hand as I replied. "I'm looking forward to it."

The end of April 1945 was a season of killing. Multitudes of prisoners arrived daily, evacuated from other camps as the US military approached. The gas chamber was filled and emptied as quickly as possible to reduce the population and relieve the overcrowding. It didn't help. Typhus and starvation killed more prisoners than the Nazis.

On one hand, I was elated at the possibility of freedom. On the other, appalled at the devaluation of human life. Reality was more brutal than any nightmare the alps could conjure. I hoped to see Herr Smith again soon. I knew his return would herald our pending freedom.

In early May, Herr Muller left for a meeting with Colonel Ziereis. He never returned to the lab. Considering Ziereis' reputation as a temperamental hitsiger, I assumed Herr Muller dead. His guards disappeared, with the exception of the nachzehrers. They remained, guarding the lab. The fenced portion of the camp grew quiet. Soon, a group of Viennese men showed up around the perimeter of the camp. That evening, Herr Smith snuck up to the back door.

"Mr. Mayr, is it safe to come in?" he murmured.

"Yes, but stay hidden. The Nazis may have left, but nachzehrer guards are still on patrol."

Herr Smith slipped through the door and hid back under the table. "Can we take them out after the caged creatures?"

"Their last orders were to protect the lab. They would prevent anyone, including me, from destroying the beasts."

"That's bad news. Do you know where they are?"

"Two of them are upstairs. The other two are making their rounds outside."

"Good, we will get the two outside first."

"We? Are the Allies nearby?"

"My allies are. I brought a couple of buddies to help me out." He crept back to the door and replied over his shoulder. "I'll introduce you when we come for the others." He checked both directions before heading for the woods behind the lab.

Shortly after he disappeared, one of the nachzehrers walked around the corner. He headed for the woods, aiming for the spot Herr Smith faded into. I hoped Smith remembered about the coins. If not, he and his friends are going to have a tough time of it. Shortly after the guard disappeared into the woods, I heard scuffling and muffled curses in the trees. It drew the attention of the second guard making rounds. He trotted from the opposite side of the lab and vanished into the woods. This time, the commotion drew the attention of the guards upstairs. As they descended, I ran to the bottom of the stairs.

"What is going on outside?" I asked as I stood on the bottom step. "Did you see who is causing that racket?" I rocked back and forth, trying to look nervous while blocking their path.

The first guard grumbled and pushed past me. He headed for the door. I grabbed the arm of the second guard and bombarded him with questions. "Where are the Nazi soldiers? Why don't they handle this problem? Do I need to hide? What should I do with the experiments?" My goal was to delay the second guard long enough to give Herr Smith and his colleagues time to dispatch the first one. I backed slowly towards the door, still spouting questions. "How will I protect myself and the lab if you leave?"

The ruckus outside grew to shouts as the second guard shook off my grasp. He grunted and pointed to the cages before he charged out the door.

"Wait! What do you mean?" I yelled after him, trying to warn Herr Smith that he had another adversary coming.

While they were handling the guards, I started assembling the data about the creatures. I collected every notebook I had written in. Then I went upstairs to see if Herr Muller had left anything behind. I found a few files in a cabinet, some photographs in a drawer, and a briefcase under the bed. I gathered all I could find, tucked it into the case, and went downstairs to add the rest of my data.

As I squeezed the notebooks into the briefcase, Herr Smith and his associates came in. One gentleman, who he called Herr Grabowski, wore a similar uniform and sounded American as well. The other, a stocky red-haired man with a bowler hat, carried one of the nachzehrer's heads.

"Alright, Gerry boy," he called in an Irish brogue, "give me back my challenge coin." He set the head on the table and started prying at the jaws with his pocketknife. After several minutes of curses and fumbling, the coin finally came loose. It had distinct teeth marks in the surface. "Now there's no wondering which one is mine," he crowed.

"O'Brian, you are one crazy SOB." Herr Smith shook his head and turned to me. "How long will it take you to be ready to leave, Mr. Mayr? LT wants us to destroy all the evidence of this lab and bring you back to him."

"I don't have much for personal belongings, just the clothes on my back. I can leave whenever you are ready." I pointed to the briefcase on the table. "I have all the data I have collected on the creatures packed into that case. I would prefer to take it with us. It could be useful in the future."

"Fair point," he replied. "Alright, O'Brian, time to torch this place."

Herr O'Brian giggled manically. "About bloody time I got to burn something."

"Wait," I interjected, "there are a few things we should do first."

"Like what?" he scowled.

"Well we should bring the nachzehrers bodies in here to burn with the rest of the creatures. You wouldn't want anyone to find them. I would also like to sedate the animals."

"Why in the world would you want to do that?"

"It's more humane." I countered. "And I won't allow you to burn this place until I can."

Herr Grabowski chimed in. "He's right. You wouldn't want to be trapped in a cage and burned to death, would you, O'Brian?"

"I don't know," he argued, "I've never tried it."

"Well, I doubt you would," Herr Grabowski replied. "You can help Hollywood and I bring back the bodies while Doc handles the animals."

"Doc?" I asked.

"You remind me of the old guy at the factory that would doctor people when they got banged up. We called him Doc." He pulled Herr O'Brian out the door, following Herr Smith who was heading for the woods. "You do your *doctoring* while we do the grunt work."

I gathered the supplies to sedate the creatures. I disliked that the beings had to be destroyed, but I understood the need to keep them secret. I had seen an astounding variety of reactions from prisoners sent to help me in the lab. Most people could not handle the knowledge that such creatures exist. I gave the creatures treats as I said my goodbyes and put them to sleep. The alps and nachtkrapps settled quickly. I pocketed a feather from the nachtkrapp cage. But the kobold fought the drug. It took several minutes before the solution finally took effect.

As I was finishing up, the gentlemen returned with bodies in tow. Herr Smith and Herr Grabowski went back out to gather the remaining bits, while Herr O'Brian prepped the lab for burning. He muttered to himself while he piled everything flammable near the kobold cage. Then he tromped up the stairs and returned with an oil lamp and bedding. I helped him position the lighter cages around the kobold cage. He wrapped the bedding around the cages and stuffed pages torn from the few abandoned books into every available crevice. Upon their return, Herr Smith and Herr Grabowski heaved the bodies onto the stack. Herr Grabowski broke the table and chairs, tossing them on for good measure.

"Alright, laddies. You head out while I light this thing," Herr O'Brian told us as he carefully drizzled the lamp oil onto the pile.

Herr Smith grabbed the briefcase full of notes as Herr Grabowski started out of the door. I followed them to the yard. Herr O'Brian backed out the door, lighting the wick on the lamp. He tossed it into the lab and chuckled.

Fire bloomed in the far end of the kitchen and grew rapidly as it reached the oil-soaked pile. The ceiling lit, then the second floor brightened. Soon, the entire building was engulfed in flames. Herr O'Brian danced merrily towards us, giggling as he approached. Herr Smith shook his head again and barked out orders as we started walking. "You take point, Ski. Doc and I will follow. O'Brian, you cover the rear."

Fire and Ice

By: William Joseph Roberts

It was only September, and we'd already seen our fair share of action after arriving in Europe. Since the invasion of Normandy, the regular Army had been pushing eastward into France against the Nazi forces. While they handled the war, we'd been dealing with everything from gremlins to harpies to massive bridge trolls.

Never in my wildest dreams did I ever expect to be issued orders to hunt dragons, let alone hunting dragons on the Soviet eastern front. The worst part was that even if we could talk to anyone in the regular army about any of this, they'd look at us like we were insane.

Maybe we were. Everyone in the unit seemed to thrive on the strange and weird. But that was just another normal day as part of Task Force Thirteen, I suppose.

We'd been loaned out to the Red Army and Mother Russia because they'd had full units mysteriously disappear in their push into Czechoslovakia and the Carpathian Mountains.

Lieutenant Rustay had assigned us the designation of *Whiskey Mike Bravo*, or the Widowmakers B-team since he and the rest of the Widowmakers unit were on special assignment behind enemy lines. Since *Jumpin' Jess*, our P-61 Black Widow pursuit craft was down, waiting on parts for repairs, the LT had requisitioned the use of one of the Army's newest A-26Bs straight from the factory back in the states. Hell, she still had that new-plane smell to her. With only thirty-six hours on her airframe, they'd barely even broken her in.

She wasn't near as pretty as *Jess*, in my opinion, but she'd sure do in a pinch. Equipped with six .50 caliber M2 machine guns and two 20mm auto-cannons in her nose, as well as two M2's in the remote-controlled dorsal and ventral turrets and a bomb bay loaded to the brim, we set out to upgrade her to the Widowmakers standard.

In under twenty-four hours, we had her equipped with two new five-round rocket racks under each wing, four new blister pack gun pods on the fuselage, as well as two gun pods on each wing at the outer positions, adding a total of sixteen extra M2 machine guns to the inventory.

Warrant Officer James Pierce, our lead aviator, was worried that she'd steer like a dead cow *if* we could even get her off the ground.

I wasn't too worried about the weight. She wasn't near as heavy as *Jumpin' Jess,* and she was equipped with the same Pratt and Whitney R-2800 Double Wasp radial engines.

Fully fueled, we stowed our personal gear and loaded up. Private First-Class Kenny Doyle manned the gunner's position in the rear, while I strapped into the copilot's seat beside Pierce in the cockpit.

We'd traveled for days, taking the long way around. Crossing the Mediterranean we stopped for fuel in Turkey before heading north across the Black Sea to Crimea and Soviet territory.

Shortly after arriving, the call came in from the front that a column of Soviet T-34 main battle tanks had encountered a small German convoy and went in pursuit of what they thought was an easy target.

To us, it just sounded like a whole lot of crazy talk, but none of us spoke the first bit of Russian. Per our liaison and translator, Major Artyom Popov, the sporadic radio contact afterward mentioned a freak blizzard and what sounded like *great wyrm* to him.

Word of the new encounter spread like wildfire across the small forward operating base and in minutes, most of the personnel had gathered outside of the radio tent. A heated argument started between the men, and Major Popov explained the debate. Some thought it was Chudo-Yudo from Slavic mythology, returned because of the noise of the war, while others claimed it was Yilbegän, a multi-headed man-eating monster to the Siberian Tartars.

Regardless, we launched as a five-ship flight with four of the Soviet squadron's American-built Douglas A-20G medium attack bombers, which were the predecessor airframe to the A-26B that we were in.

Nearing the last reported coordinates, Major Popov ordered that we take up a high-altitude position to observe and advise only. It was apparently a point of pride with the crews, especially if the threat turned out to be of German origins.

"Copy that, Major," Pierce responded into the mic set. "Taking up overwatch position. Good hunting, Major."

I watched the snowy Carpathian landscape slowly pass by below as the Major responded with something in Russian that I didn't understand. Pierce broke away from the flight and banked east, angling our nose to climb. We reached the heavy gray clouds of the low-flight ceiling in what seemed like no time at all.

Nearing the mountains on the eastern side of the valley, we banked north along the deep river valley, lazily following behind the four Soviet attack bombers.

"That doesn't bode well," Pierce said.

"What?"

Pierce pointed at a storm forming in the distance ahead of the Soviet aircraft.

"When was the last time you saw snow like that, Sullivan?"

"Never," I responded.

"Not like we'll be able to do much if that gets any thicker."

"Hey, Doyle," I said into the intercom.

"Yeah, Sarge?"

"The snow's getting heavy up here. How's your visibility through the turret scopes?" The hydraulic motors of the A-26's remote-controlled gun turrets hummed.

"Seems fine so far," Doyle responded. "As long as I don't let the snow build up on the lens, we should be golden."

Broken Russian radio chatter erupted. The plane shook. A sudden frigid gust rocked us, and we dropped like a rock.

"What the hell did we just hit?" Doyle shouted.

Pierce pulled back on the steering yoke and replied through gritted teeth. "I don't know! Hang on!"

I grabbed the copilot's yoke and assisted. Crosswinds buffeted us, gusting from multiple directions. The tail of the aircraft suddenly slid out from under us. A sheer crosswind struck, sending us spiraling earthward.

"We've got to get out of this chop!" I shouted.

Pierce rolled the wheel left and kicked the right rudder pedal to the stop before rolling right and pulling back hard on the yoke once again. "You think I don't know that?"

The blinding flash of a fiery explosion to our right drew our attention.

"The hell was that?"

"I don't know, but that'll be us if we don't get into some clean air," Pierce said. The airframe shuddered as if on cue. Pierce pushed the throttles to the forward stop and banked us hard to the west; the overpowered Double Wasp radial engines sloughed us out of the turbulence-induced tumble. We leveled out roughly five hundred feet lower than we originally were.

Flashes off to our right caught my attention. Small arms fire mixed with an exchange of tank fire signaled the position of the ground forces through the flying snow. Just above their position, three of the four Soviet aircraft struggled against the buffeting storm.

"There's three of the Soviet birds," I reported, pointing toward the friendly aircraft.

Tracer rounds lit up the sky, peppering the Soviet flight. More than a dozen ruined tanks from both sides burned. The Soviets banked and dove, escaping the fully automatic fire.

Pierce nosed us up, rolled to the right, and dove before pulling a slow barrel roll left, getting us well clear of the tracer fire.

Another arctic blast of wind and snow drove into us, slamming both Pierce and me forward against our shoulder harnesses. The hum of the engines increased to the point that I thought they were going to fly apart.

Pierce laughed. "I think I'd rather take on a dragon than deal with this storm for much longer. There's too much turbulence."

I grunted a laugh. "What if we…" That's when something that sounded like the winds of Niflheim escaping into this realm screamed, the sound echoing across the Carpathian valley.

I looked over at Pierce and punched him in the shoulder. "You had to say something, didn't you?"

"How the hell did I know it was real?"

The three Soviet A-20 Havocs unleashed a firestorm of rounds further up the valley from us.

With another roaring scream, the icy blue head of a massive serpent appeared from the snowstorm at the far end of the valley.

Heavy turbulence struck us, and we suddenly dropped, losing lift. Icy blue wings emerged from the storm to either side of the massive head. It flapped and drove another frigid gust in our direction.

Pierce cut the throttle on the number one engine to idle and kicked the rudders hard to the right, spinning us free of the fall. Going back to full throttle, he nosed her up to climb out of the chop. The beast spanned the width of the valley where it choked down to a narrow canyon. With opalescent colored claws, it clung to the stony granite cliffs on either side. It roared, blasting the ground forces with another swath of arctic wind.

The line of Havocs strafed the line of German armor, dropping a string of bombs onto the German lines before turning their guns to the massive ice dragon.

The beast roared again, aiming its breath weapon at the Soviet aircraft furthest to its left. Covered in a heavy layer of ice, it tumbled and fell from the sky.

"Come on! Pull out of it," Pierce shouted.

"I don't see any parachutes," I reported.

But I knew it was already too late for that. They were too late for anyone to survive the drop, even if they did manage to bail out. The Soviet Havoc exploded on impact.

Doubtful that anyone survived, as the aircraft exploded on impact and seemed to all but disintegrate. The two remaining Havocs pulled up and banked hard to escape the dragon's breath weapon.

"What the hell is going on up there?" Doyle asked.

"The Soviets were right," I said. "It's an ice dragon."

"What?"

Pierce banked left, beginning a circular pattern of the area.

"Ho-ly shit," Doyle said over the coms.

"Yeah…" Pierce gasped. "So, what do we do?"

I laughed and looked over at Pierce. "You expect me to know? I don't have the faintest clue. Hey Doyle."

"Yeah, Sarge?"

"Do you know how to kill a dragon?"

"No?" Doyle replied.

Pierce let out a long sigh and shook his head with a smile. "Situation Normal, All Fucked Up."

"Just another day for the Widowmakers," I said with an agreeing nod.

The two remaining Soviet aircraft strafed the German armor lines once more, staying clear of the dragon's breath weapon. It looked like it wanted to leap away from its perch and give chase to the A-20s, like a hawk tracking a pigeon.

"Did any of the Soviet rounds hit the thing?" I asked.

"I don't know," Pierce answered. "I really couldn't tell." He keyed the radio on the Soviet frequency. "Apensky one one nine, Widowmakers Bravo. Did your rounds have any effect, Major?"

"Nyet, comrade," Major Popov replied. "We did not get close enough."

"Can you *get* close enough to try?"

There was a long moment of silence, followed by a reluctant sigh. "We do not feel that our training is adequate to handle this threat, comrade. You are the experts in this sort of situation. We will deal with the German tanks while you deal with the beast. Popov out."

"Oh, hell…" I wiped my face in frustration. "Well, that's just great."

"What?" Doyle asked.

"The situation just shifted," Pierce said. "We've gone from SNAFU'd to fucked up beyond all recognition."

"How the hell do we take down a dragon?" Pierce asked me.

"Overwhelming force?" I questioned.

"Do you really think we can do any damage to that thing?" Doyle asked. "It's huge!"

"We won't know until we try," I said, then thought for a long minute. "The fifties might do something if we're close enough. The twenty-millimeter auto-cannons will most likely do some damage since they're loaded with armor-piercing rounds. I'm not really sure what the rockets will do besides piss it off."

"At least they explode," Pierce interrupted.

I nodded in agreement, then continued. "The five-hundred-pounders would probably be our best bet if we can get close enough to hit it. We need to unload everything we've got on that thing on our first pass. Think we can get your buddy Popov to distract the dragon?" I asked Pierce.

He shrugged. "I doubt it, but it sure won't hurt to ask." He keyed the mic once more. "Apensky one one nine, Widowmakers Bravo."

"We are currently occupied, Warrant Officer," Major Popov growled. "Make this quick."

"Can you distract the dragon while we make our approach?"

"Da," was the only thing he replied before the remaining A-20's banked north in the dragon's direction, and the line of Soviet armor concentrated their fire on the snowy beast.

Pierce pushed our throttles to full power and nosed high to gain altitude, veering left toward the western side of the valley. The Soviet line continued their barrage as the A-20's fired a salvo of rockets at the beast on their pass.

Closing the distance, Pierce fired our rockets. The beast let out another bone-chilling roar as a cluster of rockets struck the beast square in the chest. Frigid wind blasted the Soviet aircraft, covering its wings and fuselage in a heavy coating of ice, and it dropped like a rock.

"The crazy Russkies might have just given us the chance we needed," I said, then flipped the switch to open the bomb bay doors and arm the payload.

"No kidding," Pierce replied. "Let's just do our best to not become ice cubes like those poor bastards."

Pierce fired the remainder of our rockets and unleashed hellfire on the creature. Our entire forward-facing arsenal of .50 caliber and 20mm cannons fired, raining hell down onto the dragon. Doyle added fire from the upper and lower .50 caliber turrets to the onslaught as I adjusted the bombsight.

We were so close to the thing that I could see the star-shaped pupils of its eyes when I looked up from the Norden bombsight. The plane jumped suddenly in altitude when I released the six, five-hundred-pound incendiary bombs from our payload onto the beast.

We were flying so low at the point of impact, that the conflagration left in our wake rocked the aircraft to the point that I thought we'd taken damage. What I thought was the sound of tearing sheet metal turned out to be the shrieks of the beast.

"Are you guys trying to get us killed?" Doyle screamed over the comms.

"No, *Private*, we aren't," Pierce answered.

"Well, I saw the thing's teeth from back here. And looking down the throat of an honest-to-God dragon was not on my list of things to do today."

Pierce banked us in a long, turning arc that would roughly bring us back around to where we started our attack run.

The thing had lost its grip on the rocky cliffs and fell from its perch. It lay limp on the roadway that coursed through the valley, covered in stone and rubble.

I could barely contain my excitement and belted out a full bore, *"Yee Hawww!"*

"Shit!" Doyle shouted. "No! Go, go, go, go, go!" I heard the dragon's roar before I could turn back to look at it.

Pierce rose up in his seat to see over me, then settled back in and nosed us over into a dive.

"It's in the air and heading right for us!"

"We know, Doyle. We have eyes too," I said.

The radios crackled with static, then keyed. "Comrades! You have the beast on your rear!"

"Tell us something we don't know, Major," Pierce replied.

"It… is… on… top… of… us! Doyle shouted between hyperventilating gasps. Horror lacing every word. "Do something! Please!" he begged.

"Hang on," Pierce said.

"Doyle," I shouted. "You have control of the turrets. Keep that thing busy."

Pierce pulled the nose up, rolling right and banking hard before rolling left and pulling enough Gs in the opposite direction that my vision blurred, tunnel visioning down to nearly pinpoints.

Major Popov's voice crackled over the radios again. "We have disabled the German armor, gentlemen. Can we be of assistance to you?"

"Yes!" screamed Doyle! "For all that is holy in this world, *yes*! We want assistance! Tell him we want assistance!"

Both dorsal turrets opened fire. Flashes of tracers reflecting in the side mirror drew my attention. The reflection of the massive wingspan grew larger by the second amid the string of tracer fire.

"Yeah… we might could use a hand." I said.

"Copy that," Pierce said. "We'll take any assistance that you can provide, Major."

Pierce rolled and dove, turning back on our original course, then banked, bringing us around in a wide arc. The dragon continued on course over us. Major Popov and his remaining A-20's came in high, strafing across the dragon's back. Holes and tears formed in the dragon's leathery wing membrane.

The beast rolled, dropping clear of the gunfire, then spread its wings and began flapping hard, coming in behind the Soviet A-20. It let out another echoing scream, sharply banking with the Soviet aircraft as they turned.

Our turrets continued firing, the tracer fire tracking along with the beast as we banked opposite of it and the Soviet aircraft.

One snapping bite and the ball turret on the backbone of the Soviet A-20 came away, breaking the backbone of the aircraft. Radio frequencies filled with Soviet screams and swearing. The tail section of the aircraft broke away, sending the crew tumbling earthward in two pieces.

Pierce banked and got us into position for another run. Leveling out, he nosed over and opened fire with everything we had, strafing the dragon across the length of its neck as we banked, rolled, and dove away, heading back toward the Soviet lines.

"It's turning!" Doyle reported before both turrets opened fire once again.

I looked back as we banked once more. The beast seemed to recoil in pain from rounds striking it in the mouth.

"Go easy, Private," I shouted over the comms. "You'll run out of ammo or melt the guns if you don't slow down."

The turrets suddenly went silent.

"Holy shit!" Doyle shouted. "No! No! No! Dammit! I'm out, Sarge! I'm out of ammo!"

I looked over to Pierce. "Think we can outrun it?"

"No clue," Pierce said, shrugging. He pushed the throttles to the forward stop. "Only one way to find out."

"It's gaining on us!" Doyle reported. "Twelve O'clock high!"

I glanced back through the canopy just as it folded in its wings and dove for us.

The plane pitched forward suddenly as the world around us became a snowy blizzard that engulfed us. Frost formed at the edges of the cockpit glass and grew rapidly, blocking out almost all visibility.

"We're losing altitude," Pierce shouted just as engine number two came to a screeching halt and engine number one exploded.

"Mayday! Mayday!" Pierce shouted into the radio. "Widowmaker Bravo going down! I repeat! Widowmaker Bravo going down!"

Pierce fought against the frozen controls. "Hang onto something, boys and girls, this is going to be a bumpy landing."

There was no time to bail out; we were too low and going entirely too fast. Luckily, we were low enough that we didn't have a whole hell of a lot of distance to drop, which meant our glide path looked much better than an overweight boulder dropped from ten thousand feet.

I braced myself, seeing the ground rushing up to meet us as Pierce angled our descent for a mostly open field.

We slammed hard into the frozen earth and skidded across the snow-covered field. Pierce pulled back on the control yoke in a futile attempt to steer our out-of-control skid. We bounced, listing to the left and the wing tip caught. It dug into the snow and soil. Crumpling, the left wing ripped away at the engine nacelle and sent us spinning into a tail-first slide.

We suddenly veered right and came to a stop near a small stand of trees dividing two large open fields. When I tried to open the canopy, it wouldn't budge. That last blast of the dragon's icy breath had apparently coated the outside of our A-26 invader with a heavy layer of ice, essentially turning us into a flying ice cube.

Other than a little shaken, I was alright. Pierce must have banged his head against the canopy frame during the crash; I could see a small trickle of blood on the left side of his head when he turned to look at me.

While Pierce went through his safety procedures, I pounded my fist against the canopy frame. Standing in the copilot's seat, I braced my back against the canopy and stood, forcing the ice to break away and the canopy to open.

Climbing down, I rushed to the rear, where I found the gunner's compartment door in a similar condition. Using a broken wing spar I'd found lying nearby, I chipped away the ice and freed Doyle from his icy prison.

When I opened the door, I found Doyle slumped over, still strapped in his seat and unconscious.

"Doyle! Hey Doyle! Wake up," I shouted while lightly nudging him. The dragon roared and Doyle suddenly sprung to life, unstrapping himself.

"We gotta go! We gotta get out of here!"

"We can't just run, Doyle," I said, placing a calming hand on his shoulder. "We have to get rid of that thing so our Soviet friends can do their part to get rid of Nazis."

"What the hell are we going to do, Sarge?"

"We join up with the Soviet ground forces and tell them to shoot everything they have down the thing's throat."

Pierce appeared about the time that Doyle finally climbed out of the gunner's compartment and handed me my survival pack from the cockpit. Real quick, I checked my gear, slung my pack, and regardless of how much good it would do against a dragon, I reassured myself that my revolver was fully loaded.

The dragon raced by overhead at treetop level. Its roar echoed across the cold mountain valley.

We could hear the raucous of small arms fire combined with the deafening blasts of Soviet armor.

"Let's get to the Soviets before that thing decides to stop for snacks," Pierce said, then turned, heading in the direction of the gunfire.

We hoofed it across the snowy fields, hiding behind anything we could anytime the beast came near. After what seemed like an eternity, we arrived at the Soviet forces, who were quickly running low on ammunition and patience. None of them paid us any mind as we ran up behind their lines.

A number of the Soviet tanks had been disabled, covered in a thick layer of ice from the dragon's breath weapon.

The beast swooped low, coating yet another tank with an arctic blast of breath before dropping to the ground and gulping one Soviet soldier down whole. Soldiers immediately broke and ran, deserting their posts at the sight of one of their own being devoured.

I spotted a Soviet officer yelling into a microphone attached to another young Soviet soldier that carried a portable radio unit on his back.

Even though we approached with our hands and weapons up and in plain sight, the officer had spotted us and drew his sidearm. He holstered his weapon once he realized we were the Americans sent to aid them.

We must have pissed off Lady Luck before this mission because neither the officer nor the radio man spoke a lick of English. Pierce tried everything he could think of to pass along the message that the beast was tender in its mouth, but nothing seemed to work.

In a momentary lapse of either brilliance or insanity, I drew my revolver and pointed to it, then to the commander's pistol, the soldier's rifle, and then to a nearby tank before pointing at the dragon and then aiming my revolver into my opened mouth and pantomiming firing the weapon.

Even though Doyle and Pierce froze with looks of absolute horror plastered across their faces, the Soviet officer comprehended what I was trying to convey. Just as he started yelling into the microphone again, the Great Ice Wyrm pounced, landing on the tank nearest to us.

It ripped the tank commander from his position and swallowed him down in a matter of seconds. We sprinted and dove behind another nearby tank, firing shots at the beast as we ran.

The blast of frigid arctic wind buffeted us from around the Soviet tank we huddled behind. I could feel the near-instant pain of frostbite trying to set in where the icy wind struck my uniform. We huddled closer together, trying to stay out of the deathly wind.

Once the gale had subsided, I carefully leaned around the end of the tank. The dragon's attention had been drawn to the other end of the Soviet line. Small arms fire rang out with no outward effect on the beast.

The Soviet officer and radio man were both frozen in place, like statues of warriors who had looked upon the face of the gorgon Medusa. The tank commander hung there suspended from the top of the tank, leaning out from the command hatch and frozen solid.

"Well, that didn't go well," I said as I leaned against the rear of the tank and pulled a cigarette out of my left breast pocket.

"The officer?" Pierce asked. I nodded and lit the partially crumpled smoke, then took a long drag and inhaled deeply before responding.

"Frozen solid where they stood."

"What?" Doyle barked, then glanced around the edge of the tank. "We can't stay here. We have to get out of here."

"We don't have a choice, *Private*," Pierce said, accentuating Doyle's rank. "This is what we do, and you know it!"

"But it's a dragon!" he shouted, exasperatedly pointing toward the massive beast.

I shrugged. "Just another day in Task Force Thirteen."

Pierce sighed, then patted Doyle on the back of the shoulder. "Yup. That's the job, kid."

The Soviet T-34's engine momentarily stumbled, then surged, as if starving for air. Black smoke belched from both of the exhaust ports on the rear plate of the tank.

I turned and stared blankly at the machine when the realization suddenly hit me. "This thing is still running."

"Like that does us any good," Doyle said. "Do either of you know how to drive it?"

I laughed. "We don't have to drive it as long as the gun and turret still works." I looked over to Pierce. "Get in there and see if you can figure out the controls. I'll check the barrel to make sure it isn't blocked with ice."

"Sounds like as good a plan to me as any," Pierce said, climbing onto the back of the Soviet tank. I followed right behind him and helped him gently lower the tank commander to the ground as quickly as we could. Pierce dropped into the hatch and disappeared, while I clamored out onto the barrel. Straddling the tank's primary weapon, I locked my ankles together and scootched my way to the end of the barrel, carefully leaning down to peer down the rifled barrel.

"The rest of the crew are dead," Pierce reported, reappearing from the top hatch like a jack-in-the-box. "Looks like they froze to death."

I started my slow slide back to the turret of the tank. "The barrel is clear. Just frosted over from the dragon's blast. Does the gun look functional?"

"As far as I can tell, yeah. I really wish O'Brian were here. As much as he likes anything that goes boom, I'm sure he'd know how to operate it."

"Well, he isn't," I said.

The turret of another tank farther down the line suddenly soared overhead, crashing to the ground a few hundred feet behind us.

"Hey, come on, guys," Doyle said. "Can we do something or get the hell out of here already?"

"The job's not done, Private." I motioned for Pierce to make room for me to climb down into the tank.

Pierce climbed out onto the top, then leaned over into the hatch. "We have to pull the gunner out first before you can get in there."

We hoisted the frozen gunner from the hole, followed by the loader on the right side of the turret, before I climbed down through the commander's hatch.

I'd driven my fair share of heavy equipment over the years and seen the inside of several M4

Shermans since arriving in Europe. I even had a few crews show me the finer points of operating the M4 Sherman medium battle tank. Everything from how to get the best fuel efficiency out of the engines, to how that particular crew had streamlined their firing and loading process, so they'd be faster than the other crews.

I lowered myself into the gunner's position and surveyed the controls. Two hand-cranked adjustment wheels, similar to what was used in the M4, were easy to spot. I adjusted each, testing which controlled elevation and position, squeezing what I thought was a lock on the lower wheel.

The world erupted in a violent cacophony of motion and sound, louder than anything I'd ever witnessed before. My insides shook from the force of the round firing and ejecting from the breech.

"I guess it still works," Pierce shouted over to me from the loader's seat.

"Guys!" Doyle suddenly leaned in from the commander's hatch. "You got its attention! It's coming this way!"

I glanced into the sights but couldn't see the beast. "Which way?"

Doyle climbed back out and pointed. "Over there and getting closer!"

"In relation to the direction of the barrel?"

He leaned back into the hole, then looked back up. "Uh… to your right, maybe off to your two o'clock position."

"Copy that!" I started to crank on the position wheel when it suddenly stopped. I reversed the direction, which stopped just as suddenly.

"What's wrong?" Pierce asked.

"I don't know. It's like the turret is frozen in place." I snapped my fingers. "Frozen! Doyle!"

"Yeah, Sarge?"

"Is there a lot of ice around the base of the turret?" He disappeared once more from the opening, then reappeared.

"Up around the front. It's covered pretty heavily."

"Can you break it loose?"

"With what, Sarge? My bare hands?"

I glanced around the compartment and spotted what must have been the commander's gun dangling from just under the inboard side of the hatch. Reaching up, I unhooked the strap and gave it a quick once-over. It was a compact submachine gun with an underslung drum magazine and a folding stock. I handed it up to Doyle.

"This should make quick work of the ice."

"What? You want me to shoot you?"

Pierce exploded in a fit of laughter. "Do you really think that thing is going to penetrate the few inches of steel separating you from us?"

A look of utter embarrassment fell over the private's face. "I suppose you have a point," he said before disappearing from view of the hatch.

Tiny pings striking the hull resounded inside the compartment in time with the sound of automatic gunfire coming through the hatch.

Doyle suddenly dove into the hatch, pulling it closed behind himself. "It's right on top of us!"

"Did you get the ice free?"

"I think so."

"You *think* so?" Pierce shouted.

I tried adjusting our position, and the turret turned easy enough. "Looks like we're good. Get a fresh round into the breech."

Pierce unlatched one of the oversized-looking rifle rounds secured along the wall beside him and easily slid it into the breech. "How do I close it?"

I pushed myself upward and leaned over the gun, looking the mechanism over the best I could from my position. "Grab that lever right there and push it up. That looks like it should close the breech."

"Hurry!" Doyle shouted. I looked up, and he was peering through the commander's viewports at the top of the compartment. "It's right in front of us!"

I dropped back into the gunner's seat and spun the position adjustment as fast as I could, bringing the gun to bear.

Peering through the tank's gunsight, I adjusted the elevation and centered the targeting reticle on the dragon's head.

"Clear!"

"Clear," Pierce answered.

"Fire in the hole!" I shouted, then pulled the trigger again. The concussion of the blast rattled every part of my being.

"Not good!" Doyle shouted. "Fire again! Fire again!"

I couldn't believe what I saw when I looked back through the gunner's sights. Smoke roiled around the dragon's thick neck where the round connected but failed to penetrate the thick scaley hide.

"Reload!" I shouted at Pierce, who had already detached another round from the wall behind himself and was loading the gun.

"Loaded!"

The beast's head rhythmically swayed as it approached. It stopped, letting out a frigid roar. I made a final adjustment, bringing the reticle to the center of its forehead, and yelled, "Clear!"

I pulled the trigger the moment I heard the first letter escape from between Pierce's lips.

Doyle let out an excited cheer, quickly followed by an angry, "Dammit! The round basically glanced off its face! Fire again! It's right on top of us!"

The tank rocked and lurched as if something had suddenly pushed us sideways.

Pierce detached another round, reloading the gun as soon as he'd regained his footing, and shouted, "Clear!"

Fire and Ice

Frost blossomed across the front wall of the compartment, growing like a living thing. A frigid wave of cold permeated the compartment.

Frost encroached across my view when I returned to the targeting sights, and the targeting reticle sat square down the open gullet of the Great Ice Wyrm.

I squeezed the trigger just as frost completely obscured the viewfinder, and the world shook. The Soviet tank suddenly shifted sideways with an excruciating acceleration, then stopped as suddenly and rolled onto its top.

I fell up, Doyle cushioning my landing against the top of the turret. Upside down and completely in the dark, we skidded to a stop.

A keening howl, like some great cosmic leviathan, thundered from beyond our steel coffin.

"Could you get off of me?" Doyle asked. "This isn't exactly comfortable."

"Stow it, Private."

"Are you two alright?"

I did a quick once-over of myself for any fresh injuries. "I think I'm good here."

"Same," Doyle replied.

"Good," Pierce said. "Now, how do we get out of this tin can?" he asked as he worked his way upright in the small loader's space.

"If they were smart," I said, turning myself around upright again, "the Soviets would have put an escape hatch in the bottom somewhere." I climbed upward into the driver's compartment. Both the driver and the forward gunner were still strapped into their seats and dangled like frozen sides of beef in a meat locker. Luckily, the tank had landed in such a way that it slanted toward the rear, leaving the driver's hatch off the ground. We lowered both of the crew members out of the way and exited through the unobstructed hatch to find the dragon sprawled out across the ground maybe one hundred feet or so away.

"Hell yeah!" I shouted. "Got that dirty SOB."

Doyle crossed himself, then said a quick, quiet prayer. "Let's not do that again, please."

"I'd second that," Pierce added.

The thing looked just like the fairytale descriptions of dragons; horns, wings, scales, the works. The dragon's tail and legs spasmed sporadically as it lay in the icy mud. I stepped closer to inspect the creature. The final round had apparently sent it tumbling backward, snapping its neck at an odd angle. The back of its head was completely missing, and the edges of the newly formed orifice smoldered from the blast. The smell was odd, similar to fresh frog legs right out of the skillet.

No sooner had we reached the dead beast than two trucks pulled up to the scene and unloaded at least two dozen soldiers who rushed to surround the beast.

"Otstupit'," one soldier said, motioning for us to back up with his rifle before shouldering it and sighting us in.

"Doesn't that just beat all," Pierce huffed. "We go to all the trouble of killing the thing, and you just want to up and take it?"

"Otstupit'!" A second Soviet soldier repeated the order and stood shoulder to shoulder with the first.

I held up my hands and backed away. "Alright, alright, we get the hint." I looked around at the soldiers for anyone that looked like an officer. One thing we'd failed to familiarize ourselves with was Soviet field ranks and their insignia.

One man stood out among the rest; tall, broad of shoulder, who directed soldiers with ropes and tarps toward the corpse of the beast.

We approached, and no sooner had we gotten within spitting distance, than four soldiers surrounded the man and leveled their weapons on us.

"Hey, now guys," Pierce said, laughing slightly. "That's not exactly called for, is it?"

"Hey!" I shouted and pointed at the guy who I was sure was an officer. "Do you speak English?" He squinted with a perturbed look on his face.

"You know, English…," Doyle said, drawing out the word. I slapped him across the chest and glared at him.

"We were sent here to help with the flying threat," Pierce said, jabbing his thumb over his shoulder in the beast's direction.

The man said something in Russian, then motioned the guards away before stepping toward us. "I am very well aware of and capable of speaking English."

"So then, how about you explain what your goon squad is doing with our dragon," Pierce blurted out. "We didn't almost get ourselves killed for nothing. We need to study this thing and learn everything we can about it."

The Soviet officer let out a laughing snort while removing his gloves. "Your assistance has been greatly appreciated, gentlemen. But we will take over from here. You will be returned to your higher command once transportation can be arranged."

"What? That's bullshit," Pierce shouted and took a step toward the officer. I grabbed him by the arm and restrained him. At the same time, six rifles were up and aimed at us.

"Sarge…" Doyle said, stepping closer to the pair of us.

The Soviet officer stepped forward. "Is there a problem with this arrangement?" He cocked his head sideways and a conniving, backstabbing smile crossed his face, daring us to do anything.

"No, that'll do," I said. "Just point us where we need to go."

The officer pointed to one soldier and said something in Russian before turning back to us. "Follow this soldier, and he will direct you to where you need to be."

"Just play along, and we'll get out of this alive," I said quietly to Doyle and Pierce, then turned and nodded to the soldier. "Thank you. Let us know if we can be of any more assistance."

The officer nodded then turned back to the corpse of the Great Ice Wyrm we'd almost died to defeat.

I would have loved to mount the things head on a wall back home, if I could find one big enough. But it wasn't worth arguing about. The Soviets had made up their mind who the dragon's remains belonged to, and we were just shit out of luck.

But that's just another day in Task Force Thirteen.

The End

Fire and Ice

Jason Cordova

Providence's Player

By: Jason Cordova

Somewhere behind me in the dark Ecuadorian jungle, a demon was in pursuit. It's a startling thing, changing from predator to prey. Even more alarming was that there was an actual fucking *demon*.

I was down to six rounds for my handgun, a slightly bent machete, and a canteen half-filled with brackish, questionable water.

The local men who'd been guiding me through the jungle?

Dead.

My sat phone, which could have signaled the extraction team to pull me out? Broken, and long since discarded. My supposed waterproof boots? They were soaked through with mud and water, raising the risk of gangrene setting in, and squished with every step. Food? What a joke. The rotted *aguaje* fruit I'd scrounged up from the jungle floor had been absolutely disgusting, but it kept me going… barely. Other than some weird pasty vanilla plant I'd found, it was the only thing I'd eaten in almost a week.

To put it mildly, I was in a bit of a bind.

Working as a member of the CIA's Special Activities Division, I was used to having the odds stacked against me. More often than not, I'd be inserted into some Latin American country for tasking, then after completing the op, the extraction typically would be quick and I'd be back at Langley within a week, two at the latest. Though nothing about the job would be classified as "routine", I'd sort of lapsed into that mentality of late. Of course, all of that came to a screeching halt when the demonic *thing* slaughtered my guides in seconds.

I needed to stop, to breathe, if only for a moment. Everything hurt. However, stopping meant dying. I pushed on. The monster pursuing me gave truth to the definition of dogged pursuit. He'd gotten a taste for human flesh—not mine, though he had caught my left arm. Those razor-sharp claws had left nasty furrows running down the bicep. Odds of an infection were likely if I didn't get some antibiotics on them soon.

"To hell with dying tired," I muttered and slowed my pace. I wasn't giving up, no. Mama didn't raise a quitter. But there was no point in me being exhausted when the demon came for me once again. Glancing around, I spotted a shaded place beneath a few trees. There were multiple approach vectors surrounding it, but the lack of undergrowth would keep the monster from sneaking up on me–unless the demon could climb like a monkey. Something I wasn't discounting, mind you, but it was the only place I saw where I could be safe for a short while. Long enough to catch my breath, at least.

Listening to the surrounding jungle, there was nothing. Not a single bird was chirping, no animals screeching and calling out into the hot, humid morning. Inwardly, I shivered. They were afraid because a predator was close, and it wasn't me. The demon was still out there, somewhere close by. It was an unnatural creature which caused even the dumbest of animal in the jungle to go silent. Swallowing, I resisted the urge to take a small sip of my pungent, probably infested water and looked around.

The moriche palm trees towering above me didn't quite blot out the sky, but they were numerous and grew in dense clusters, which allowed me some shade. This alone told me plenty about the area I was in. Locals in more populated areas harvested the trees regularly. Judging by the size of these trees, these hadn't been touched in years, if ever. I sniffed the air. No hint of fires. No smoke. Nothing to indicate people nearby.

I was completely alone, and nobody was coming to rescue me. On the plus side, at least the creature couldn't kill any innocents way out here.

Shifting on the balls of my feet, I weighed my options. The temptation to simply eat a round and call it a day was brief, but there. I wasn't stupid enough to believe I was walking out of here in one piece, if at all. However, if I just gave up, who knew what sort of damage the demonic little beast would do to any locals it came across? It had already slaughtered my guides. There was no telling what it could do if it found its way into a larger metropolis. Or worse, one of the small villages which the governments of South America always seemed to ignore.

No, it was up to me to stop it, or die in the process.

"I'm gonna die," I quietly acknowledged as I felt a blister on my heel pop. It was the third one in as many days. If the demon didn't get me, infection would. One of the very first things I'd learned during my SERE–Survival Evasion Reconnaissance and Escape–training in Panama, was to take care of your feet. There was no grading scale when it came to taking care of yourself while on the lam. Everything was pass/fail.

Pass? Survive. Fail?

I shook away those thoughts. There was a huge difference between knowing you were about to die and expecting it. The mind could do many great things when it still thought there was a chance at winning. Entire wars had been won or lost with a simple switch of mentality. Yes, I was going to die, but it didn't have to be right now. I could starve to death in another week or so, lost in the jungle after killing the demon.

But that was the point. Kill the demon first, then die.

Easier said than done.

I looked around at my surroundings, trying to get my bearings. In order to defeat this monstrous creature, I needed an advantage. So far, my handgun had provided nothing more than comfort and loud, empty promises. I couldn't even blame poor shooting skills on my part. While no Billy the Kid, I was more than proficient with all types of small firearms, and even some rifles. Any agent within the Special Activities Division of the CIA had to be intimately familiar with all possible weapons they might come across in the field.

There was a spot twenty feet away which looked promising. A small cluster of trees created a natural chokepoint along what looked to be a wild animal path. It was as good a place as any. The problem was, I needed to lure the mock creature into my kill box. But how?

"I can always bleed," I grunted, looking down at my leg. Somewhere along the line, something had punctured my calf. A small trickle of blood had dried on my pants leg. Which was impressive, really. The whole point of wearing the same outfit as the local terrorist operations was to protect against the natural elements. The green khaki pants weren't made for the dense jungles of Colombia or Ecuador. Someone had lied to me.

However, ruined pants aside, the cluster of trees looked perfect for what I needed. Grabbing a large, wide leaf from a nearby bush which towered over me–it probably could have been a tree itself, I wasn't certain–I hastily wiped any blood I could find on my pants with the leaf. It wasn't the best job, and most of it was already dried, but it was what I had. I didn't want to tear my khakis any further than they already were.

There wasn't much blood, but it was enough for what I needed. Maybe.

Taking the leaf, I tried to wipe as much as I could onto the tree trunk. It took a few tries—including the use of some of the brackish water in my canteen—before I could get enough blood onto the tree. If the demon was tracking me by scent, then this would look very appealing. If it was following me through the jungle using other means, I was well and truly screwed.

I chastised myself. *Stay positive*, I thought as I looked for somewhere to hide. There was a large tree nearby which had fallen sometime in the past few months, rotting on the ground. It wasn't much, but it was the only thing I could find. Doing my best to keep the small wound on my leg from splitting, I slithered over to the other side and waited.

It didn't take long for the demon to find the blood. I shivered as I watched it approach the narrow path between the trees. The shadows cast by the leaves above distorted the shape and form of the demon, but I could see the scaly red skin as clear as day. Even though the monstrosity stayed in the shadows, its eagerness to take my life had drawn it into the light for the first time since its initial attack.

The beast was just as hideous as I remembered. Batlike ears protruded from its head. Long, muscular arms nearly dragged along the jungle floor. Across the shoulders were orange hieroglyphics, all of which seemed to glow with an unnatural heat. Its legs and lower body were hidden from view, which I was thankful for. If the demon had some sort of prehensile reproductive member, I would have been scarred for life.

More so than I already was.

Six rounds left. I needed to make every single one count. I tried to clear my mind as the demon approached the trunk where I'd smeared my blood. Focusing on my breathing, my heartbeat slowed. I'd always been calm and collected in a firefight. Until this… *thing* had come along, I'd never lost a single man on my team. It was time for a little bit of payback.

The demon stepped into my kill box. Raising my pistol, I squeezed off four rounds in less than a second. The recoil wasn't bad, not as bad as I remember at least. The demon dropped, shrinking before it scampered behind another tree for cover. I leapt over the downed log I had been using to hide behind. My foot caught on a straight branch I hadn't seen, and I fell flat on my face. Fortunately, I didn't have my finger on the trigger and did not waste a round.

I scrambled back to my feet, my eyes scanning the jungle floor. The demon was around somewhere. I could hear its petulant whining and groaning. I must've hit him. Not a kill shot, but he knew he'd been kissed. Satisfaction came over me.

It was time to finish the job. Sprinting in a wide circle, I tried to flank the demon where I guessed he was hiding.

He was gone. Or rather, he'd moved. Cursing, I whirled around and just barely managed to get my arm up in time to block the demon's attack. Razor-sharp claws laid into my forearm, cutting through the tissue and deep into the muscle. I howled in pain and managed to pistol whip the demon across the face. I switched my gun to my offhand–the damage from the attack had affected my grip–and aimed towards the creature. It was wily, though, and used the very log that I had been hiding behind to protect himself from me.

I tried to get another round off but was too slow. Howling in pain and rage, the demon disappeared into the jungle. Panting, I quickly checked my magazine. Two rounds left. A fierce grin split my face. I'd hurt the little bastard, which meant normal weapons would work on whatever the demon was. My arm stung and blood flowed freely, rivulets running down the long cuts. I didn't know who won the exchange but, unless the bleeding stopped soon, I knew who would lose it.

"This was a lot easier when it was just a recon mission," I muttered, thinking back to the parting words from Deputy Director Stein. The man wasn't stupid. Far from it, actually. However, sometimes he was a bit on the optimistic side. I'd allowed his calmness to allay some of my more natural worries, focusing instead on the resurgent FARC terrorists. To be fair, I don't think anyone thought demonic entities were rampaging through the South American jungles.

The low clicking of the demon returned. The sound felt muted and muffled by the oppressive humidity of the jungle. A terrifying noise in the surrounding stillness. I jerked my head around, trying to spot the red-skinned beast. The pistol grip felt slick in my hand, a combination of sweat and muck covering the composite material. I quickly wiped my hand dry on my pants. It helped some.

I hated being prey. It wasn't me. My training, my very nature, demanded I rise up, meet the challenge, and defeat it. The time to be the apex predator was upon me once more.

Before I could troop off into the jungle and die of malaria, though, the demon spoke. It was not a pleasant experience.

<<You are very persistent, Director Cole. Why will you not die?>>

I jerked.

The voice had come from somewhere nearby, yet also resounded loudly in my head. Foreign. *Evil.* Something in the tone bespoke legions, a vastness not of this world–or this universe, if I was being honest with myself.

My throat constricted as something *pushed* against my psyche. I was under attack once more, only this time it wasn't physical. It was worse.

A pressure formed right behind my eyes. It felt as though a giant sponge was being pushed through my brain. I gritted my teeth and tried not to scream as the pressure grew. There wasn't much I could do but take the abuse. More and more, the pressure became focused on a spot just above my left eye, like a horrifying migraine, which felt as if it would never end.

Rolling my thumb over the spot, I leaned back against the moriche tree and tried to fight the pain.

After what felt like an eternity but was probably only a few seconds in reality, the pain ebbed. The steady beat of my heart replaced the overbearing pain in my head. Once more, I felt human.

The pain remained, but it was no longer blinding and debilitating. I wiped my eyes, which had grown watery from the pain, and tried to monitor my surroundings. The pain eased, but it was still enough to make my vision waiver. Instead of the vibrant colors of the jungle, everything around me looked ashy and gray. A virtual wasteland, bereft of life. The normal sounds of the jungle remained silenced. Now, even the wind had disappeared. Everything was absolutely still. Nothing moved.

<<I grew weary of this game we play. Will play. Have played. End it now. Take up your pistol, do what you must do, and many will live… thanks to your selfless sacrifice.>>

The voice was insistent. There was a deep and dark undertone which I had not noticed before. Every word reverberated through my mind, my being, and even my soul. When the voice spoke, all sense of self left me. There was nothing left. Nothing except the Legion. The millions upon millions of wasp-like voices buzzing at the very edge of my sanity.

I needed relief, anything to counter the pure evil of what I was hearing, feeling. Typically, training suggested I dispose of a problem with extreme force should it become this much of an issue. Two rounds to the chest, a follow-up to the head, just as we were trained. However, no amount of training could have prepared me to fight a demon.

So instead of shooting it again and probably missing, I tried half-witty banter. It was better than anything else I could think of.

"You… speak? Impressive. I was expecting grunting and half-coherent words, like a marine or something." I looked around. There was no sign of the demon, but if it could get in my head, that was bad news. The creature had already proven just how deadly it was. If the thing was more than a mindless beast?

My chances were already slim. There was no need to remind myself of this.

<<I speak. I see. I know all. I am the beginning, and the end. There are many like us, but none are of us. I am your death, Director.>>

"You can't be my death," I replied lamely. My wit was at an end, it seemed. "I'm not ready to die yet."

<<You seemed more than ready to die not too long ago, Director,>> the voice countered. I shivered slightly at the tone. It was, after all, true. Even if for a brief instance, I had been prepared to end it all.

"Why do you keep calling me Director?" I asked, focusing instead on the mundane and not the overbearing pressure the voice was putting on my mind. The dark entity's voice faded into the background. I could feel it considering my question. Freaky, I know. I tried to rationalize the creature's existence. There had to be some reason it chose this area, this region. Hell, even this time. There was nothing here. Nothing… except for me.

<<Time is merely a construct. You are the Director.>>

"Look, buddy, I have no idea what the fuck you're talking about."

<<You have wasted enough time.>>

"I thought time was just a construct," I mocked it as the pain slipped below a tolerable threshold. Once more I could feel the comforting grip of the pistol in my hand. I knew how many rounds I had left. I also knew the demon had to be close, close enough for me to end this battle once and for all.

The demon did not reply.

I ran my sweaty palm across the stubble on my chin, grimacing at the pain in my wounded arm. I definitely looked like a local now. There were a few small abrasions on the back of my hand. Odd, I thought. I didn't remember that happening. Everything else hurt, though—even the hair on top of my head. I inhaled deeply, and slowly let the breath out. Pain blossomed in my chest. Ignoring it, I prepared for the demon's next attack. There had been a finality in its words. The monster was coming. I started counting backwards in my head. *Ten. Nine. Eig—*

The demon dropped to the jungle floor out of a nearby tree, the red skin wonderingly invisible against the leaves above. Somehow it had gotten close enough without me spotting it, or even hearing it, moving like a skilled monkey through the treetops. I mentally amended the capabilities of the demonic entity.

Finally, I could get a better look at the creature which had spent the better part of a week trying to kill me. It was all muscle, scales, and claws. So sure of its victory, the demon slowly stalked towards me. One step after another. The beast's eyes were black, dark pits of an abyss I did not want to descend into. Fangs longer than my hand jutted from its upper jaw, while a vicious horned chin jutted angrily at me. It had a tail, albeit a small one. Unfortunately, it lacked the wicked barb on the tip I'd always been told demons had.

Mr. Clark, my Sunday school teacher, really dropped the ball on this one.

The demon showed no fear. If it could smile, I'm pretty sure it would have. There was a swagger to it which would have made any ring-knocker from the Naval Academy proud. The creature knew it had won. Or at least, thought it did. I blinked. Did it think I was out of ammo? No. The thing had been in my mind, seen my thoughts. Surely it knew I had two rounds left.

Right?

I did my best not to smile. Instead, I slumped my shoulders and looked at the ground. Everything in my body language had to suggest that I was defeated. There would be only one shot at this. If ever there was a time to fall back on my CIA training, this was it. Not only did I have to convince the demon, I had to convince myself that I had lost. There was no hope.

I was going to die.

The demon must have felt my despair, for its disgusting face split into a wide, mocking grin. <<Yes. I can taste your anguish. Your death will save millions. With you gone, the others cannot stop me.>>

"What others?" I asked, risking a look at the handgun in my tightly clenched fist. While I knew I was a good shot, I'd already missed multiple times while shooting at the demon. Okay, I tagged it once, but the damn thing showed no ill-effects. With only two rounds left, I could not afford to miss again. I needed to delay, lull the demon into coming closer. Close enough that even in my dehydrated, fugue-like mental state, I could not miss.

<<Do not concern yourself with them. The others will no longer matter.>>

"Yeah, I think I'm going to have a problem with this 'dying' thing," I stated in a firm, commanding tone. Well, as firm as I could make it. My throat was bone dry. I raised my firearm. Cracking a small smile, I realized the demon had not seen that coming. The handgun became nothing more than an extension of my arm, of my will. For the briefest moment, I saw something other than darkness in those eyes. I saw… *fear.*

Satisfied, I squeezed the trigger. Even in my weakened state, the recoil wasn't nearly as bad as one would've expected. Once, twice, the handgun barked. Founts of yellowish-black blood exploded out of the back of the demon. Two tiny, neat holes were directly over where I thought its heart would be. More of the discolored blood began flowing from these wounds.

The demon was tough, but there was almost nothing in this world which could stand against .45 caliber hollow points punching directly through the heart. Not even an otherworldly creature from the bowels of Hell.

The last echoing remnants of the gunshots disappeared into the jungle. A deep, shuddering breath left my body. Had I won? Sure didn't feel like it. It felt more like I'd simply survived. I gave a slight shrug. I didn't need to convince myself, not yet. The shock of the past week would hit me soon enough. For now, I relished the fact I was still alive. Survival was good enough.

It stared at me, clearly confused. Maybe it didn't understand pain?

The demon hissed quietly and took a step towards me, then another. The claws dragged along the floor of the jungle, leaving tiny, shallow grooves in the soil. I swallowed and grasped the hilt of my bent machete. Yanking it from the sheath, I readied myself. If gunfire hadn't been enough. I doubted the machete would do much against the demon–especially if hollow points barely slowed it down. But I swore I wasn't going to die easy.

The demon stopped fifteen feet in front of me and raised a single claw. Pointing it directly at my chest, it spoke in the voice of a hundred thousand locusts.

<<You have made a fatal mistake, human. Millions will suffer because of you.>>

With that, the demon toppled forward, dead.

Not trusting my own eyes, I waited for any sign of the demon to twitch, that its death was nothing more than a ruse to lure me forward. After several minutes, I was convinced that it might not just be faking after all. Slowly, and with the trust of a high school nerd getting hit on by the head cheerleader, I approached the corpse. My eyes remained locked on the dead red demon the entire time. If it so much as twitched, I was out of there.

Nothing. It was well and truly dead.

Just to be on the safe side, I hacked the head off. It took a few dozen blows. My aim was off, and quite a few times the machete struck the monstrous face.

Oh well.

Exhausted, I made my way to a moriche tree. I opened up my canteen and, ignoring the horrid stench of the water inside, took a small sip. It was just as disgusting as I remembered. Spitting it back out, I dumped the contents and let the jungle have it back. I wasn't going to need it. I sat down at the base of the tree and leaned back against it. The adrenaline rush of the kill was wearing off quickly. Exhaustion was calling, and I answered.

Just a quick nap, was my last thought as the darkness closed in.

"Is that him?" a voice from the darkness woke me up. My eyes were crusted shut, and I felt too weak to move. No, I realized a second later. I was just stiff. I'd fallen asleep leaning up against the trunk of a moriche palm tree. The jungle was chilly, but not horribly so. The sun was either down or well on its way. I wasn't twenty anymore and couldn't just sleep anywhere. Try to take a nap while using a tree as a pillow? Especially after being chased by—

Memories came flooding back to me, causing my entire body to jerk. I groaned softly in pain as blood began to circulate. Had I dreamt it? Was the demon, everything I'd suffered through, been nothing but a horrible nightmare?

"This is where the divining said he'd be," a second man replied. "So yeah, it's him."

"What's so important about this guy, anyway?"

"No clue. But the diviner said he was important."

"You know that man's a kook, right?"

"Stop playing with fire, you idiot. Hey, check this guy out. Looks like something chewed him up and spit him out. Is he alive?"

"I think so. Ugh, that smell… oh wow, okay. A dead furcas demon, class two judging by its size. Damn, this guy's a badass, taking one down solo. Hey, look. Our boy's breathing. Definitely still alive."

"He's waking up."

Groaning softly, I pulled myself up to my feet, using the tree as support. Standing was far more difficult than I remembered it being. However, once I was up, I began to feel a lot better. Using my fingers, I tried my best to dig the grime out of my eyes. Dried blood and rheum made seeing difficult, but after a few moments, I was able to get most of the gunk out.

Finally able to see, I looked around for the two voices who'd woken me up. I blinked. There was nothing but trees, some undergrowth on the jungle floor, and a very dead demon. Giving my head a little shake, I checked behind the tree I'd been sleeping against. Again, nobody. Frowning, I scratched my chin. There had been two voices there, I was almost sure of it. Had they been nothing but a dream?

Checking my holster, I found the empty handgun I'd used to kill the demon. A quick check confirmed I'd fired the last two rounds of the magazine. Odd. I didn't remember putting the weapon back into its holster. Then again, I wasn't really tracking. There were a lot of things going on. Forgetting a minor detail like this was, in the grand scheme of things, very minor indeed.

Had I hallucinated the voices? It was possible. My dreams were pretty vivid at times. Still, it felt like the two men had been right there with me, watching over me. I shook off the haunting sensation. The last thing I wanted to dwell on were my dreams. I'd survived the demon, sure. But would I survive the jungle, as tore up as I was?

Unlikely.

I heard a branch snap in the shadowed jungle. My entire body tensed. I carefully slid the empty Baretta from its holster. I couldn't shoot anything but, if it were some locals, then perhaps I could bluff my way out of trouble. It wouldn't be the first time I'd miraculously survived an excursion into hostile territory.

"Stop!" I called out in Spanish. "Identify yourself!" I hoped it wasn't a demonic jaguar or something. There was no way I could get lucky a second time and survive another encounter. Fortunately for me, it wasn't.

"Cole?" a man asked in unaccented English as he stepped out of the shadows. He held a weapon in his hands, but the barrel was not pointed directly at me.

I recognized the weapon instantly. It was a small carbine, a cut-down version of the AK-47. I'd seen enough of them over the years throughout Latin America, thanks to Fidel and Cuba depositing them all over for their fellow Communist revolutionaries. *Viva la revolucion* and all that bullshit.

"Connor Cole?"

"What did you say? I didn't understand you," I responded in Spanish, raising the empty pistol towards him.

I was out of ammo, but maybe I could bluff him. It was that or simply surrender. I discarded the idea before I'd even finished thinking it. The last thing I wanted after surviving some demonic entity was to be tortured by drug lords, so I remained leery, as every intelligence officer in the field should be. More than one asset in the field had been burned because they allowed their mask to slip, and their cover being blown.

"The storm has ended," the man said, flipping to Spanish with practiced ease. "The sun will be out soon. Best get inside in case the weather changes."

I stared suspiciously at the new arrival. He'd given the extraction code, but there was no way anybody should have been able to find me. I'd lost my sat phone, and I didn't have any tracker on me. Sure, our satellites were high quality, but unless someone had tasked a reconnaissance satellite to search for me–at the cost of a couple million dollars–there was no way they could have found me so quickly. Hell, neither of the station chiefs in both Quito and Bogota knew I'd been in-country.

"Good thing I lost my umbrella," I replied with the proper code phrase. Seeing his affirmative nod, I continued. "What the hell is going on? How did you find me?"

"I'm glad we did, Mister Cole," the man said as he motioned towards the corpse. "Well done, by the way. This class of demon is notoriously tough to handle. I've never seen someone take one down alone before. Hell, never seen one outside of Europe, come to think of it."

"The fuck is going on? Who are you? How did you track me down?" I repeated. He grinned and slung his carbine over his shoulder. His demeanor was relaxed, completely different from my own unsteady nerves. It was clear he was used to dealing with oddities more than I was.

"Captain Alex Leon," he replied. "I'm with JTF-13."

I'd never heard of his unit. "What are you, Ecuadorian? Are you with some spec ops group they have?"

"We're not Ecuadorian, sir," Captain Leon shook his head. "Everyone on my team is a devil dog. Oof, okay, sorry. Bad terminology, all things considered. We're a multi-service special operations unit called Joint Task Force 13. We're American."

"Never heard of you. Wait… what?" I looked around. "Your team?"

"Yes sir. I brought friends, sir," the soldier said as six more similarly camouflaged men appeared from the nearby tree line. They'd blended in so well, even my experienced eye hadn't spotted them. They were similarly armed and, if I hadn't known better, would have placed them as either Colombian or Ecuadorian. Whoever this JTF-13 was, they were of a similar mindset as I was. The captain tipped his boonie hat back, revealing the traditional high-and-tight the Marines loved so much. "You SAD types usually know who we are. I mean, the CIA's run ops with us before, sir. At least the agents over at Subic Bay did. Granted, we really don't come down here very often, but if we're getting incursions in this part of the world, then that's probably going to change in the future.

Probably have to base out of Roosevelt Roads. Fuck, I hate that place…"

My head spun.

Incursions? JTF-13 and SAD working together out at Subic Bay? These guys knew about the demon… it was too much. Nothing made sense anymore. Dizziness threatened to make me throw up. Fiery visions danced in my head, fleeting. They were too many, too fast for me to see anything more than glimpses. I was supposed to be dead, killed by a demonic creature. I could almost *feel* a split in my soul. I wasn't a believer of fate or destiny, but something changed when the demon failed to kill me. The captain grabbed my arm as I started to weave on my feet. Everything felt unsteady. For a brief moment, I understood what the demon had been taunting me about—many worlds, split apart, with my death bringing them together sooner rather than later. The fire, and blood. So much blood. Icy fingers squeezed my heart. Leon's voice sounded far away as he continued speaking.

"Sir? You okay?"

"Yeah, I think so," I gasped, as the sensation faded. Clarity returned. My sense of balance went back to normal. My arm stung. Grimacing, I glanced down and saw the scratches were oozing a particularly ugly yellow color. It wasn't blood. Frowning, I dipped my fingertip into it and brought it up to my nose. The yellow pus smelled *wrong* somehow. Able to stand upright on my own once more, I turned and thanked the young officer for his help. He glanced down at the cuts on my arm and nodded understandingly. "I don't know how to explain this…"

"You hallucinated," the young captain acknowledged. He must have been able to read my face. He laughed, then explained. "The poison from one of the red ones makes you see stuff, sir. Must have been a light hit if it wore off already. You got lucky, sir. I've seen men get taken down by one and suffer for days."

Was I lucky? I didn't feel it.

"You never did explain how you found me," I reminded him. Captain Leon shrugged and passed over a canteen. I unscrewed the top and drank greedily. It was warm, but after so long with the nasty crap I'd been forced to keep down? Clean water never tasted so good.

"It was weird, sir. We got a call about an incursion of demonic entities around these coordinates from a forward observer stationed in Quito. After we verified, we found the bodies of some locals and saw their wounds. The yellow pus is a clear indicator. We started tracking from there and found your trail, then you."

"That doesn't sound weird," I admitted. Captain Leon chuckled softly.

"There's only one small problem, sir. We don't *have* a forward observer in Quito. The codes were authentic, and clearly there was a demonic incursion, but… nobody knows who made the call, sir. It was simply providence we found you."

"Okay, that's weird," I allowed.

Who'd made the call, I wondered.

Glancing back down at my wounded arm, I grimaced. My arm looked like something had chewed it up and spit it out. The cuts were deep but, with some medical attention, they'd be nothing more than ugly scars in six months at the latest.

However, with my contacts in Ecuador dead thanks to the demon, nobody would want to stick their necks out for me anymore. It was an unexpected problem.

My time with the Special Activities Division was clearly at an end. After seeing the demon and knowing creatures like this lurked all around the world, there was no way I could go back to gathering intel or simply making mid-level cartel bosses disappear. It sucked, too. I'd worked long and hard to get into SAD after being nothing but an intel weenie for my first five years at Langley.

Sometimes, though, we have to put aside our own wants to ensure the safety of others. Or in this case, our world. These demons were not of it, which meant they were coming from elsewhere. "Incursions," Captain Leon had called them. Where were the demons arriving from? How were they entering our world? I looked over at Captain Leon. He and his men were chatting, their heads pressed. I couldn't quite hear what they were saying, but the gist of it was easy enough to decipher. Our ride was on its way.

"Captain?" I interrupted their quiet discussion. Captain Leon turned and stared at me. I took another hit from the borrowed canteen. It was still heavenly. Clean water and a shred of hope can change a man. Swallowing the mouthful of water, I continued. "Who do I talk to about joining this JTF-13?"

Captain Leon smiled. "I'd hoped you'd be interested…"

Above and Beyond

By: Steven Lord

Flashing red lights were going off all over the cockpit. Matthieu took a deep breath and weighed up his options. He had about five minutes of hydraulic pressure remaining before the system vented completely and he lost control of the aircraft. He could make it. Probably.

"Sarajevo Tower, this is Sabre 61. Mayday, Mayday—I have a hydraulic leak and need to land as soon as possible."

"Roger, Sabre 61. You are cleared for immediate approach. Call short finals."

Fighting the increasingly sluggish controls, Matthieu lined his Etendard IV fighter up with the threshold of Runway 29 of Sarajevo International Airport. It was a moonless night, and the lights on the ground provided his only references. "Sabre 61, short finals, gear down."

"Sabre 61, you are cleared to land. Good luck."

As he approached touchdown, he felt that familiar yet disconcerting sensation of the runway rushing up to meet him. He pulled back on the stick to arrest his rate of descent. Nothing happened. The aircraft slammed into the tarmac with a sickening thump, but the undercarriage held. *Dieu merci.* He squeezed the balls of his feet into the top half of his rudder pedals to apply the brakes. Again, nothing.

"Sarajevo Tower, Sabre 61 has a brake failure. Request you raise the barrier immediately."

Nothing but silence in response.

He was now traveling down the runway at over a hundred miles an hour with no way of slowing down. The far end of the tarmac rushed towards him, a line of bright red lights signifying the end of the road for him and his aircraft.

He shot past the red line into the darkness of the overshoot. Suddenly, he felt an immense deceleration as his aircraft careened into the arrestor barrier like a silver fish caught in a giant net. He came to a halt a few feet from the end of the tarmac.

"Sorry Sabre 61, we had some radio problems there. Barrier is up, report vacating your aircraft."

"Better late than never, Tower. Vacating now."

He jumped out of the cockpit to a reception party of flashing lights and worried faces. Brushing aside the attentions of an eager medic, he identified his flight engineer among the onlookers.

"She has taken some heavy fire, Corporal. Good luck patching her up," he said to the mechanic. Then he removed his helmet and took a deep breath. Safe.

"Excuse me, monsieur." It was the engineer standing by the aircraft's right wing, pointing a powerful flashlight towards the ground. "What did you say happened?"

"I told you. Ground fire. Dushka heavy machine gun, I think."

The engineer looked at him, then shone his torch back towards the fighter. Five ruts ran along the length of the fuselage, deep and jagged, as if someone had raked the aircraft with a huge, clawed hand.

"So, tell me again about this monster," Flight Lieutenant Mike Travers asked his wingman, a glint in his eye.

"Don't look at me like that—I'm not making this shit up. Just ask the engineers. They won't stop talking about it. They say a French aircraft was attacked last night near Gorazde, barely made it back to base. And when they checked for damage, they found…" Dave 'Boomer' Reynolds paused for effect, lowering his voice to a whisper. *"Scratch marks."*

Mike looked at him for a second. Then he exploded into laughter. *"Scratch marks?* Jesus… You've got to love the French. Did you know they still have a glass of red wine with lunch? *Before* they go flying!"

"You sound jealous," Boomer observed.

"Damn right I am," Mike said. "You do realize there's another explanation for this mysterious attack—the hundred Dushkas parked between here and Gorazde. Seriously mate, you've got to stop watching those horror films with the engineers. What was it last night? Pumpkinhead?"

"Pumpkinhead 2, actually. Except someone had taped over the last twenty minutes. We ended up watching some dodgy Eastern European porno." Boomer fell silent for a second of contemplation. "Plot was better, to be honest."

The two Harrier pilots chewed their meals for a few moments, contemplating the risks of buying bootleg videos from the local market. They were sitting in the main UN PROFOR canteen, a fancy name for what was a dingy, cramped shed made of corrugated iron. The United Nations Protection Force had been camped out here in Sarajevo for almost two years. As the customers regularly pointed out, the UN really should have sorted themselves out with a better canteen by now.

Mike raised another spoonful of, what someone optimistically labeled, chicken soup to his lips when Boomer nudged him. "Seen the new arrivals? Came in on the Stuttgart flight last night."

He turned his head to follow his flight lead's nod. At the other end of the canteen, five burly men were sitting down to breakfast, shuffling awkwardly down the long wooden pews to make room for each other. All five were wearing identical black jackets. The expensive kind. *Only Special Forces could make civilian clothes look like uniforms*, Mike thought. Mind you, the selection of weapons dangling from their shoulders also gave the game away. The soldiers were chatting loudly to each other, occasionally breaking into guffaws of laughter which drifted across the floor to where the two aircrew sat.

"Delta, blending in as always," Boomer said, rolling his eyes.

As Mike watched, one of the black-suited giants caught his eye and blew him a kiss, lips pursing under a bushy ginger beard. "I'm not so sure, mate. These guys seem to actually have a personality."

"Really? Maybe they're not Yanks after all," Boomer mused. "You done? We're crewing in in thirty minutes, and I need to take a shit before the met brief."

"Diplomatic *and* eloquent. I really have been crewed up with the finest of Her Majesty's Royal Air Force."

"And you've got the pleasure of my company for the next six hours," Boomer grinned. "Lucky you, eh? Right, let's roll."

The two men got up from the table. As they dropped off their used plates and crockery at the kitchen hatch, the door swung open and a tall woman with cropped black hair walked in. She wore the same clothes as the men at the table. As she walked past the two pilots to join her comrades, Mike gave her a winning smile. "Evening, ma'am. Cold out tonight, isn't it?"

"Fuck off," she growled, brushing past him without making eye contact.

Boomer slapped him on the back, laughing. "Wow, mate. I think you're in there."

"You can fuck off too, Boomer," he muttered.

The two men reached the door and stepped out into the fresh evening air of the Balkans spring. It was time to earn their pay.

Above and Beyond

Mike had only been in Bosnia for a month, but he was already counting down the days until he could go home. His arrival in-theater felt like a lifetime ago, the nervous anticipation he had felt on starting his first operational detachment a distant memory. He remembered almost running down the steps of the hulking Tristar aircraft that had delivered him into Sarajevo, he was that eager to get started. Now he would run straight back up those steps given half a chance.

It wasn't fear that had eaten away at him, nor any kind of homesickness. Hell, he loved getting away from the UK any chance he could, and it wasn't as if he had anyone waiting for him back in Norfolk.

His problem was with the job itself.

When he signed up to the RAF all those years ago, he'd been sold a particular vision: flying hell for leather, inches from the deck, ground fire lighting up the sky around him. His fast jet training had fed this myth: an intense two years spent above the mountains of Wales, screaming through steep-sided valleys on the way to the bombing ranges. With every sortie, the challenge grew and with it, the enjoyment. Until he finally found himself deploying on ops and… flying orbits ten thousand feet above the Serbian countryside for six hours at a time like a glorified tanker pilot.

At least the view was good tonight. The full moon hung low against a starry backdrop, casting a silver sheen on the forested countryside so bright that it looked like daylight through Mike's night vision goggles. Nothing was stirring, the radios were quiet. At times like this, he thought, you could forget you were flying above a war zone.

He was sat just off Boomer's wingtip, the two Harriers tracing a wide, lazy orbit ten thousand feet above the treetops. They'd arrived on station a few hours ago and they were only halfway through their patrol.

"God, I'm bored," Mike transmitted over the interplane frequency.

"You're flying a twenty million dollar single-seat fighter over enemy territory. It doesn't get any more exciting than this." Boomer's tone of reproach was audible over the crackle of the radio.

"Mate, we've literally been flying in circles for the last three hours. Trust me, I'm bored."

Boomer's reply was drowned out by an incoming transmission. "Poison formation, this is Magic. Send sitrep, over."

Mike toggled the transmit switch on his radio. "Magic, this is Poison, on station at Flight Level one hundred. Ops normal at this time, over."

"Identified, Poison. We have no trade for you at this time. Report going off-station. Magic out."

Great, thought Mike. *No trade, no fun. And I bet that guy's just gone off to get a sandwich.*

"I bet that controller's gone off for a sausage roll." Boomer's voice sounded in Mike's headset. "Bastard."

Mike was about to reply when a flashing light far below caught his eye. "Hey Boomer. Looks like an IR strobe, low level, just left of the nose. Shall we listen in?"

"Nothing better to do. Switch box three to TACSAT."

Mike took his hand off the throttle for a second and clicked a rotary switch right a few turns to select the aircraft's tactical satellite receiver. The crackle of a blank carrier wave came through his headset for a few seconds, before an American voice cut through the white noise. "Broadsword 6, this is Razor. Offload complete, we're lifting off and heading home. Good luck down there, guys."

Another American voice replied, this time a Texan drawl so relaxed it was almost horizontal. "Copy that, Razor. Safe flying, see you on the flipside." The radio returned to static.

"Guess that's all the excitement for the night," Boomer said. "Three hours left on station. Shall we do states again?"

"Sure," Mike sighed. "Alabama—one down." This was going to be a long night.

Hours passed. The moon traced a slow arc through the night sky as the two Harriers continued to circle on their lonely patrol. On night sorties like this, you could forget there was anyone else alive on the planet, save you and your flight lead. Tonight, Mike's flight lead seemed determined to make up for that deficit through sheer weight of personality alone.

"I'm telling you, we've already had Virginia. We're still one short." Boomer had been fixated on getting the 50th state for some time now. If the man was anything, it was tenacious.

"No, we've had *West* Vir- Fuck!" Mike's reply was cut short by an electronic squeal over the TACSAT that had him fumbling for the volume.

The squeal wavered for a second, then resolved into that same Texan drawl Mike had heard earlier. All composure had vanished; the voice now sounded urgent, almost frantic. "All callsigns, this is Broadsword 6. We're taking incoming, Metal Plutonium Gold and Aluminium Bronze. Requesting immediate fire support."

Mike could hear the distinctive rattle of small arms fire for a second or two before the transmission cut out. Just as he was about to ask Boomer about the unfamiliar codewords, his primary radio crackled into life. "Poison, this is Magic. We have troops in contact three-five nautical miles north-west of your position. Are you able to assist?"

Boomer replied before Mike could. "Magic, that's a negative. We are approaching bingo fuel, unable to assist at this time."

Mike couldn't believe his ears. "What the hell, Boomer?" he asked on the interplane frequency. "Are you kidding me? Those guys need help."

"Yes, they do. And we don't have the fuel to help them. By the time we reached their location, we'd have to turn back. Our replacements are coming on station in five minutes. They can take this one and actually do something useful."

"What if that's too late?"

"Dammit Mike, I'm flight lead tonight. We're going home. We'll discuss this on the ground."

Mike could feel his face heat up underneath his oxygen mask. Four weeks on deployment without a single iota of excitement. Now, something finally happens, and they ignore it? Fuck that. "Magic, this is Poison 2. Disregard last, Poison formation is heading to that location now."

"Magic copies, Poison. Contact JTAC direct on TACSAT Channel #6, callsign Excalibur 6. Magic out."

"Mike, what the fuck are you doing?" Boomer's voice was measured, but dripped with cold, controlled anger.

"Something, Boomer. I'm doing something." He smacked his stick full right, rolling his Harrier inverted, then pulled back hard. The aircraft's stubby nose pointed towards the ground, its height dropping rapidly as its speed increased. Mike ran through figures quickly in his mind. Six hundred knots, that's ten miles a minute. Thirty-five miles to the firefight—he'd be there in three and a half minutes. Lots to do, not much time to do it.

He glanced quickly over his right shoulder. As he'd hoped, Boomer was following him, his aircraft sitting just off Mike's starboard wing. The guy might be pissed off, but he wasn't about to abandon his wingman. Although Mike guessed he was flight lead now. "Poison formation, go switches live."

"Copied, Poison 1 switches live."

Mike tried to ignore the anger still present in Boomer's voice. The weapons systems on both aircraft were now fully activated, safety systems disengaged. The Harriers weren't carrying bombs or rockets—they were up there to deter Serbian aircraft, not provide ground fires—but they each had a pair of Aden 30mm cannon pods tucked under their bellies. More than enough firepower to ruin someone's day.

Twenty miles to run. Time to check in with the Joint Terminal Attack Controller—the JTAC.

This was the person who would direct them during the strike. If Mike's job was tough, the JTAC's was much, much worse: they had to spot the two aircraft rushing towards them—tiny points of light in a huge sky—then direct them towards the enemy and do all this while in the middle of a firefight. Mike hit transmit, "Broadsword 6, this is Poison formation, pair of Harriers currently two-zero miles south-east of your location. Guns only. Request target location and bearing for run-in."

"Poison, this is Broadsword 6." It was the Texan. "God, I am happy to hear you guys. Target designation will be laser strobe. Run in on a bearing of 270."

Mike read back the information, then jinked the nose of the aircraft right by a few degrees. He'd be running in east to west, using a lazy left turn to line up with the target.

Ten miles. One minute to go.

"Poison, this is Broadsword. I am visual with your formation. Confirm you have target in sight?"

Mike looked down through the left side of the canopy. By now, the aircraft had dropped to a thousand feet. Treetops streaked past, a blur of black and green through his night vision goggles. He scanned the terrain, looking for the telltale wink of a laser strobe. *There!* On the aircraft's ten o'clock, a semi-circular gap in the blanket of trees like a giant bite ripped out of the vegetation. On the northern edge of the clearing, a bloom of light was flicking on and off. He started his left turn. "Broadsword, Poison is visual with the target. Setting up for guns run now."

"Copy that, Poison. Be aware, this will be danger close. Friendlies are one hundred meters to the south of the target."

Shit! One hundred meters? That wasn't danger close, it was danger on top. Just one degree off heading and his shells would be hitting friendly troops, not the enemy. He forced the thought to the back of his mind. *Focus.* He rolled out of his lazy turn heading due west, the laser strobe sitting dead center at the top of his Head-Up Display. This was it. Behind him, Boomer had pulled into a tight right-hand orbit—he'd wait for Mike to complete his run before he took his turn.

Two miles. "Broadsword, Poison running in hot." He slid out his air brakes, slowing the aircraft down so he'd have more time over the target. The laser strobe started tracking down the glass of his HUD towards the gunsight symbol. Off to the left, he could see flashes of small arms fire from inside the tree line—the Broadsword team fighting for their lives. Around the strobe itself, dark shapes were flitting around like moths around a candle. What the hell was he about to fire at?

His gunsight slid over the strobe. Mike squeezed the trigger and fire spat from the belly of the aircraft, two glowing arcs of tracers reaching out to the ground. The aircraft buckled beneath him from the recoil as four hundred high explosive rounds launched from his gun pods at twice the speed of sound. In a few seconds, the cannons were dry. He slammed the throttles forward, pulled back on the stick, and put the aircraft into a steep climb, eager to get away from any threat on the ground. Too late.

"SAM, SAM! Missile on your six." Boomer's voice rang out over the roar of Mike's straining engine.

Mike's head whipped round. Behind him, a dark shape was reaching toward his aircraft. He slammed the stick full right, converting the climb into a tight barrel roll. The shape streaked past his port wingtip, missing the control surfaces by inches.

He fought the G-forces pushing him into the seat and looked down at his radar warning receiver. The little screen, designed to pick up and display emissions from enemy SAM sites, remained disconcertingly blank. Whatever had just been fired him, it wasn't radar-guided.

Mike eased off the back pressure on the stick and rolled the aircraft level. He scanned the night sky in front of him for any sign of the threat. *There!* 2 o'clock high. As soon as he spotted it, the shape started to turn. For a second, it was silhouetted perfectly against the full moon.

It wasn't a missile. It was alive.

Framed against the pale light of the moon was a huge winged creature, its narrow body arching down between a pair of slowly beating wings. It hung there for an instant, a falcon scanning for prey. And then, with a twist of its torso, it was coming straight for Mike's aircraft like an avenging angel.

He squeezed his trigger in panic. Nothing—the guns were dry. The shape was almost on him. He tried to jink left, far too late. The whole aircraft shuddered as razor-sharp claws the size of kitchen knives ripped through the fuselage.

Mike's cockpit lit up like a Christmas tree, warning lights casting an eerie red light on the canopy.

ENGINE FIRE.

"Shit!"

That wasn't good.

He looked behind him. The shape was disappearing back towards the ground, almost lost behind the hungry flames erupting from his four, engine exhausts. As he watched, the fire spread to his wings. He had seconds before the whole aircraft fell apart around him.

"Mayday, Mayday. Poison 2, engine fire. Ejecting."

Mike took one last look around. Boomer was still behind him, powerless to help. His wingman couldn't even stay overhead to protect him as he parachuted down to the ground—as predicted, both aircraft were nearly out of fuel.

Shit shit shit. Here we go.

He reached between his legs and pulled the handle of his Martin-Baker ejection seat, triggering a precise sequence of events over the next two seconds. Above his head, a web of miniature detonating cord ignited, shattering his canopy into tiny pieces. Restraint cords that had previously hung loose tightened in an instant, pinning his legs and arms to the seat. A heartbeat later, he felt an incredible force pushing up on him from below as his seat exploded into life. Then everything went black.

"Higher, Daddy," Mike squealed in excitement. He loved the swings, loved the feeling of freedom as he rose towards the sky, wind rushing through his hair. "I want to go higher!"

It was dead of night, and the playground was deserted. Abandoned equipment lay rusted and cracked in the moonlight: to the right, a plastic swing, snapped in two by an invisible hand; to the left, a roundabout creaking a slow death rattle. Nature was reclaiming this place, grass forcing its way up through gaps in the tarmac. Beyond the playground fence, a dark forest loomed, stern legions of trees hiding terrors in the shadows between them. But behind him, he could feel the reassuring presence of his father and he knew everything would be alright.

The swing slowed down to a gentle rock. "Sorry, Son," his father whispered. "Time to wake up."

Mike opened his eyes and saw the lush green forest floor swaying six feet below him. Morning sunlight was streaming through the trees, casting dappled shadows on the foliage that shimmered and rippled in the light breeze. He checked his watch, mild confusion creasing his forehead. 0600 local time. That felt like it should be important somehow. Then the events of the previous night came back in a rush.

The strafing run. The ejection. *The creature*. It was still out there somewhere. And he'd been hanging in these trees completely defenseless for hours.

He glanced around to get his bearings. Above him, his parachute was hopelessly entangled in the treetops, multiple lines of cord connecting the silk canopy to two thick nylon risers on his harness. He reached down to the leg of his flying suit and drew his aircrew knife from its sheath. The blade was designed to cut through the risers with one smooth motion, and it did its job well. Too well, perhaps. The risers gave way under the blade, and he felt a moment of exhilarating freefall before hitting the ground with a bang that knocked the wind out of him.

As his mind cleared, training kicking in, replacing the fog of shock with a well-rehearsed series of priorities. He checked himself from top to bottom for serious injuries. There were parts of his body aching that he didn't know existed. Martin-Baker designed their ejection seats to save lives, but they didn't guarantee a smooth ride. He'd heard stories during training of ejectees leaving their kneecaps behind when they banged out. No broken bones, no serious bleeds, just cuts and bruises. Maybe he wasn't so unlucky after all.

He reached down to his hip and drew his Walther PPK, ejecting the magazine and pressing down on the exposed top round. A full mag, seven rounds. He slapped the magazine back into the pistol and the ghost of a smile flickered on his lips. Just holding the weapon made him feel better, like he could take on the world.

Then he sat down next to the tree he'd been hanging from and started going through the many bulging pockets on the combat survival vest he wore. A button compass, tiny and difficult to read, yet crucial. A silk map, tightly folded, the scale large enough to cover the entire Balkans. Not particularly practical for anything other than the crudest of navigation, but around the edges were pictures of local edible plants and useful phrases in Serbo-Croat. Flares, the big handheld type. When activated, they would burn with a fierce light that rescuers could see for miles, even in daylight. A secure radio, his lifeline and ticket out of this mess. He carefully put it aside—he'd need it in a few minutes. Lots of 'high energy rations', which to the casual observer would look just like regular chocolate bars. Water, stored in small plastic pouches, each containing just enough to quench thirst.

He had everything he needed to survive, and the forest was a friendly environment anyway, ripe for scavenging. All he had to do was avoid whatever the hell it was that had taken down his aircraft. Best not to think about that too much. He wasn't ready to deal with that particular problem just yet.

He repacked his vest and turned on the secure radio. It was a matt green brick of a device, built to survive a crash landing, with a small digital screen inset above a line of rubber keys. After a few minutes, a light on the side turned green, telling him that the inbuilt GPS had fixed his location. Perfect—now to sort out his pickup and get the hell out of Dodge. He tapped out a quick message, held the radio in the air and hit send. An electronic message in a bottle winged its way upwards through the atmosphere, an encrypted databurst complete with position accurate to a meter, heading straight into the waiting receiver of an overhead satellite. Now all he had to do was wait for the cavalry to arrive. He settled down against the trunk of the tree and cradled his pistol.

Thirty minutes passed before the radio chirped. He had to read the message three times before he could believe his eyes.

Airborne extraction is not possible due threat. RV with ground troops 2 miles east of your location for land extraction.

No helicopter was coming for him. No friendly bird of freedom would take him home to his bunk tonight. Instead, he was going to have to trek through the forest, meet up with a bunch of soldiers-probably the same guys he saved last night-and then walk out of the woods to a safe location. This was definitely *not* what he'd signed up for. Still, it wasn't as if he had a choice. Sighing, he stood up, checked his compass, and headed east.

There it was again.

The rustling had started about half an hour ago, a suggestion of motion deep in the thick branches. At first, he thought it was the wind moving the leaves, or perhaps a bird hopping through the undergrowth. Now he was pretty sure whatever was causing the rustling was bigger than a bird. Much bigger. And it was following him.

The cool dawn had turned into a beautiful morning, liquid gold sunlight streaming through the forest canopy, but a light breeze keeping the temperature comfortable. Despite that cool wind on his face, he had worked up a good sweat. He'd been walking for the best part of two hours, his progress constantly hindered by patches of dense foliage. The GPS on his radio was keeping him more or less on track, but he'd covered about six miles already and still hadn't reached the rendezvous. His legs were aching, the bruises he'd picked up in the ejection were screaming out for attention, and he had a bitch of a headache. The last thing he needed was a stalker.

A branch snapped behind him, the crack echoing through the calm of the forest and sending flocks of birds screeching into the air.

Something inside him snapped at the same time. The rational part of his brain was yelling at him to run, but he ignored it. He was tired, aching, and pissed off. It was time to take back control of the situation. He drew his pistol and stomped over to the source of the noise.

"Right, you bastard, come on out," he yelled into the bushes, waving his gun in what he hoped was a threatening fashion. His training hadn't covered invisible stalkers—a major oversight, he felt—so he was making this up as he went along.

A minute passed. Nothing happened. He realized he hadn't really thought about the next steps should his stalker not respond to his reasonable request. Another minute passed. He wondered whether he'd been mistaken, whether the rustling *had* just been the breeze, in which case he'd been threatening a (presumably) innocent tree. He was about to walk away when, thirty yards ahead of him, a nightmare emerged from the branches.

Above and Beyond

When Mike was a child, his parents had taken him and his sister to a local zoo. As part of the 'Birds of Prey' exhibition, a grim-faced keeper had coaxed a huge bald eagle onto their outstretched arms. His sister had loved it, but the memory of that experience had haunted Mike's dreams for weeks afterwards. It wasn't the sharp talons digging into his arm that had scared him, nor that cruel, hooked beak. No, it was the eyes, those uncaring, black eyes that looked deep into your soul. Eyes that you knew would remain lifeless even as their owner chased its prey down and ripped it apart.

Those same dead eyes stared at Mike now, bulging out of a leathered mockery of a human face. The creature's nose was hooked and broken, its mouth a jagged red tear lined with diamond-shaped teeth. It wore no clothes, body covered in that same thick leathery skin as the face, and wicked-looking claws protruded from its stubby fingers and toes. It was hunched over slightly, yet still stood at least as tall as Mike. Huge, feathered wings sprouted from each shoulder-blade, stretching out a full four feet in each direction, like a perverted angel. The right wing had a hole the size of a basketball ripped through its center, blood still dripping from the wound.

As Mike watched, mouth open in disbelief, the beast took a step towards him. Then another, and another, until it was loping forward at speed, clawed hands reaching out.

Hands shaking, he raised his weapon, pointed it at the terror bearing down on him, and snatched at the trigger, once, twice. The rounds impacted harmlessly into the branches above the rapidly approaching creature. Tossing the gun down, he turned to run. He'd only taken ten steps when his foot snagged on a tree root, and he fell hard.

Breathing heavily, he flipped himself around, desperately scrabbling backwards with his hands, his fingers sinking deep into the soft loamy soil of the forest floor. The creature was looming over him now, jaws drooling. Time seemed to slow for Mike, his senses sharpening in the face of impending death. His attacker raised its clawed hands and screeched a terrible cry of victory. *This is it*, he thought, his mind strangely calm. The creature's claws plunged down towards his belly.

Suddenly, the air filled with the aggressive *braapp* of automatic gunfire. As Mike watched, the monster's head exploded, showering him in blood and gore. The corpse remained standing, headless, for a long second before it collapsed in a heap next to him.

A familiar Texan drawl rang out against the echoes of gunfire. "Mike Travers, I presume?"

"So I'm not going home?"

"You're going home, son. Just not yet."

Mike closed his eyes and took a deep breath. This wasn't over yet.

The Texan had introduced himself as Troy, fitting for a man who looked like he'd stepped straight out of a Greek myth with his olive-tanned skin and bulging biceps. "I'm in command of this bunch of reprobates. You've got Zoltan over there, our heavy weapons specialist." He nodded to a bear of a man whose face was largely hidden behind a bushy ginger beard. He was resting the barrel of a light machine gun against his shoulder as if it were a lady's parasol.

"Doc, our intel analyst, and team medic." A tall, balding man wearing wire-frame glasses nodded at Mike.

"And this is Cherish, our sniper."

The dark-haired woman from the canteen was standing some distance away from the rest of the team, leaning against a tree trunk. She had scowled at Mike, lip-curled. "You sure we have to take him with us, Sarge? He's just going to slow us down and we're running late as it is."

"Orders is orders, Cherish. He's coming with us."

She'd deliberately turned her attention back to her weapon then, a long-barreled rifle nearly as tall as she was. "He's probably going to die anyway," she'd muttered.

That had been five minutes ago. Mike had taken that long to come to terms with the news. He still hadn't really come to terms with it. He was just too tired to care anymore. He opened his eyes and nodded at Troy. The warrior turned to his team.

Here comes the stirring motivational speech, Mike thought.

"Alright losers, let's saddle up. We need to take out this nest before sunset or we're screwed."

Well, that was one kind of motivation.

"Zoltan, you're on point. Cherish, take up the rear. Mike, are you armed?"

"Sure," he said, reaching down to his holster. His empty holster. Feeling warmth rise to his cheeks, he stepped over and picked up his pistol from where it had been tossed to the ground in his panic.

"Is that a Walther?" Cherish asked, her eyebrow arched.

"It is indeed," Mike replied with a wan smile, completely misinterpreting her expression. "Like it?"

"Sorry, wait, I've got an incoming message," she said, touching her outstretched finger to an imaginary earpiece. "It's the museum. They want their peashooter back."

"Enough, Cherish," Troy barked. "Mike, stay close to me. Let's go."

With that, the team started moving through the forest, keeping a loose formation as they wound through the trees. They walked in silence, weapons lowered but ready, each knowing instinctively when to shift to cover another's arc of fire. A well-oiled machine. Mike just hoped he wasn't the grit that jammed the gears.

After a few minutes of silent movement, he risked asking a question. "So what the hell was that thing that attacked me?"

Troy looked over in surprise, as if he'd forgotten the pilot was there. "Doc, do you want to take that one?"

"Sure thing, sarge," Doc answered. He was walking about thirty yards behind Mike, but his East Coast twang carried clearly.

"The JTF-13 scientists call them *Homo Cathartes*. We just call 'em harpies. Real nasty bastards they are, too. Not too intelligent, barely sentient really—but they're cruel sons of bitches. They like to torture their prey, see, watch them die slow. When they're not killing things, their hobbies include chasing bright lights, collecting shiny things—they're obsessed with anything that glitters, basically. Evil magpies, for want of a better phrase. Oh, and they're nocturnal. Daylight makes them sluggish. Lucky for you."

"That was a sluggish one?" Mike shuddered. "Hey, what was that about JTF-something?"

"JTF-13. That's us," Troy said. He shook his head. "We're going to have a hell of a time sorting your clearances out when you get back."

"Not if he dies first," Cherish called out happily from the back of the column.

"The conflict drew the harpies here," said Troy, ignoring the sniper. "They've been torturing and killing civilians. Only a matter of time before they start on the UN troops. That's why we're here. Plan A was to lure them into the open last night, then take them out with an air strike. You know how that went. We lost two good men last night."

Mike paled. "Blue on blue?"

"Amos was shredded by those flying bastards. Brett... Well, there are always inherent risks in calling in strikes when it's danger-close. I knew the risk. I took it. Don't beat yourself up about it."

Mike's heart dropped. He felt physically sick, a toxic mix of shame and guilt flooding through him like a tidal wave.

Troy grabbed him by the shoulders. "Park it, son. I've said it's fine and I don't have time to put up with your self-pity. Last night went wrong, so we're onto Plan B. These harpy bastards hide out during the day. They like cool, dark spaces. We got confirmation this morning that overhead surveillance has located their nesting location in a cave about six klicks from here. We get there before nightfall, blow the cave entrance, and bingo. Threat neutralized."

"Wait," Mike said. "Whatever attacked my aircraft last night was bigger than that harpy today. A lot bigger."

Troy glanced back at Doc. "We'd heard rumors that there may be a Queen involved."

Mike stopped dead in his tracks. "A Queen? Harpy? A Queen harpy?"

"Yes, Mike, a Queen harpy. We'll deal with it. It's what we do. Now come on. We've lost too much time already diverting to pick you up. Sun sets in three hours. If we don't blow the cave by then, we're all screwed."

Mike took a deep breath and started walking again. This day just kept getting better and better.

It took them another two hours to get to the cave. Zoltan, the point man, spotted it first, raising his right fist in the air. It took Mike a second to realize everyone else in the team had stopped.

"What have you got, Z?" Troy called out.

"Looks like our target, sarge. Can we get some optics up here?"

Troy motioned to Cherish. The tall woman jogged up to join Zoltan, then took a knee and raised her weapon's scope to her eye. After a few long minutes, she finally gestured to the rest of the team to come up and join them.

The three of them moved forward, Mike sticking to Troy like a shadow, Doc a few feet behind. As they got closer to Zoltan and Cherish, the soft forest soil transitioned into a loose gravelly scree.

Through the thinning trees, Mike could see a sheer cliff-face erupt vertically from the shale about a thousand yards ahead of them. The rocky barrier stretched left and right as far as the eye could see, an uncrossable wall stretching into the sky.

Dead ahead, at the base of the cliff, a black hole opened. It reminded Mike of a gaping maw, one wide enough and tall enough to swallow a bus. A few oddly shaped sticks were scattered around the entrance, blanched white by the sunshine. The breeze picked up and for the first time, the smell hit him, a combination of ammonia and rotting flesh powerful enough to bring tears to his eyes. This was the place, alright.

"What do you think, Z? Can we do this?" Troy asked.

"It'll be tight. Real tight. But it's doable."

"OK then, don't waste time talking to me. Get those charges placed. Doc, we'll cover Zoltan from there," he said, pointing towards an enormous boulder, ten feet high if it was an inch, about halfway between the trees and the cave entrance. "Cherish, can you get up a tree or something? Give us some top cover."

"Sure thing, boss," she answered. She slung the huge rifle across her back and started to shimmy up a nearby tree with astounding grace. After a couple of seconds, she called down. "In position."

"OK," said Troy. "Go, go, go."

The four of them jogged towards the boulder, weapons in the high ready, Mike clutching his Walther as if his life depended on it. They reached the rock, Troy and Doc smoothly taking up firing positions on either side of the stony edges while Zoltan ran on to the cave entrance. In the absence of further orders, Mike stayed close by Troy's side.

The next forty-five minutes seemed to last an eternity. As the rest of the team provided cover, Zoltan moved around the cave mouth, placing rectangular lumps of gray plastic at regular intervals along the edge of the entrance. The soldier was clearly a skilled free climber, scaling the rocky cliff face then clambering left and right above the opening like an oversized gecko. By the time he had set the last charge, the sun was dropping behind the horizon.

"Hurry, goddammit," Troy muttered under his breath.

Zoltan picked up his weapon from where he'd propped it against the cliff and slung it over his back. It looked like a child's toy across his broad shoulders. Then crouching over, he backed towards the boulder where Mike and the others waited, unrolling a command wire as he went. The bare metal of the wire glinted as the evening sun hit it, a glimmering line of light that twinkled in the dusk half-light.

Finally, the big man made it back to the safety of the boulder. "This is going to be one big bang," he warned as he handed a detonator to Troy.

The sergeant called up to Cherish. "We're clear. Get your ass down here and take cover."

"Already on it, top." The sniper was already swinging down from the lowest branch of her tree. She dropped to the ground in a crouch, then sprinted to the boulder and the rest of the team. "Clear."

With everyone now lined up safely behind the cover of the huge rock, Troy raised the detonator. It looked like a militarized staple-gun to Mike. "OK," Troy said. "On three. One... Two... Three..." He squeezed the handle...

Nothing happened.

"What the fuck?" said Troy, looking at Zoltan for answers. The big man just shrugged his shoulders.

Mike peeked around the corner of the boulder, then pulled his head back quickly. "I thought you said those things weren't intelligent, Doc."

"They ain't."

"Then why has one of them just ripped up your wire?"

"Shit."

The entire team came out from behind their cover. About halfway between them and the cave entrance, a harpy stood astride the command wire. It had picked up the metal cord in clawed hands, tearing and ripping at the bare steel. It looked like it was currently trying to eat one end of the twisted strands.

"It's the sunlight glinting off the wire," Doc said, disbelief in his voice. "It's attracted to the damn sunlight."

"Fascinating," Cherish said, deadpan, as she raised her rifle to her shoulder. She took a second to aim through the big scope, then squeezed the trigger. The harpy's head vanished in a spray of bright red blood. "It's not attracted to it anymore

"OK," said Troy. "We can still make this work. Zoltan, get out there and patch up the wire. Call me when it's done."

"On it." The big man took off at pace towards the breach in the wire just as the last few rays of sunlight slipped beneath the horizon. He dropped to his knees for the last few feet like a baseball player sliding into base.

Mike's ears were ringing from the sound of Cherish's shot, but under the buzzing, he could hear something new; a screeching, growing in volume until it reached a terrible crescendo.

"We're too late," said Doc.

The cave mouth erupted with activity, an immense black wave emerged into the night sky; swarms of harpies screaming furiously, with their claws outstretched.

"Keep them off Z," Troy yelled, gesturing towards the big man caught out in the open.

The darkness lit up with multiple muzzle bursts as the team opened fire. Harpies dropped from the sky, but for every one that fell, another two took its place. The monsters were circling overhead the squad, diving towards the ground whenever they saw an opportunity to attack, raking out with those vicious claws. Zoltan, still focused on splicing the command wire, was taking the brunt of the attack. "Nearly there," he called, as another dead harpy smashed to the ground next to him, a smoking hole in its chest from one of Cherish's .50 cal rounds.

Throughout the firefight, Mike stood with his back pressed against the boulder, trying to avoid the attention of the harpies while staying out of the way of the JTF-13 shooters. His gaze was dragged left and right, as creature after creature flew past. Suddenly, one was in front of him, its horrible leathery mouth opened in a scream, black eyes fixed on him. He fired off a couple of rounds from his Walther. One hit the creature in the wing but seemed just to aggravate it. He felt a fiery line materialize on his left arm, looked down in surprise to see blood dripping from deep grooves in his biceps. The harpy screeched in triumph, licking the gore off its claw. He hadn't even seen the attack. It had been so quick.

A knife tip burst through the beast's mouth, like a second tongue. Wet gurgles sputtered from its throat, and it slumped to the ground, sliding free from the combat knife tightly clutched in Cherish's hand. "Next time you're on your own," she hissed.

Gradually the firefight seemed to turn in the JTF's favor, the hordes thinned out by sheer weight of the team's combined fire. Then Mike felt the earth shake underneath his feet. He peered round the boulder to see two clawed hands, each the size of a family car, grasp either end of the cave entrance. A huge leathery face emerged, followed by a misshapen body, as the Queen crawled out of the cave on shortened limbs, like a winged lizard. It was easily twenty feet from head to toe. Once clear of the cave, it launched itself into the air, moving with surprising speed for something so big. Then it twisted and dove for Zoltan.

Rounds ricocheted off its flanks as it plunged through the night sky, but its thick leathery skin acted as natural body armor. With a screech that split the air, it passed low over Zoltan, scooping him up in clawed hind-legs like a field mouse and carrying him a hundred feet into the air before letting him drop, screaming, to the ground.

Mike felt his whole body shake. There was no way out. It was over.

"Hey, Sarge," Doc yelled out between bursts of fire, "I think Z might've fixed the wire before he got snatched."

"No use now, Doc. These bastards are all out. We'd be blasting an empty cav-*arrrghh*!" Troy's voice became a yell of pain as a harpy skewered his leg. He collapsed, drawing a pistol from a hip holster as he did, putting two shots into his attacker's brainpan. The harpy fell on him, pinning him to the ground.

Mike looked around in a panic. Cherish had three harpies closing in on her as she slashed wildly with her knife, the sniper rifle lying empty at her feet. Doc had taken a wicked-looking injury to his right leg, and was now shooting from a prone position, occasionally rolling over on his back to take shots at those harpies directly above him. As Mike watched, the queen circled round again and plunged for the medic, skewering him through the shoulder with six-foot-long claws.

The team was all down. Mike realized he was the only one still standing. He didn't think he'd last long against these odds. Then he remembered what was in his survival vest.

Fuck it. If we're going to die, better to go down fighting.

"Get that detonator ready!" he shouted to Troy. Then he reached into his jacket and produced one of his flares. He struck the flare and held it high in the air. The thick tube burst into incandescent red light, the flames casting flickering bloody shadows around the killing ground.

From high above, the queen harpy screeched its approval.

Here we go.

He sprinted as fast as he could towards the cave entrance. After twenty seconds, his lungs were on fire. He could sense the queen swooping down behind him, lining up for a killer strike. He put on an extra burst of speed, drawing on reserves he never knew he had.

The entrance grew bigger, and before he knew it, he had burst into the darkness of the cave. He kept sprinting blind, eyes not yet adjusted to the sudden change of light, until he smashed into a wall at the far end of the cavern. He sank to the rocky ground and turned to watch the queen enter the cave, stomping towards him, the red glow from the flare reflecting the rage and blood in its black eyes.

Why hasn't he blown it yet?. Oh God-the wire is still snapped.

The entire world exploded.

He was back in the playground, but this time he could feel the warm summer sun on his skin.

"Well done, son," his father said from behind him. The unmistakably familiar Texan twang added, "You killed the monster."

The sunlight grew ever brighter. He squeezed his eyes shut, but still the light grew more intense, like a laser beam drilling into his brain until…

His eyelids fluttered open. He was lying in complete darkness, save for a single beam of dust-studded daylight stretching from a point in the black. Mike pushed himself into a seated position, the point expanded into a crack, then a bright white circle. He heard voices, quiet murmurs, as if coming from a great distance.

"I can see him, Troy. Looks like he's alive."

"I don't fucking believe it. Well, keep going then. Let's get him out of there."

As his eyes adjusted to the growing light, dim shapes in the darkness resolved into recognizable objects. A rock here, a pile of bones there, and- *Jesus!*

He pushed himself backwards in shock until he slammed up against the cave wall. Just a few feet in front of him lay the head of the Queen harpy. Its face was a rictus of pain, a gaping maw displaying rows dagger-like teeth. It was big enough to devour him in two bites. Behind the head, the supine body of the immense beast disappeared underneath the rockfall that had crushed it to death.

"Mike Travers, I presume?" The voice still sounded distant. He looked up. Troy stood next to him.

Mike nodded, choked with emotion. His shoulders shook as huge sobs of relief racked his body.

"It's alright, son. You're safe now. Sorry it took us so long to reach you—after the queen went down, we had to mop up the rest of the grunts." He flicked his powerful flashlight upwards. The cave extended a hundred feet straight up, reaching high into the bowels of the mountain. "At least we know there aren't any left in here. Otherwise, I wouldn't be talking to you now."

Mike started to answer, then realized he couldn't hear his own voice. His eyes opened wide in panic.

"It's ok," Troy said. For the first time, Mike noticed the sergeant was shouting, even though his voice sounded quiet as a whisper. "The blast damaged your eardrums. They'll recover. And so will you. You up to walking?"

"Hell yes," Mike yelled. He clambered to his feet and put his arm around Troy's shoulder. The two of them walked to the gap in the rockfall and clambered out of the cave that had become a tomb. Outside, Mike could see Cherish crouched over Doc. The tall man had bandages over most of his body, but he was still breathing.

"Helo inbound. ETA 30 mikes," Cherish called out to Troy. Then she looked at Mike, and for the first time since he'd met her, flashed a smile. "Good job, soldier. Ever thought about a career change?"

Mike smiled weakly. Time to go home.

THE END

R. L. Parker

Incident at Tarok Kolache
By: R.L. Parker

Nothing felt better than climbing into a Hawk after a mission. No matter how many times he did it, that feeling never went away. There was always a risk that he wouldn't return, or that he'd have to be carried on board someday. No matter the injuries—and there had been plenty in the past—he always made every attempt to climb into their ride home on his own power.

This time around, he'd avoided any real injuries. That wasn't too uncommon for a typical mission, but what they'd just been through wasn't what he'd classify as typical. Intel had been wrong; the downed team was much farther behind enemy lines than they'd been told, and damned if it wasn't another ambush. They'd made it out and achieved their mission; but the cost had been high. Two of his men were injured, and another had paid the ultimate price. All to save a Seal Team that'd strayed off course.

Incident at Tarok Kolache

It was hard not to be petty when things played out so poorly. Special operators were only as good as the information they received, and clearly both teams had gotten bad intel. It was a clusterfuck, and the men piled into the Pave Hawk around him had paid the price for it. What was worse was that it wasn't the people who made the mistakes that had to stand in front of Tech Sergeant Braden's wife and tell her he served his country honorably. No, that would be his job, and he'd have no good explanation for her when he did it… at least nothing he could legally share with a civilian.

A voice came over his headset, breaking the stream of thoughts that were threatening to go toxic. "Colonel Archon on board?" the pilot asked. His voice sounded frantic.

"I am, what's up?" answered Archon.

"Gotta drop you off, sir, we-"

"You gotta be shittin' me. We were literally just picked up. Half my men are down!"

"Sorry, sir, but this came from HQ. Team nine reported a Metal Door situation, and you're the closest unit."

"What the fuck is a 'Metal Door'?"

"Sorry sir, I got nothin' else. Orders are to drop you off to hold the position. Another team is inbound, but they're ninety minutes out. If I don't get you down there, it's a total wipe."

"Fuck!"

"We doin' this Colonel?" asked TSgt. Conwell.

"Grab what you can, boys… we gotta hold out for ninety," he ordered. "Doc, throw me that bag," he added, pointing next to the medic's knee. He started filling the bag with supplies as soon as it was within reach.

"So much for the nap, eh Colonel?" joked Staff Sergeant Maddox, fishing around for anything useful.

The three of them spent the next few minutes checking their ammunition and ordnance. Their last firefight had depleted a large portion of what they'd brought with them, but with two of their own badly wounded, another deceased, and all four of the Seals they rescued similarly out of commission, they had plenty of pockets and pouches to dig through. The one Seal the doc hadn't already dosed with morphine handed over his own ammo, and a few grenades.

"Ain't got enough, Colonel," said Conwell, holding up his last remaining M4 magazine.

"Maddox, sling your M4 and pass your mags to Conwell. Grab that SCAR," said Archon, pointing at the assault rifle before tossing the Seals' magazines to his best shooter.

"Hell yes, sir!" chimed Maddox.

"Runnin' light on 9mm," added Archon, checking his M9 rounds. "Fight better not get personal."

"Thirty seconds to drop off, sir," called the pilot.

Archon swiveled on his heel and grabbed the edge of the side door, peering out to get a look. They were moving fast and low, dangerously close to the random poles and pipes that jutted up from the sand-colored buildings and rubble below. Most of the town seemed to have been destroyed sometime prior. Only a few buildings were still standing, and those were just barely hanging on. "What's hot?"

"I believe all of it, sir, or none of it. We aren't sure," answered the pilot.

"You're droppin' us in with zero intel? We can't clear the whole damned city, son."

"No choice, sir. Captain Ferris was our intel, and he's gone dark. All we got was a 'Metal Door' and some coordinates."

"Fuck," sighed Archon.

A few seconds later, the chopper slowed and came to a hover just above an intersection in the cramped streets below. Dust and sand whipped through the air violently, making it difficult to get a good view of what was waiting for them at ground level. The only peace of mind Archon could find in the situation was that they hadn't yet been fired upon.

"Mad, you've got point," he said, his arm out and urging his man forward.

The Staff Sergeant complied. As he stepped to the edge, the three of them tossed their headsets to the floor and hooked into their rappelling lines. One by one they descended to the street below and fell into a defensive formation. Once they were free from the ropes, they ducked into a nearby alley at Maddox's lead, and stopped to gain their bearings.

As the rapid thump of rotary blades and the angry roar of their ride's engine faded into the distance, one thing immediately struck them all. "It's way too fuckin' quiet, Arc," said Conwell, giving voice to what they were all thinking.

"Where're we headed, Arc?" asked Maddox.

"Sit tight and listen," answered Archon.

After a few moments, the Hawk was fully out of range. The only regular noise they could hear was small gusts of wind moving through the buildings, and the occasional piece of fabric or paper fluttering in the distance. It was eerily quiet. Archon could feel a slowly building warmth in his gut as his anxiety heightened. This was supposed to be an active war zone. Nothing unnerved him more than a quiet, damned-near peaceful, war zone.

"I don't th—" started Maddox.

Archon cut him off with an abrupt shush. A very faint hum was emanating from a building not too far away. It was barely perceptible, but out of place none-the-less. With nothing else to go on, that strange sound would have to act as their only clue.

He identified the building with a few tilts of his head, isolating the direction the sound was traveling from. Turning his head toward Maddox, he gave a quick nod and pointed his index and middle fingers toward the location. Maddox nodded back and moved around him to take the lead.

Each movement was precise and well-orchestrated as they advanced from cover to cover, studying their surroundings from each new location for a few brief moments before crossing open ground again. As one of them arrived at the teammate in front of them, they put their left hand on the other's shoulder, sending them into motion and then taking their place.

Eventually, they found themselves at a small opening in the south wall, located in a side alley. Some form of small ordinance had blown the wall out from the inside, leaving only remnants of the upper window frame in place, and a gaping hole near ground level. Maddox studied the interior briefly before entering, then stopped a few paces inside, slightly crouched and ready, his SCAR scanning the room methodically.

Archon entered next and moved to the far side of the room, checking every crevice, and behind every large piece of debris for signs of an enemy.

Conwell entered last, and took up Maddox's position, freeing Maddox to move to the base of the stairs.

The hum was much more noticeable inside the building. Maddox caught Archon's attention and put his hand to his ear, indicating that he had identified the source of the strange noise. He then pointed two fingers twice toward the stairs in a rapid motion. Archon nodded and moved in behind him. Conwell fell in at their rear and kept his attention behind them as they moved upward.

When they reached the first landing, Maddox came around and pointed his weapon up the stairs, but hesitated. A strange blue glow was sending pulsating shadows into the stairwell from the room beyond. The hum was oscillating. There was a certain metallic taste to the air that none of them could put their finger on.

Archon's anxiety hit a new high. Something bad was about to happen, he was certain of it. A falling sensation in the core of his gut accompanied that feeling, and the hair on his arms standing on end.

The wall above them blew open. A gaping, crumbling hole replacing the space where the door should have been. There were no pieces of door lying about, and no evidence that one had ever existed, aside from the stairs they were ascending. A pulsing blue and white light that matched the rhythm of the strange humming noise illuminated the room. A faint sound of electric discharge cut through the deep, resonating hum at sporadic intervals, further raising Archon's concern and apprehension.

He placed his left hand on Maddox's shoulder, signaling him to stop and crouch. As he went around him, Conwell fell into place beside Maddox at the top of the stairs and kept his attention on the path behind them. His soldiers ready and waiting, Archon took a few steps forward and leaned, ever-so-slightly, around the crumbling opening's edge.

All the walls and rooms on the top floor of the poorly constructed building had taken similar damage as the door through which he peered. Several soldier's bodies lay strewn about the center of the room ahead of them, their feet pointed toward a shimmering blue light floating a foot and a half above the floor.

Keeping his eyes on the room, Archon held up four fingers on his left hand, and pointed down abruptly, signaling to his men that they had four casualties. He then raised his hand back up to shoulder height and pointed two fingers quickly toward the room. They stood and fell in behind him without a word.

As they entered the room, they each kept their weapons pointed in front of them, scanning their sector of the area for any sign of the enemy. Archon stopped a few feet from the fallen men, then turned to face the stairs while Maddox and Conwell finished clearing the floor.

A few moments later, Conwell calmly called out, "Clear." When neither of his teammates responded, he realized he hadn't spoken loud enough to cut through the almost deafening sound of the hum. "Clear!" he repeated as he approached Archon's position.

"Cover the stairs!" ordered Archon.

Conwell nodded in the affirmative and took the indicated defensive position.

Maddox slung the SCAR over his shoulder and knelt beside one of the fallen soldiers. "Uh, Arc? You ever seen this patch before?"

As Archon turned to face him, he saw a military patch flying through the air toward him, having been tossed by his man. He caught the patch as it slapped him in the chest, then turned it over to see the insignia. "JTF-13?"

"They Delta?" asked Maddox.

"I don't know *what* they are."

"Well, they're definitely operators."

"And this must be their 'Door'," added Archon, thumbing toward the blue light beside them. When they entered the room, the blue light appeared as a thin line above the floor. From their new angle, it was almost as large as a small car. The outside of the anomaly was a stark blue with tiny white bolts of lightning dancing across its surface. The inner expanse between the edges looked like an oily pool of blue liquid, rippling in reaction to the white bolts of energy. "Let's get these men away from that thing."

Archon slung his M4 and grabbed one of the men by the ankles. Maddox followed suit, and they proceeded to pull them toward the stairwell, next to Conwell. After retrieving the other two, they checked the men for signs of life.

"We're too late, Arc," said Maddox.

"We aren't here for them. We're here for that thing," answered Archon. "Whatever that is, we're here to hold this position because it's here. Otherwise, their recovery could wait for the next bird."

"I don't like this," said Conwell.

"Yeah, this is fucked, Arc," added Maddox.

"It is what it is, boys. See if you can find out what killed these men, and if you find any M9 mags, toss some my way."

"On it," said Maddox.

Archon stood back up and started walking slowly toward the anomaly. He only made it a few steps before Maddox called out to him.

"Got a brick, Arc, and it's hot." He reached up to hand the radio over, then continued checking the fallen men.

Archon grabbed the radio and stepped away from the anomaly to better hear what might be broadcasting. He didn't know anything about a

JTF-13, their command structure, or even what branch of the military they served. What he did know was that his team had been sent to help them, and he needed to report the men down. He pressed the transmit button firmly and calmly stated, "Area secure."

A few seconds later, the radio chirped, and a gruff voice came across. "Identify yourself."

"I could ask you to do the same," retorted Archon.

"I asked first," returned the voice.

"You want the status of your men, or we gonna dance all day?"

"Are you a member of the PJ unit diverted to help our men?"

"Ah, so you're JTF-13? Lieutenant Colonel Darren Archon, CRO from the 38th. And yes, half my team was dropped here to hold this position. Your men were down when we arrived."

"You're a long way from Moody, Colonel."

"Shit hit the fan; we came to help clean it."

"Well, I hope you boys are as good as they say you are. Assault team is inbound. ETA seventy-five minutes. Your position can not fall."

"What the hell are we protecting, here?"

"That blue shit still hanging around?" asked the voice.

"That an official term?" joked Archon.

"Is it still there?" huffed the voice on the other end, clearly not entertained.

"Affirmative."

"If anything steps through, kill it."

"Steps through?" asked Archon with a slight chuckle. He wasn't sure he believed what he was hearing.

"Confirm receipt of your orders."

"Confirmed. What about your men?"

"They aren't your concern."

"What?"

"They never existed."

"Uh," he started, then collected himself. "Affirmative." He hooked the radio to his belt and returned to Maddox and Conwell. "Black ops, boys. These guys were never here. Take what you need and line 'em up along that wall," he said, pointing toward the wall beside the stairwell opening. "Conwell. Stairs aren't important, our enemies aren't coming from outside. Apparently, they come through that blue light."

"They what, sir?" asked Maddox.

"Don't look at me," shrugged Archon. "Let's just arm up and get in position."

"It's wide open, sir. Nowhere to take cover," said Conwell.

"Use the stairwell. Set up behind the hole in the wall and stay focused. We'll watch it from the thin edge. If something comes through, it'll be easier to see."

"What the hell are we watching for?" asked Maddox.

"Unclear," said Archon.

"Well, *that's* just awesome," complained Maddox.

"Didn't say it was gonna be fun, just what we have to do," said Archon.

"Maybe a new girlfriend will climb out and introduce herself to ya, Mad," teased Conwell.

"Already got yer sister, Con. You can have her."

"Stow it. Stay focused," repeated Archon.

"These guys are covered in burn marks, Colonel, and they've all been stabbed through the chest.

Not a bullet wound in sight," said Maddox. "Whole room's littered with casings, the walls have been blown out… but there are no other bodies. What the hell were they fighting, sir?"

"Guess we'll find out the hard way," answered Archon. "Let's just get these guys out of the way and take our positions."

After they moved the bodies, Maddox and Conwell collected their remaining weapons, ammunition, and ordnance then organized everything within easy reach at the top of the stairs. Conwell laid down on the stairs with his feet braced against the sides and propped his M4 up on his elbow on the landing. Archon took position on the left side of the opening with his elbow braced atop his right knee, his weapon aimed at the light.

Maddox was last to take his position. He stopped next to Archon for a moment on his way to the right side of the opening and handed him a hand-sized metallic cylinder he'd found in one of the JTF-13 agents' bags. Archon turned it over in his hands a few times before giving Maddox a puzzled look.

"Remind you of anything?" asked Maddox.

"It seems oddly familiar, but nothing comes to mind," said Archon.

"Kinda looks like a miniature version of those portable EMP bombs the DARPA boys were toying with a few years back."

"I don't think they can make those things this small. At least not powerful enough to be worth anything," said Archon.

Maddox shrugged. "Ask your friend on the radio."

"I'll stow it for now. He's not very chatty. Besides, I still don't know who JTF-13 is."

"Don't trust 'em?" asked Conwell.

"HQ sent us here, so *somebody* up the chain recognizes them. I just don't trust agencies I know nothing about."

"Well, I-" started Conwell.

"Holy shit!" interrupted Maddox.

Everyone returned their attention to the strange blue light and watched closely. After watching for a while with no activity, Archon was about to ask what Maddox had witnessed. Before he could form the words, a small pair of pointed ears poked out of the blue light, emerging out of its left side.

A tiny, furry head followed shortly after, complete with dark, black eyes and a dog-like snout. After a few short seconds, the little head ducked back through the portal and out of existence.

"That was a fucking scout," said Maddox. His words were short, low volume, and almost rushed. His adrenaline was high, and he was ready to engage.

"If it pops out again, end that little fucker," said Archon.

"You sure, Arc? This seems like a world-changing event; meeting a life from another world. Shouldn't we-" started Conwell.

"You a fucking scientist now, Con? We have a mission. Orders are to kill whatever comes through. So…"

"We kill whatever comes through," said Conwell.

"Mad, Con, then me. Make your shots count."

"Check," said Maddox.

"Check," said Conwell.

They waited for what seemed like hours; long enough at least for Archon and Maddox's left arms to start growing weary of their firing positions. Just as Archon lowered his arm to stretch the joints, another small head poked through the portal.

Maddox fired one shot and hit the creature directly between the eyes. The rest of the being's body tumbled through and onto the floor. It was a small humanoid with dog-like rear legs and snout with black leathery wings on its back. Its fur seemed to be brown but was coated in a thin layer of soot. The stench of sulfur and ash filled the air as its corpse came to rest, carried to the men by an ironically timed breeze through the crumbled holes in the exterior walls.

"The fuck is that thing, Arc?" asked Conwell.

"Why would I know?"

"You're supposed to be the smart one, sir," joked Maddox.

Just then, dozens of the creatures poured through the portal. Some took to the air and hovered just over the portal, the rest turned directly toward the stairs and rushed the soldiers. Maddox and Archon immediately flicked their thumbs to put their rifles into three-round burst mode and opened fire. Conwell focused on precision fire against any targets that made it past their barrage and approached the firing line.

As bodies littered the floor between the stairs and the portal, the small creatures started throwing balls of fire toward the men from their tiny fists. Tiny bursts of flame erupted all around the men, scalding the flesh of their faces and hands, singing their clothing, and covering the entire stairwell opening in a layer of short-lived flame and smoke.

Archon ejected his empty magazine and slammed a new one into place. He resumed firing as fast as he could, and covered Maddox's side of the room while he reloaded the SCAR. The swarm was thinning. All they needed to do was hold out a little longer. Once the ground forces were down, they turned their fire toward the ones flying near the top of the room.

"They're quick as fuck!" blurted Maddox as one of his shots narrowly missed its target.

"Can't lead them, Arc, they're too erratic!" yelled Conwell.

"Mad lead, Con follow, I'll call," answered Archon. He followed one with his sights for a moment, then called out, "top right!"

Maddox fired ahead of the creature, Conwell fired behind it, and Archon fired directly at it. Conwell's round ripped through its chest, and it fell dead to the floor. They continued the firing pattern until their targets had dwindled to just a handful, each flitting in and out of the room into the open air outside the building, through the various holes in the walls.

"What the hell?" yelled Maddox.

Archon focused his attention on the portal. Two large hands reached through; each nearly the size of Archon's center torso. Their blood-red flesh seemed to hiss as they turned and gripped the sides of the shimmering blue energy, black nails digging into the border as if it were a solid material. With a great heave, the creature pushed the portal's edges back, widening it and sending sparks of its strange, electric energies shooting across the room.

A pair of large, black horns slowly pierced the veil between their realities. The head that followed was unlike anything they'd seen before; human-enough that they could recognize similarities, but as far from human as their minds could perceive.

Deep, black eye sockets glared at them, somehow able to see despite their lack of eyes. Its nose was missing, or had never developed, and in its place was a pair of gaping holes that seemed to lead straight into the creature's brain cavity. Its lips seemed permanently peeled back into a grimace, revealing its black, pointed teeth.

They fired at the horror's eyes, nose, mouth, and eventually its neck as it slowly passed through the portal. Their shots seemed to do very little harm to the creature, if any at all.

"Cover!" yelled Maddox. Archon ducked back behind the wall at his words. Conwell slid down a few steps and lowered his head below ground level. Maddox pulled the pins on three frag grenades and tossed them toward the new arrival.

The monster's upper torso was through the portal when the grenades landed. The building shook violently as the ordnance exploded, sending fragments and chunks of the small creatures' bodies flying in all directions. Archon whipped his head back into the opening to see the results. The creature's flesh was peppered with tiny wounds and flash burns from the explosion that began healing before his eyes. A strange green smoke seeped out from the corpses scattered about the room and streamed toward the large, muscular beast. It entered his wounds, swirled about atop them, and left nothing behind but fully healed flesh.

"Fuck!" yelled Maddox, witnessing the aftermath.

Conwell pushed himself back up a few steps and immediately began peppering the creature's torso with rounds. He emptied an entire magazine before Archon, frustrated, waved him off. Conwell's 5.56 rounds didn't seem to have an impact on the creature whatsoever, and any damage they were doing internally was being healed by the effects of the green smoke that continued to flow toward it.

When the firing behind him finally stopped, Archon noticed the frantic voice coming from the JTF-13 radio on his belt. He grabbed it and backed away from the opening a few paces before answering.

"Colonel Archon, are you still there?" blurted the distant voice. It wasn't the same man he'd spoken with before. The rumble of a helicopter's engine was roaring in the background every time the person's mic keyed up.

"Hope you boys are close," said Archon.

"We heard an explosion from your end. What's going on?"

"You heard that?"

"Passive listening mode is built into our radios… for various reasons, which I'm sure are obvious by now."

"Lose a lot of operators, do ya?" It was hard to hide his sarcasm when faced with what seemed like certain death. He hoped the man on the other end of the radio understood.

"What's the status of the portal?"

"Well… it's bigger than it was. Something huge just pried it open and pushed its way through."

"Huge? Describe it, fast!"

"Uh… red skin, black horns, approximately twelve feet tall? It just cleared the portal. It can't stand up all the way. Oh, and cloven hooves and huge black wings."

"Fuck!" belted the man on the radio. "HQ, cancel Priority Red Metal Aluminum. Set Priority Black Metal Iron Gold! Metal Door active!"

"Someone wanna clue us in, here?" demanded Archon.

The floor and walls shook as the creature roared. Its voice fluctuated slightly, varying in pitch and stuttering at points, as if its voice were cracking and breaking while it yelled.

"See the big thing in front of you? Keep it near the portal. If you recovered any of our team's ammunition, use it. Incendiary rounds are your only option."

"How's that? The thing shrugged off our grenades. It's feeding off the little corpses all over the room."

"The big ones secrete this slimy shit that acts as a kinetic dampener. You've gotta burn it off or your rounds won't penetrate," answered the voice.

"Sir," came another voice over the radio. "We've translated the invader's roar. It said, *Incursion secured. Proceed.*"

"Colonel, get your men out of there! Without the football, you've got no chance of survival!" added the first voice.

Archon retrieved a few incendiary magazines from the wall to his left and tossed one to Conwell a few feet away, and another to Maddox across the opening. Maddox dropped the SCAR and swung his M4's strap up and over his head. Reloaded with the new magazines, they started a fire barrage.

White streaks cut through the air as the white-phosphorous-tipped rounds raced toward their target. Each round hit the creature's flesh with an audible hiss, followed instantly by the expected somewhat squishy thump of a metal slug impacting muscle. Unlike their previous attack, the incendiary rounds actually penetrated the creature's skin and embedded into the muscle and softer tissues beneath.

The creature roared again and stomped forward, fighting with the ceiling above in an attempt to move faster, its wings, spines, and horns snagging as he lunged and lurched.

"Football?" yelled Archon, his left hand pressed firmly over his non-radio ear. "You mean that little silver thing we found with your men?"

"Yes!" yelled the man on the other end. "It's experimental, but if it works, it could save your lives!"

Archon fished it out of his bag and turned it over in his left hand. "Flip this little red switch and toss it, I assume?" His thumb moved toward the switch as he waited for a response.

"No! No, no, no! Don't touch that yet! You have to calibrate it to the portal first. Pop open the flat side. You'll see a dial, and an LED. Stick the round end partway into the portal and turn that dial until the LED turns green. Then you can flip the switch and listen to the beeps. When the beeps are one second apart, you toss it through the portal. If you time it right, it'll go off as it crosses the threshold and collapse both sides, sealing the doorway."

"How the hell-"

"You wanna debate the science behind controlled-burst-halon and small-scale, attuned electromagnetic pulse waves on interdimensional portals, or you wanna take action and save your teams' collective asses?"

"On it," answered Archon. He tossed the radio toward Conwell and loaded his own incendiary round magazine, then sent two more skittering across the floor toward each of his men. "Cover me!"

Archon crouched low and moved around the wall into the room beyond. The demon swung its right arm toward him far quicker than he expected and slammed its massive fist into the back of his right shoulder, sending him sprawling across the floor to the far wall.

Maddox swapped magazines, stepped forward, crouched, and flicked his M4 into full auto. He held the trigger down for several long bursts, back to back, trying his best to keep all the rounds clustered in a tight grouping at the creature's left breast. Each round found its home less than an inch from its siblings, slowly burrowing a hole into the dense monster's muscle fiber toward what he hoped would be its heart.

Conwell followed suit, climbing the stairs to take a similar position. As he arrived, however, the demon swung its great horned head toward Maddox. Flames erupted inside its empty eye sockets, and when it leaned down to roar at the nuisance, a jet of magma spewed forth and engulfed Maddox fully.

The frightened Tech Sergeant pulled his weapon to his chest and spun around to put his back to the inside wall of the stairwell while Maddox screamed in a gurgle of pain and horror, slowly dissolving into the floor.

Archon forced himself back to his feet with his left arm. His right was sagging lower than it should be, the shoulder forced from its socket, and likely shattered in several places. He wasn't feeling the pain yet, but knew that was coming, and fast.

"Lure it downstairs!" yelled Archon.

"It melted Maddox!" yelled Conwell while the creature grunted and pounded at the walls trying to get at him.

"Get the *fuck* downstairs, and fire as you go! Lure him out!"

Conwell bolted down the stairs to the first landing, then spun and fired back at the demon. He targeted the creature's neck and face, peppering it with incendiary rounds as fast as he could in three-round burst mode.

The demon hunched further and pushed its way into the opening, then pressed its arms outward and stood as forcefully as it could. The wall and ceiling cracked violently and crumbled all around him. Several large pieces of debris tumbled down the stairs toward Conwell, forcing him to cease firing and dodge. The creature let loose a roar as it rose to full height for the first time.

"Fuck! This!" yelled Conwell as he resumed firing and began sidestepping toward the last flight of stairs leading toward the ground floor.

Archon took advantage of the creature's distraction and stumbled toward the portal nursing his right arm and leg. When he arrived, he flipped the flat end open and found the dial and LED as the man had described. He spun the device in his left hand so that he could turn the dial with his thumb while supporting the rest of it on top of his other four fingers, then held the rounded edge of the device precariously against the water-like surface of the portal.

The creature began pushing its way through the ceiling above the stairs, fighting its way toward Conwell.

As Archon turned the dial the LED blinked, brightened, and dimmed in an array of colors. Within a few seconds, it turned a pale green. He slowly adjusted it using as little pressure as he could on the dial until it brightened and became a vibrant, nearly neon, green.

He withdrew the device and pulled it into the crook of his arm while backing away. He closed the lid on the flat end, and then flipped the little red switch at the center of the device and placed it near his ear. It was difficult to make out with the roaring creature still so near, but he was just able to make out a very faint *beep* followed about half a second later by another faint *beep*.

Conwell bolted for the ground floor. He turned around halfway across the room and aimed at the stairs. He wasn't sure if the creature was going to fit down the stairs, or fall through the floor, but he wanted to be ready in either case.

Enraged, the demon flailed at the building around him and stomped at the floor with all its might. Cracks formed in the floor and walls around him. He drove his hooves into the floor even harder, sending chunks of debris falling into the cavity below. Conwell backed further away.

The device's beeping hastened to the point where the two beeps had almost blended into one. Archon held it back in his left hand above his shoulder, as if he were about to throw a football. As the beeping nearly blended into a single, *beedeep*, he lobbed the device toward the portal as best he could, considering he was throwing it with his off-hand.

Brushed aluminum reflected the portal's light in an eerily beautiful display as the device tumbled end over end toward the watery surface in slow motion. Its flat end crossed the plane, sending ripples toward the portal's edges. The explosion that followed was louder than that of all three grenades Maddox had thrown earlier. A white mist instantly filled the area directly around the portal, creating a sphere of smoke, and the air seemed to suck inward toward it with a hiss.

It only took a second for the mist to dissipate and the portal was no longer present. In its absence, Archon breathed a sigh of relief, but the feeling didn't last.

The floor crumbled beneath the demon, sending him crashing to the floor below. Conwell jumped backward to get clear, but his efforts were not enough. Large chunks of the ceiling and several cross-beams fell atop his legs, pelvis, and lower torso. The demon fell as well, landing atop the debris with a ground-shaking impact. Conwell screamed briefly, but his cries were cut short when a final chunk of the floor above fell on his chest.

Archon fell backward as the floor gave way, landing on his rear up against the wall, barely out of harm's way. He heard Conwell's outcry, and its abrupt end, and knew without a doubt that he was alone with the horrific monstrosity before him; now shoulder deep inside the building's first floor.

He got to his feet as quickly as he could and grabbed his fallen M4 with his left hand, still unable to make use of his right. After a moment of adjustment, he braced the weapon's stock between his elbow and hip and fired quick bursts at the creature's exposed head. It wasn't an ideal firing scenario, but it was certainly more stable than trying to aim down the weapon's sights.

The demon turned toward him in lumbering fashion, fighting with the building that was still crumbling all around it. When its face came into line with Archon's position, it inhaled deeply, and its eye sockets filled with flames.

Archon glanced back over his left shoulder to the window he'd seen nearby. He bit back on the fear within him that insisted his plan was stupid, turned, and sprinted for the window as quickly as he could. His head crashed through the remnants of the thin wooden bars that had once held single panes of glass, as he rolled mid-air to land on his back, rather than his face. A wave of heat burst past him as his feet cleared the outer edge of the window and the room he'd just left erupted into a bright orange flame.

His fall was stopped short by a pile of debris from the neighboring building, felled by an earlier bombing run. He rolled to his side, the wind slightly knocked out of him, and looked for an easy way off the pile. As his head came level with the eastern horizon, he could see an Apache helicopter closing in on the village.

"Fuck yes!" he blurted as he clamored toward the edge of the debris. Just as he cleared the edge and slid on his belly toward the ground, two rockets burst out of the launch tubes on the sides of the helicopter and slammed into the building to dramatic effect.

The western face of the building evaporated into a cloud of rubble and smoke, exposing the now-heavily wounded demon. Incendiary 30mm rounds streaked through the air with deadly accuracy, pinning the demon back against the eastern half of the building's debris pile long enough for two more rockets to fire directly into its torso.

When the firing stopped, all that was left was bloody chunks of oversized carcass, soon buried under the rest of the building as it finally gave way to gravity. The chopper moved off a safe distance on overwatch while a Blackhawk circled overhead, searching for a clearing in which to land. Archon's adrenaline was wearing off, and he was in too much pain to get up and walk toward them.

Instead, he simply waved his left hand at them to let them know there was a survivor and sat back on his haunches to await retrieval.

A few minutes later, four men entered the clearing. Three were heavily armed, and moving in a synchronized, practiced manner. The fourth walked ahead of them, and–while armed–seemed rather at-home in the detritus; carrying himself fairly casually, unconcerned with what might be around the next corner, or under a nearby pile of debris.

As they arrived at Archon's position, the leader turned to his men. "Scout for any remaining Imps. Remember to look up." He turned back to Archon as his men dispersed. "Need help standing?" he asked, offering his hand. His voice was the last one Archon had heard on the radio.

"Yeah, that'd be great," grunted Archon as he took the man's hand and pulled himself to his feet, favoring the left side of his body.

"Quite impressive, your survival. It's rare for someone untrained in our particular style of warfare to make it through even a simple encounter; let alone a demonic incursion."

"A fucking demon? Imps? What the hell is JTF-13?"

"Your new outfit, if you're willing. We need people like you."

"You mean you fight this kind of shit all the time?"

"For longer than you'd think. This world isn't safe; far from it. Help us fix that."

"I'll have to think about it," sighed Archon.

"No, you won't," the man retorted with a smile. He extended his hand in greeting. "Colonel Mark Johansen, JTF-13."

Archon shook his hand. "What were you before that?"

"Force Recon. Got caught in a little fairy situation back in Desert Storm, and JTF-13 recruited me… just like I'm doing with you."

"I said I needed to think about-"

"That's bullshit and you know it. I'm down four men, your team is mostly deceased. You can stay where you are and fight in little skirmishes all over hell and high water with no end in sight, or you can join us and fight what really matters. I know what you'll choose."

"Look, I have a family. It's not that easy. Hard enough leaving on missions as it is."

"Listen, Darren, I-"

"Arc. I go by Arc."

"Okay, well... listen, Arc. I have a family too. Most of my guys do. Fact is, we need you. We need your field experience, and we need your instincts."

"Well, let me think about it while you give me a ride to a medic, and then your headquarters. I need to meet with whoever is in charge before I make my final decision."

"Fair enough," said Johansen.

The ride out of Tarok Kolache couldn't come soon enough. After waiting for Johansen's men to return from their scouting mission, they climbed on board team's Blackhawk and were finally underway. Despite his injuries, and the crushing loss of his men, Archon climbed into the chopper under his own power, and left the battlefield, on his own terms, his future decided, and the fate of the world now in his hands.

Desperate Ground
By: David W. Hensley

*On intersecting ground form communications,
on heavy ground plunder,
on bad ground keep going,
on surrounded ground make plans,
on desperate ground fight.
- Sun Tzu-*

The fish weren't biting, and that was perfectly fine by Oscar. He sat near the bank of Spruce Creek, close enough to cast a line and yet not so close his shadow would spook the fish swimming in the deep, shade-dappled pool. He leaned back in the old lawn chair stretching and smiled. *'Like Grandpa says, a bad day fishin' is better than a good day doin' nearly anything else."*

The deep howl of a small block V8 shattered his reverie. Its dual exhaust roared with a determined grunt.

Jimmy Hake. Great.

Turning his head, Oscar looked down the mountain canyon. There, through the trees, roaring along the old mining road was Jimmy's 1970s Chevy pickup. It was painted a jarring shade of orange, accented with metallic blue flames. The old four by four sped past, its oversized tires kicking up a cloud of dust. Birds startled from the spruce trees at the shrill, blatting cry of Jimmy's train horn.

The driver's arm was out the driver's window, his middle finger extended. "Screw you, Rockwell!"

There was a passenger with Jimmy, she leaned across the roof with both middle fingers extended.

Oscar shook his head.

Crying shame, what Jimmy's done to that truck. I wouldn't paint my dog's ass that color.

He turned back to the deep pool and the fish that weren't biting.

The sounds of mountain summer had not fully returned to Oscar's little slice of heaven. Some of the songbirds were back at it. A chipmunk scolded something downstream.

Wait.

Oscar stood quickly. He glanced about, eyes and ears taking in every detail.

What is that chipmunk going on about?

Something or someone was moving through the willows and brush downstream. Oscar froze and listened.

Definitely someone, no sensible animal would make that much noise.

Oscar faded away into the spruce trees upstream. He could hear them clearly now. Two sets of footsteps trying to be quiet and failing. The crack of dead twigs and crunch of dried leaves beneath heavy feet announced their presence more surely than a bullhorn. Oscar worked his way up-slope towards the road, away from the creek and his fishing gear.

Probably The Douchebag Twins. Jimmy never leaves home without 'em.

Oscar shook his head and settled down in the dry needle-covered dirt, low crawling forward to a vantage where he could watch the fishing spot unseen.

It didn't take long before two figures blundered from the willows lining the bank of the creek.

Tommy Gillette and Brice Rogers. Yep, Douchebag Twins. I bet Jimmy's looking for payback.

They stood staring at Oscar's empty chair, his fishing rod propped on a stack of rocks, a coffee can of worms next to the open tackle box.

Oscar closed his eyes and sighed. It might have been a mistake to face off with Jimmy last fall. He didn't see where he'd had much choice in the matter. If he continued to take Jimmy and the other upperclassmen's abuse, then it would only have escalated. So, Oscar had done what Grandpa advised. The very next time Jimmy started in, Oscar went to war. That he had been wet and naked when he did it didn't hurt.

"Come on out Rockwell!" Tommy, hollered.

"Yeah! Come on out Rockwell!" Brice repeated.

Tommy walked over to the deserted fishing spot. He looked around the small meadow, head swiveling. He was big, man-sized. Oscar figured him for six foot five or six and probably two hundred sixty or two hundred seventy pounds. Word around the campfire was that Tommy had been held back three times in the past six years. Oscar thought three a bit high. But where Tommy lacked academic ability, he made up for it in physical prowess. He was a two-time state champion wrestler in the heavyweight division and a fixture on both football and basketball teams at Spruce Bend High. Clearly a city boy from the way he moved in the woods.

"Come on Oscar." Tommy called. "We just wanna talk."

"Yeah, we just wanna talk." Half again the size of Tommy, Brice was ginger-haired, fair-complected, and only slightly smarter than Tommy. Well, that's the way he let on. Oscar knew for a fact that he was an A-student, in addition to being an all-conference running back.

Talk my ass. These two clowns are here to keep me from escaping. Jimmy and his girl are probably working downstream right now trying to box me in.

"All right, have it your way Rockwell!" Tommy gave the open tackle box a solid kick, upending it, scattering its contents into the tall grass. Next came the fishing rod which he broke across his knee and tossed into the deep pool.

"Shit Tommy. Why'd you go and do that?" Brice asked.

"Pussy won't come out and talk?" Tommy upended the bait can and tossed it into the creek. "I break his shit."

Oscar eased back deeper into the clump of spruce trees, their cool evergreen aroma counterpoint to the white-knuckled anger boiling up from deep in his gut. He'd bought that gear with his own money. Money earned working after hours in Grandpa's shop. Good gear didn't come cheap, and money didn't come easy.

Keep cool, Grandpa always says 'angry decisions are bad decisions'.

Oscar breathed deep.

Two-on-one is bad odds.

He took another calming breath. Shrugging, he looked around, picked a path through the trees, and headed up towards the road. Listening, creeping quiet and careful.

He squatted down in a thicket of chokecherries near the edge of the old mining road. A plan began to form.

Trash my gear? Screw with my day, on my ground?

He could hear Jimmy and his girl calling back and forth to each other, cawing like crows—

or, what they *thought* crows sounded like. One was doing a passable job.

Probably Shannon.

Oscar waited. The rest of the birds had gone silent. The only other sounds were chipmunks, scolding the two faux-crows.

One will be on the road. The other down by the creek.

Minutes crawled past, the crow calls growing closer bit by bit. The crow on the road stepped into view, Shannon Mutz. Oscar gave himself a mental high-five.

She kept to the middle of the rut-filled road where the going was easier. Tall grass and yellow clover not-quite obscuring her sturdy hiking boots. She was tall for a girl, probably six-foot, if Oscar had to guess, neither heavy nor lanky. She was dressed for the mountain weather in faded jeans, a Greenday t-shirt with a denim jacket tied around her waist, and her coal-black hair pulled back into a no-nonsense ponytail.

If he was honest with himself, Oscar had a deep and abiding crush on the senior. She was smart, hot, articulate, and best of all she was a mountain girl.

Why's someone like her into a douchebag like Jimmy?

She cawed twice. Jimmy's response echoed from somewhere behind Oscar, downslope, where the going was easier. Oscar waited till she was ten or fifteen yards past his position and quietly broke cover, heading up the canyon along the road.

"Pssst!"

Oscar whipped around.

"Wrong way, Rockwell." She stood hipshot; arms crossed. Half a smile tugged at the corner of her mouth.

Downslope, Jimmy cawed. She returned the call.

Oscar blinked. "Can't be wrong if it's away from your asshole boyfriend."

"You can't get away that way." Her smile was gone.

"Wasn't getting away I was plannin' on." It was Oscar's turn to smile.

"No?"

"Douchebag-twins trashed my gear. I'm returning the favor." Oscar turned and sprinted up the canyon road—away from Shannon, and toward Jimmy's truck.

"Jimmy!" Her voice rapidly faded, drowned out by Oscar's pounding feet.

The Turnaround was practically a legend. Surrounded by miles of wild mountains, it sat at the end of the Spruce Canyon mine road in the shadow of the sealed and abandoned mine. It was the end of the line, hence the name. The Turnaround was where the teens of Spruce Bend High came to cut loose and engage in all manner of risky behavior as young people on the verge of adulthood are wont to do.

Jimmy's garish four-by-four was parked at the Turnaround, just past the blackened circle of ash and cinder left behind by a hundred party fires; its bed filled with pallets and used tires. The steel door of the old mine was not far off. Oscar pulled out his knife and cut the valve stem from both rear tires. Air hissed, chastising him for the vandalism.

Wreck my gear? You pricks can walk home.

He knew they wouldn't be too far behind. Not with Shannon calling for Jimmy like she had. Oscar jogged back to the mine entrance, pulled Grandpa's keys from his pocket, unlocked two deadbolts and three heavy padlocks.

Overkill Grandpa.

He pulled open the heavy steel door and stepped into the cool, velvet darkness of the mine.

Step one complete. Now it's time to wait.

Jimmy had the numbers, which gave him a significant advantage. However, Oscar knew the ground, and according to Grandpa, knowing the ground did a lot to even the odds.

Oscar had been checking on the old mine since he'd turned thirteen. That was when his grandpa had brought him up here and told him about the mine's dark secret. That Great-Great-Grandpa Rockwell, along with an old Navajo medicine man, and half the men of Spruce Bend went down into the mine, to put an end to a terrible creature that had been stalking the woods and mountains around Spruce Bend. The old Navajo called it *Hodichin Chaha'oh*, the Starving Shadow. Great-Great-Grandpa Rockwell had called it by the name he'd learned fighting the same thing back east. Wendigo.

According to the tale, thirty men went down into the dark that day; only four came back. Great-Great-Grandpa Rockwell and the medicine man had collapsed the lowest level of the mine, to keep the creature trapped in the dark where it belonged. Afterwards, Great-Great-Grandpa had spent most of his considerable fortune on that collapsed mine and sealed it up tight.

Grandpa told Oscar that he came from a long line of men, who served in the Marine Corps, as part of a special unit. He'd shown Oscar the tattoo that night; a gold dragon, and the number 13 on a red shield. He'd told Oscar that his daddy was part of that unit too and hadn't come home 'cause he'd died on a mission, standing the line between heaven and hell.' One day, Oscar too would stand that line, and Lord willing, would come back to Spruce Bend and keep the *Hodichin Chaha'oh* sealed up tight down in the belly of Spruce Canyon Mine.

Oscar grabbed a headlamp from the hooks near the door, strapped it to his head, and clicked it on. Over the past three years, he and Grandpa had regularly walked the tunnels of the Spruce Canyon Mine, eyes peeled for mice, rats, and other crawly things. Grandpa always said that *Hodichin Chaha'oh* would take them first. After that, when it was strong enough, it would come up through the tunnels in search of larger prey. Oscar wasn't sure about Grandpa's stories. They were probably just ghost stories, meant to scare him from wandering the deeper tunnels alone. He kept an eye out for rats and mice, just the same.

"What the hell!" Jimmy sounded pissed.

Oscar peaked through the cracked door.

Jimmy stood next to his truck, hands on his head, staring in disbelief at the flat tires. Tommy and Brice shook their heads. Meanwhile, Shannon leaned against the tailgate, her half-smile back.

Oscar grinned.

Show-time.

"Hey, douchebags!" Oscar kicked the steel door open with a screeching bang. *"Heard you wanted to talk."*

All four of the teens jumped. Their heads whipped around; eyes focused on Oscar.

"Shit, Rockwell." Jimmy stomped toward Oscar and the door. "You ruined my tires."

"Only two." Oscar stepped back. "Consider it payback for your idiot friends trashing my fishing gear."

"Who you calling idiot? Pussy." Tommy stood two steps behind Jimmy, fists clenched.

Brice followed a step or two behind Tommy like a dutiful watchdog. Shannon stayed leaned up against the orange tailgate, watching.

"Well, since Shannon didn't bust up my gear that pretty much leaves you and your red-headed lady friend." Oscar shifted his weight to the balls of his feet. Jimmy and company were closing the gap pretty quick.

"Hey—", Brice started.

"You might as well come on out here and get what you got coming Rockwell." Jimmy stopped just outside the narrow mine entrance.

"Yeah, Rockwell. Come on out." Brice repeated. "Get what you got coming."

"Hell, I was gonna fight you straight up till you cut my tires. Now?" Jimmy grinned, his eyes cold. "Now I'm thinking we're all gonna take turns kicking your hillbilly ass."

"Jimmy." Shannon pushed off the orange tailgate and started towards her boyfriend. "You didn't say anything about jumping Oscar."

"Straight up?" Oscar asked. "You brought bigfoot and Ginger Brice along for what? To carry your ass out of here in a sling, like last time?"

"Naw." Jimmy shook his head. "Brought them along to observe, official like. You know, so you can't say you beat me again."

"Hey Jimmy, maybe we should hold up." Brice said. Maybe something in the lizard part of his brain was screaming a warning. Maybe it was the grin on Oscar's face. Either way, Oscar was done waiting.

"What for?" Tommy had stopped to the right of Jimmy. "Little pus—"

Oscar skipped forward. Snapping his left foot out and up, hard. He felt Tommy's testicles squish against the instep of his boot. Tommy's huge frame crumpled around the burning agony in his groin.

Pivoting, Oscar hammered a straight right into Jimmy's stunned face, felt lips smear under his stinging knuckles. Oscar whirled and sprinted into the narrow dark opening of the mine.

Just like Grandpa says, *'when on desperate ground, fight.'*

Oscar ran hard.

The inverted U-shapes of the mine-supports cast jumping, jittering shadows in the bobbing light of the headlamp. He passed the narrower ventilation tunnels and the first intersection; juked around an abandoned mine cart leaping the flat-bed mucker's platform, bending double to avoid braining himself on the low rock ceiling.

Coming to the first large gallery Oscar made a sharp right turn, cut off his headlamp, and stood still in the cool dark. He leaned against the hard rock wall, straining to hear any sound of pursuit over his own whooshing breath and pounding heartbeat. Breathing slow and deep, he heard them shuffling and bumbling along.

He crouched and peeked around the corner. They were slow coming down the tunnel, careful. Jimmy led; the beam of his flashlight playing along the low ceiling, over the deeper blackness of the smaller ventilation tunnels, carefully checking right and left. Cautious.

I surprised them. The next go around won't be as easy.

"Stop this Jimmy," Shannon's voice echoed. She was about a half-step behind Jimmy, one of the headlamps from the entry on her head and turned on.

Smart girl.

"Not till we make him pay, babe." Jimmy's voice sounded a little nasal.

Oscar was behind them now. He'd taken advantage of their cautious advance and worked his way around the group using the western tunnels. Crouching low, headlamp off he watched the vengeful quartet explore the central gallery.

Time Brice took some lumps.

Oscar backed deeper into the shadows of the main tunnel and duck-walked to the far wall where he could see Brice and Shannon peering into the east tunnel. A crackling, crunching sound—like someone walking on dry leaves—whispered through the chamber.

Shannon looked down.

"Gross!" she said, skip-stepping back. Her face a mask of pure revulsion.

"What?" Brice asked. "What's gross?"

"Roaches." She shined the light onto the ground near Brice's feet. Oscar craned his neck trying to see. "Lots of them."

Oscar felt a chill run up his spine. *What had Grandpa said about the bugs?*

"They're dead." Brice gave a couple of crunching stomps.

Early warning system.

"See. All dead." He turned, looking deeper into the tunnel. "Did you hear that?"

"Hear what?" Tommy walked across the gallery. *Oh shit.*

Oscar stood up, started forward.

"I think I heard something." Brice started down the tunnel. "Come on, I bet Rockwell's dow—"

A large, yellow-brown hand shot out of the darkness and grabbed Brice's face. Oscar's stomach dropped.

Oscar could see Brice's eyes, wide with panic, swiveling back and forth staring through the black-clawed fingers that dug into his face and dragged him away. The red-headed senior clawed at the thing's iron grip to no avail, his screams fading into the darkness.

Shannon stumbled back, her hand clamped tight over her mouth, a high keening leaked out around her fingers.

"Oh shit, oh shit, oh shit, oh shit…" Jimmy backed away from the tunnel.

Tommy stood there, frozen; his mouth opening and closing, like a beached trout.

"Shut up!" Oscar cut on his headlamp and stepped into the gallery. "Jimmy. *Hey, Jimmy.*"

Oscar thumped him on the chest.

Jimmy stopped his panicked mantra and stared at Oscar, chest heaving.

Shannon had stopped, as well. She stared at Oscar, eyes wide, face pale and bloodless.

"We have to go." He shoved Jimmy toward the main tunnel. "Now." Oscar shifted back to the entrance of the eastern tunnel, shining his headlamp along the walls and the floor. Blood covered the cross members of the rail system. It glistened dark and lurid in the light.

So much blood.

"What about Brice?" Shannon backed away from the blood.

"P—pretty sure Brice's gone." Oscar's tongue felt overlarge in his too dry mouth. A heavy hand gripped the back of his neck. It squeezed hard.

"What do you mean *gone?*" Tommy pulled Oscar around to face him, eye to eye, toes barely scraping the ground.

"You want to let go of me, Gillette." Oscar said, his voice tight with pain.

Tommy Gillette shrugged and squeezed harder. Oscar's vision began to tunnel.

"Okay."

He grabbed Tommy's arm with his right hand for leverage, then used that leverage to bring both legs up and kick Tommy hard in the gut.

Air whooshed out of Tommy. The force of the kick flung Oscar to the ground, where he turned most of the momentum into a stinging back roll through the crunching, desiccated cockroaches, and came up in a fighting crouch near the opening of the eastern tunnel. Tommy struggled to his feet desperately trying to draw air into his paralyzed lungs.

"You said Brice's gone." Shannon backed away from Oscar and the eastern tunnel entrance. "What took him?"

Tough girl.

"Like I know." Oscar stepped away from the tunnel entrance, feet crunching, rubbing at his sore neck. He kept his distance from Tommy, back to the northern wall of the gallery.

You know what took Brice. Grandpa wasn't trying to scare you with ghost stories.

Oscar shook his head.

The Hodichin Chaha'oh, The Wendigo. That's what took him. It's back, and you missed it.

"What took him doesn't matter." Oscar started walking towards the southern tunnel. "What matters is getting out of here."

"Not without Brice." Tommy Gillette stepped in front of Oscar, blocking the southern tunnel. The way out.

"You want to get out of my way Gillette. Now." Oscar stopped just outside of Tommy's significant reach.

We don't have time for this macho bullshit. We have to get out of here. I have to tell Grandpa.

"No." Jimmy walked across the gallery, stopped next to Tommy. "We can't leave Brice."

"He's dead." Oscar looked at Tommy and Jimmy, making eye contact.

"Bullshit!" Jimmy blustered. "That bear just grabbed him, dragged him off. It—"

"That's a lot of blood." Oscar pointed to his left, at the shadow-shrouded eastern tunnel. "He. Is. Dead."

"That was not a bear, Jimmy!" Shannon shook her head. She moved over next to Oscar, back to the northern wall. Her voice sounded scared and angry. "Bears don't live in caves during the summer, and they don't have hands."

"If it's not a bear then what is it?"

"Like I said before, I don't…" Oscar trailed off.

Something loomed in the shadows of the southern tunnel, hard to see with Tommy in the way. It filled the tunnel, floor to ceiling.

"Shit." Oscar pulled the six-inch buck knife from his belt.

The black-clawed hand snaked forward, latching onto Tommy Gillette's substantial shoulder, it snatched him back into the southern tunnel. Oscar's last glimpse of Tommy was the giant athlete being dragged off into the tunnel, clawing at that thing's arm like a toddler being snatched up by an angry mom in the toy aisle of the grocery store.

Oscar pushed Shannon towards the western tunnel, grabbed the stunned Jimmy, and shoved him in the same direction. Shadows jumped and slithered in the light of Oscar's and Shannon's headlamps.

They ran north, through the western tunnels— the same tunnels Oscar had used to get around behind Jimmy and company. That seemed like a lifetime ago. The upside-down U-shapes of the support timbers passed at regular intervals, casting their eldritch shadows along the gouged and chipped rock walls. Oscar led. Shannon followed close behind with Jimmy fifteen yards in the rear.

Say what you want about Jimmy Hake, he's no coward.

He slowed to a stop at a large junction, held up his hand, fist closed in the infantryman's signal for stop. Just the way Grandpa had taught him. Oscar motioned the other two forward. Shannon had an old pick handle she must have grabbed somewhere along their mad flight. Jimmy was carrying a three-foot length of chisel tipped, rusty steel.

Probably an old mining drill.

"Wait here." Oscar pulled his headlamp off, masking the beam with the fingers of his left hand. "I'll scout. The way out's not far." Shannon and Jimmy nodded.

Oscar crouched low, back to the wall, and peeked around the corner. To the right, the tunnel ended in another right turn some forty or fifty yards distant.

Desperate Ground

Not that way. That way is down, deeper into the dark.

Ahead lay a narrow tunnel only three feet wide and four feet high; Grandpa said those smaller tunnels were for ventilation.

To the left, the tunnel ran east-to-west. The rails and supports seemed to just fade into the darkness at the edge of Oscar's small light. He stayed crouched low and slid around the left-hand side of the junction, moving from one support timber to the next, hugging the wall. Creeping along slow and easy, only a stray bit of light escaped through his fingers, poor illumination at best. He strained to hear any sound besides his hammering heart in the damp, chill dark.

First came the smell. A pungent earthy smell all wet dog, spoiled meat, and copper.

He doused the light, plunging himself into the absolute darkness that only exists underground. Heart hammering once again, Oscar pressed himself hard against the rough rock of the tunnel wall and the nearest timber support.

This is bad. I think it's between us and the door.

He breathed in slow and deep, then out.

In *one… two… three… four.* Out *one… two… three… four.* Over and over until he could hear something other than his rushing blood and pounding heart.

Slowly, carefully, he peeked around the edge of the timber support; total darkness.

Got to see if the way out is clear.

Keeping the lens covered, Oscar clicked on the headlamp, letting only the slightest bit of illumination to leak through his fingers. *Nothing.*

Oscar slipped around the support. He moved to the next one, and then the next. No sign of the creature, just that metallic, rancid smell. He reached the junction between the western tunnels and the main tunnel, the way out. He crossed his tunnel quick, quiet. Oscar dropped to his belly and peaked his head around the support beam, his left cheek in the hundred-year-old dust. Light, distant and beautiful, leaked in from the wide-open door.

The way out.

Relief flooded Oscar like hundred-pound feed bags being lifted off of his shoulders. Smiling, he eased back into the western tunnel.

The bulk of the old mine car was a black hump in the middle of the tracks. Something about it was wrong. Oscar froze. Too big, too rounded

'Attention to detail Oscar. Details are the difference between life and death.' He could practically hear Grandpa's deep, gravelly voice.

He eased forward again, still on the ground, the dust tickling his nostrils. Oscar looked again, *really* looked. There, between the deeper shadows of the vent tunnels and the door, silhouetted by that glorious light, sat something large and hunched. It squatted on the rails like some great carnivorous toad.

Shit, shit, shit, shit.

Oscar quietly, carefully slid back into the western tunnel.

"Okay." Oscar whispered. "We have a serious problem." He had been rehearsing this part in his head all the way back to the others.

"No shit, Rockwell." Jimmy leaned against a support timber. He looked pale, washed out in the light of Shannon's headlamp. He looked scared.

"Worse than before."

"What's worse?" Shannon looked at Oscar. "What's worse than being hunted in the dark?" She seemed to be taking this better than Jimmy, more angry than scared. Then again, she would be. Word was, she'd bagged a three-hundred-pound black bear with a bow last fall.

"It's between us and the only way out."

"That's worse." Jimmy's hands twisted back and forth on that rusty length of steel, like a nervous batter stepping up to the plate. "Shit, that's way worse!" He sounded close to panic. His eyes darted around, as though he expected the creature to ooze forth from the rock. "You saw how it manhandled Tommy."

"We can't stay here either," Shannon said. "It's between us and the only door. Sooner or later it will start searching for us. Hunting us."

"You don't know that!" Jimmy looked back and forth between Shannon and Oscar. "We don't even know what it is. Maybe it'll get bored and go back to its den."

"Still not a bear." Shannon said.

"Look." Oscar stepped between the two. "We don't have time for this. Grandpa says when the unexpected happens you can't waste time. He says you have to assess the situation. Upside. Downside. Plan accordingly."

"Who's your granddad? Rambo?"

"Better than Rambo." Oscar put his hand on Jimmy's shoulder. "He's a Unit 13 Marine."

"Isn't he a little old to be a Marine?" Jimmy's hands were still wringing that steel rod.

"Once a Marine, always a Marine." Oscar said.

"No. He's right." Shannon said. "Same rules for hunting and hiking the backcountry. Something bad happens, you have to stop reacting and assess the problem. Take stock of your pluses and minuses. Reacting in panic is a quick way to die ugly."

Both Oscar and Jimmy looked at her, nonplussed.

"What? I bow hunt. My old man made me take wilderness survival courses from this retired army guy over in Durango. I think he was a Ranger or Green Beret or something."

"Okay," Jimmy brushed Oscar's hand away and pushed off the wall. "What are our pluses then?"

"We have the numbers." Shannon said.

"We're armed." Oscar reached out and tapped the pick handle and steel rod.

Worst weapons ever, but better than nothing, I guess.

"And I know my way around the upper tunnels pretty well."

"We have light." Jimmy said.

"Light, weapons, numbers, and a working knowledge of some of the tunnels. That's our upside." Oscar said. "Now, what's the downside?"

"It's bigger, faster, stronger, better armed, and between us and the door." Shannon leaned against one of the support timbers. She shivered in the chill darkness of the mine.

"Don't forget the environment." Jimmy rubbed at his bare arms. "It's cold down here."

"And it does not get warmer." Oscar said. "Jimmy and I are not equipped for the cold."

At least she has that denim jacket.

"Also, I'm pretty sure this thing can see in the dark and has an excellent sense of smell and hearing."

"How do you know that, Rockwell?" Jimmy asked. "You can't know that."

"Yeah." Shannon was looking at Oscar now. "How *do* you know that? And don't say comic books or that Dungeons and Dragons crap you and your geek buddies play."

"Grandpa." Oscar said. "He told me stories about Spruce Bend and the mine and his grandpa. My Great-Great-Grandpa Horace was a Marine too. Fought in Cuba, in the Spanish American War. Ran into something, something not normal or natural. This special unit recruited him because of it. Special Unit Thirteen."

"Special Unit Thirteen?" Shannon paced back and forth across the tunnel. "Never mind, get to the point. That thing won't sit there forever."

"Unit Thirteen was, is a special unit that hunts monsters, keeps the supernatural at bay—"

"Bullshit, Rockwell!" Jimmy stepped away from the support beam shaking his head. "Sounds like one of those games you and your fat buddy Arnold are always talking about."

"Not bullshit. Great-Great-Grandpa Horace lost a leg back east in '04, came home to Spruce Bend." Oscar crouched down, leaned back against the wall. "Sometime in '06, just before or after Great-Grandpa Earl was born, something was killing folks around Spruce Bend. Grandpa says it probably started with small things first. Said that was a bad year for hunting. No game in the mountains for miles and miles, not even rabbits or groundhogs."

"My gramps tells the same story." Shannon said. "Said his granddad's family nearly starved that year."

"So, Great-Great-Grandpa Horace, he recognizes the signs, calls it a Wendigo. He goes and finds a local Navajo holy man, one who believes him. They put together a posse and they track this thing down. They chased it into this mine, all the way down into the bottom. As Grandpa tells the story, the thing fought back and fought back hard. It killed ten or fifteen men before they hurt it bad enough that it crawled away into the bottom tunnels. Grandpa says they doused the thing in lamp oil, lit it on fire, and then dynamited the bottom tunnels; brought the roof down on its head."

"Wait. You said 1906." Jimmy had slid down the opposite wall of the tunnel. "Wasn't that when the big mine accident happened? When they closed down the mine, sealed it up?"

"Yeah." Shannon said. "We learned about it in history class. The 1906 Spruce Canyon Mine Accident. It killed mining here. It killed the town."

"Wasn't a mining accident that killed the town." Oscar rubbed his face. "It was a Wendigo."

"Okay, Rockwell. Let's say I buy this. What's a Wendigo?"

"Hunger. Pure hunger. The Navajo medicine man called it *Hodichin Chaha'oh*, the Starving Shadow." Oscar said. "It starts out human, usually an Indian, but not always. Things get bad enough that he or she goes cannibal. Betrays their humanity, sometimes betraying the tribe or village. According to Grandpa when someone goes that wrong, that dark, it leaves room for something darker to come in, take up residence."

"Like what?" Shannon asked.

"Depends. Grandpa says there are worlds next door to ours, adjacent. From time to time the barrier between them and us is real thin, and things creep through. Other times, we do terrible things that attract the dark and hungry things that live there. Killing and eating another person does that. It's an act so dark and terrible, it draws these spirits of pure hunger. Draws them like dead meat draws flies…"

"Then what?" Shannon asked.

"Then one moves in, takes over. It starts eating. Always hungry, never full."

"What?" Jimmy asked. "Do these spirits give the cannibal superpowers?"

"Kind of. Grandpa says it makes 'em strong, fast, nearly indestructible. Great-Great-Grandpa Horace told him it could see down here in the dark."

"So, what hurts them?" Shannon asked.

"Fire. Maybe. Great-Great-Grandpa Horace's Navajo friend told stories of this thing coming back every so often, no matter what they did to kill it. Grandpa thinks this one must have been around when the Anasazi were living in Mesa Verde."

"Did you know?" Shannon took a couple steps toward Oscar. Her grip on the old pickaxe handle was white at the knuckles. "Did you know this *thing* was down here? When you set this up. *Did. You. Know?*"

"No," Oscar shook his head.

How could I have known? Those roaches weren't there last week.

"I really thought those stories were Grandpa just being Grandpa. I mean—I buy the Unit 13 stories, and the story about 1906. But a thing that can come back from being burned and dynamited? *No way*. Nothing comes back from that. *Nothing*."

"You really are some kind of asshole, Rockwell." Jimmy stood up. He took a couple steps toward Oscar, the steel drill rod resting on his shoulder.

"If that ain't the pot calling the kettle black." Oscar leaned his head back against the wall looking up at the two angry teens.

We don't have time for this blame game. Shannon's right, that thing is going to get tired of waiting and come looking.

"Nobody made you clowns follow me in here." He looked Jimmy right in the eye, his gaze cold and flat. "I didn't invite you to a kegger down here. You douche bags came in here looking to give me a beating."

"You asked for it." Jimmy said. "You busted my nose last fall. I had to play in the state championship with a busted nose."

"Should have thought of that before you and your friends stole my towel and clothes from the showers" Oscar shook his head smiling now. "And you damn sure should have thought of that before trying to drag me out onto the football field naked, to roll me through the mud."

The look on his face just after I headbutted him was worth the weeklong suspension.

"It was a joke," Jimmy said. He and Shannon were both well within striking distance. "Every freshman gets the naked mudroll. Hell, Rockwell, it's practically a tradition."

"Not every freshman." Oscar said. His smile became a wolf's grin "I told you to leave me alone. You didn't listen. Not. My. Fault."

"How was I to know you were some kind of hillbilly Bruce Lee?"

"Look. We're running out of time. How about we figure a way out of this mess?" Oscar said. "You can have a rematch later. You can even keep that drill rod you're strangling there."

"Or," Shannon said, "we break your legs and leave you for bait, while we get out of here."

Jimmy stared at Shannon, nonplussed.

"You think you're that kind of tough, Shannon Mutz?" Oscar asked. "Sure, you bow hunt bear and deer and elk, and you even kicked the hell out of that handsy new kid from California. Being tough don't make you a killer."

Now I see why she's with Jimmy. She's not completely wrong though. Bust me up and run. That thing would probably be on me quick.

"Besides… you don't know the way out."

"Maybe." She pointed the old pickaxe handle at Oscar. "Maybe not. But you do. What's the plan?"

"Your idea about bait's not half-bad." Oscar said.

That caught Jimmy's attention, he stared at Oscar.

"Not the busting me up part, but the bait part…"

Jimmy's fast. Not as fast as Brice, but fast. I'm quick and I know the tunnels. Shannon's probably not that fast but she knows hunting, and she knows the woods.

He looked up at Jimmy. "I'm the bait. You and Shannon are getting out of here."

"What?!"

"Shannon and you—you're gonna use that vent tunnel to hide." Oscar, ignoring Jimmy, pointed to his right, across the east/west tunnel, to the smaller opening. "I'm going to get that thing to chase me down into the lower tunnels. Once it passes by you, keep following that tunnel. It will come out about sixty yards or so from the door. You go get my grandpa. He'll know what to do."

"No." Jimmy said.

It was Oscar's turn to look nonplussed. He stared up at Jimmy, standing there with his white-knuckle grip on that drilling rod. Wide-eyed. Pale. Scared.

"You won't be the bait Rockwell. *We* will." He looked at Shannon. "You go get Rockwell's granddad."

"Jimmy…"

"No babe, you have the best chance of getting back to Rockwell's house on foot. Remember, dingledick here cut the tires on the truck." Jimmy gestured toward Oscar. "Besides, I can't let hillbilly Bruce Lee here save my girlfriend." Shannon stared at Jimmy for a moment.

"You're not saving me, dumbass." She grabbed Jimmy and kissed him hard. "I'm saving you." She turned back to Oscar holding out a slender, well-manicured hand. "Let's get out of here."

Oscar and Jimmy huddled in the cold, dark recess of the western ventilation shaft on Level Two. The bait plan had worked—a little *too* well. Now they were trapped.

It stalked back and forth—shrieking and growling with fury—stopping every few passes to reach for Oscar, swiping and clawing into the space. With each failed attempt its howls grew louder, its shrieks more intense. The air stank of wet animal, rotted meat, and old copper. Oscar could hear Jimmy breathing hard behind him. He sounded hurt, not just out of breath. These ventilation tunnels were even smaller than the upper ones. Large enough for Oscar and Jimmy to fit, if they crawled. Small enough that the Wendigo didn't.

"How long do we have to do this?" Jimmy scooted deeper into the vent tunnel.

"Long enough for Shannon to bring Grandpa back." Oscar slashed a ropey, reaching arm. Watched the wound grow closed.

"Whoa!" Jimmy halted his backward scoot.

"What?" Oscar asked.

"There's a hole back here."

"Where does it go?" Oscar hacked desperately at the massive scrabbling hands.

"Up and down."

"Can we fit?"

"Maybe." Jimmy looked up, the hole vanished beyond the range of the headlamp. "Looks like a couple feet around. No way I can climb up."

"Why not?" Oscar asked.

"This knee is swelling like a bitch." Jimmy said.

"Knee?" Oscar watched the creature's blood spattered legs pass back and forth in front of their tunnel.

"Took a bad hit at state last year." Jimmy shrugged. "It ain't been right since."

"How far down does it go?" Oscar scrambled backward, narrowly avoiding a black-clawed swipe.

"My knee?" Jimmy asked.

"No." Oscar glanced back at Jimmy "The hole. How far down does the hole go?"

"I can't see the bottom." Jimmy said. "It slopes away."

The creature lunged forward, cramming its head and shoulders into the too-small vent.

Shit!

Panic clawed and clamored in the back of Oscar's mind. The thing dragged itself forward. Hair, skin, and flesh peeled back. Blood spurted and ran, lubricating its forward progress. Shrieking, roaring, it kept coming.

"Get in the hole, Jimmy." Oscar called over his shoulder.

"What?" Jimmy craned his neck, to see around Oscar.

"Get in the damn hole. It's in here with us!" Oscar backed towards Jimmy.

"What?" Jimmy asked.

"I'm a little busy. Get. In. The. Hole!"

Oscar braced the drill rod against a ridge on the floor. He held it low and flat, waiting. It was picking up speed, flowing forward, paying no mind to the pain.

Wait…

It was nearly on him.

Wait…

Oscar clenched his jaw tight against the urge to piss and weep. It planted both clawed hands and lunged forward, anticipation writ in its icy gaze.

Now!

Oscar snatched the tip of the rod up—felt it punch through the creature's chest. It kept coming, sliding along that rusted length of steel, roaring in agony.

It stopped short. The rod had punched through its back and wedged against the roof of the vent tunnel, halting the thing's forward momentum.

"Get in the hole, now!" Oscar scrambled toward Jimmy. "If you don't get in the hole, we die."

"Shit—shit—shit—shit." Jimmy went into the hole, feet first.

Oscar came sliding out of the hole, landing in a gasping, sobbing heap. He rolled onto his back, snatched the hunting blade from its scabbard on his belt.

Holy shit!

He stared up at the smaller hole, eyes wide. Part of him expected to see the creature dragging itself through that small opening shedding skin and meat. When it didn't, Oscar worked himself around to face Jimmy, his heart pounding like a runaway triphammer. Jimmy sat half in half-out of the cramped vent tunnel clutching his right foot, moaning in pain.

"Got to go." Oscar pointed past Jimmy down the vent tunnel. Jimmy sat there cradling his foot. "Jimmy!"

"I think it's broken."

"What?" Oscar scooted toward Jimmy. "Let me see."

Jimmy leaned back, careful to avoid the hard rock of the vent tunnel. He pushed his right foot forward, gasping in pain. The foot was turned at an unnatural angle. Oscar eased the injured boy's pants leg up. Jimmy inhaled through his teeth with a hiss. Bruising, dark and purple, ran up the injured limb; a softball-sized lump just above the low-top Adidas shoe.

"How bad—how bad is it?" Jimmy lay back in the vent tunnel panting with the pain.

"It's busted."

"Is it still coming?" The injured boy pushed himself up on his elbows, trying to see past Oscar, to the hole. The thing's unholy shriek echoed from within the black.

"No. I think it's still stuck on that drill rod," Oscar said. "We gotta get the hell out of here. If that thing gets to the other end of this vent before we get out…"

"What?" Jimmy asked. Sweat glistened on his pale face. "What?"

"It catches us in here, it'll tear us apart." Oscar pointed into the black of the tunnel beyond Jimmy. "We've got to go."

Oscar and Jimmy struggled along the mine tunnel. The air close and stale. Both boys were sweating—Oscar from exertion, Jimmy from pain. Only one direction to go. The other direction, whichever way that was, a pile of rubble filled the tunnel from floor to ceiling.

How long? How long does it take for that thing to tear free and make its way down here?

He couldn't hear the shrieking any more.

Is it because we've gone far enough, or because it's loose?

Oscar tried to pick up the pace.

"Rockwell." Jimmy said. "Rockwell… Stop… just stop."

"What?" Oscar stopped. He unslung Jimmy's arm from his shoulders, and eased him down against the tunnel wall, near a timber support. Iron tracks curved off past a narrow, glittering opening. Picks, oil lamps, and drill rods all leaned up against the opening, waiting for long-absent hands to put them to work.

The injured boy sagged against the support, pale and gasping. Oscar could see the sweat glistening on Jimmy's face, despite the damp chill.

"I'm done." Jimmy said.

"Bullshit." Oscar bent over, hands on knees, catching his breath. The rushing sound he heard didn't subside with his heart rate.

Water. That's running water.

"I can't go any further. My ankle is killing me." Jimmy gestured toward the battered limb. "No way I can climb out of here."

"Hell Jimmy, I don't even know where *out* is." Oscar shook his head. "You rest, I'll scout."

Oscar sat leaning against the tunnel wall, head back, eyes closed. He'd found the way out. Or, at least the way *to* the way out. That was the good news. The rest? All bad. The tunnel had partially collapsed and was choked with debris and rubble. A path to the other side did exist; Oscar had followed the torturous route, scrabbling and clambering along. Several times, crawling through reeking puddles of half-dried blood.

He'd even scouted the rest of the tunnel, found the inclined shaft leading up and from there Oscar knew the way out.

No way Jimmy can make that. Not now.

Oscar banged his head against the cool rock.

I could go. I can dodge that thing on my own. Get out. Get safe.

He banged his head again, hearing Grandpa's voice in his head. *'What's right and what's safe ain't always the same thing. Fear'll make you choose safe over right every damn time. You're in charge, you make the calls, not your fear.'*

Oscar banged his head against the rock again.

Almost there.

Each step felt lighter than the last. A step closer to his goal. He walked in the middle of the tunnel, no longer shielding the lamp beam. Big steps, confident.

No sense in sneaking. It's still up there somewhere.

Ahead, the tunnel widened making a sort of lazy Y-shape. No rail tracks that way, so Oscar had ignored it on his first pass through.

"Hello?" a voice echoed from within the passage. "In here. Help!"

Oscar cautiously peered into the opening.

"Tommy?" Oscar walked deeper into the widening gallery. The floor underfoot shifted and crunched like brittle twigs. He looked down.

Bones—*everywhere bones*—white and shining in the headlamp's beam. Here and there picks, drill rods, and other tools, protruding like masts of sunken ships in a macabre sea. A stench permeated the damp cold. Wet dog, putrid meat, and copper.

"Rockwell?" Tommy asked. His voice coming from the deep blackness, where the gallery narrowed.

"Yeah. Keep your voice down." Oscar made the turn. Staggered back, gagging. Saliva flooded his mouth, bile burned his throat.

The tunnel ended in an abattoir; a slurry of half-dried, half-rotted blood, offal, and bone covered the floor. Near the back, in a wallowed-out heap lay pants, coats, packs, and other assorted belongings of the creature's victims. Hanging from spikes driven into the support timbers were Brice, Tommy, and several other bodies. The creature had bound their feet and hung them upside down.

Brice—what was left of him—hung next to Tommy, the two friends face to face. Brice's stomach and chest torn open, the ends of ribs shining in the light. No intestines, no organs. Just gaping, empty ruin, from crotch to chin. Eyes wide, empty, and staring. Oscar leaned forward and heaved, adding the contents of his stomach to the rotting mess on the floor.

He must have died screaming.

Not counting Tommy, the other bodies were in a similar state. Gutted, hung to keep in the cold damp dark of the deep mine.

It must have dragged Tommy down here. Saved him for later.

Oscar wiped the sick from his mouth.

Then it came back for us.

"Got to get you out of here." Oscar drew the knife and sliced through the length of climber's rope that bound Tommy's legs.

"We're trapped?" Tommy asked, his voice was flat. He sat next to Jimmy staring off into the distance, his face a filthy mess of dirt and smeared blood.

At least he's stopped crying.

"Yeah." Oscar leaned his head back against the rough wall opposite Jimmy and Tommy. "No way we're getting over that cave-in dragging Jimmy."

"It dragged me through there." Tommy said. "If I fit, you two will fit."

"Probably." Oscar nodded.

"So what's the problem?"

"Think about it." Oscar sat up and rummaged through the neon-yellow hiking pack he had salvaged from the Wendigo's den.

"Shit." Comprehension washed across Jimmy's pain-pinched face.

"What?" Tommy looked at Oscar, then Jimmy.

"Jimmy gets it." Oscar pulled item after item out of the pack, a gallon Ziploc bag of meal bars, underwear, a roll of athletic tape, socks. "Tell him Jimmy."

"The vent tunnel," Jimmy said.

"That thing trapped us in the vent tunnel." Oscar passed around the meal bars. "It came in after us—just crammed its way in. It didn't fit, but it came in anyway." He shuddered. "I don't want to do that again someplace it *does* fit."

"So… we do what? *Wait?*" Tommy asked. "Hope your grandpa gets here before it does?"

"We can't wait here." Oscar started cutting the pack fabric away from its metal frame. "Too exposed."

"Where the hell ain't?" Tommy said around a mouth full of meal bar.

"In there." Oscar nodded past the mining tools, toward the narrow opening and the sound of running water. He scooted over to Jimmy, holding the roll of athletic tape and pack frame pieces. "This is gonna hurt like a bitch."

"How is that any bett—"

The growling shriek echoed through the dark.

"Oh shit, oh shit, oh shit…" Jimmy pushed himself onto his good leg, sliding up the tunnel wall.

"Tommy, grab Jimmy." Oscar sprang to his feet—the improvised splint forgotten. He grabbed a length of chisel-pointed, rusted-covered steel, and headed in the direction of the shriek. He pointed the tool at the narrow, glittering opening on his way past. "Go. That way."

He planted his feet in the center of the tunnel, taking a defensive stance. Waiting.

Why was it shrieking? Why announce its presence? Why not slip up on us and attack?

Oscar smiled.

I hurt it back there in the vent tunnel. It's trying to psych me out, get me to panic and run.

"Oscar!" Tommy's voice echoed from the narrow opening. "No good in here, it's a dead end."

The shrieking growl had gone quiet, but the stench…the stench of the creature grew stronger with each passing moment.

"Same here." Oscar edged back, toward Jimmy and Tommy. He peered through the narrow opening.

Three, maybe four feet. Narrow enough, one of us can hold it. Maybe.

"Did you hear me?" Tommy grabbed Oscar's shoulder. "Dead end. There's nowhere to run."

"Can't be," Oscar said. "Listen. You hear that?"

"Yeah." Tommy said. "Sounds like Bonzai Pipeline at Wate—"

It filled the opening floor-to-ceiling, wall-to-wall. Its putrid stench practically a physical presence. The eyes glowed a pale blue, cold and merciless. Winter in a gaze.

"Find it!" Stepping inside its long, stringy reach, Oscar rammed the chisel-tipped steel down through the top of its left knee. The crunching, wet pop of its knee coming apart under the blow brought a hard smile to Oscar's face, as did the creature's agonized shriek.

On desperate ground, attack.

Oscar danced back out of reach and drew his buck knife. "Sooner would be better!"

The Wendigo swarmed forward on three good limbs. It growled low and rasping, pure malice and hunger in its icy gaze.

Shit this thing is still way too quick.

Oscar stutter-stepped forward, driving the knife into the creature's head with an overhand strike. The blade tore through knotted flesh and skidded off of bone. He skipped away, desperate to dodge the blurring swipe of its clawed hand. Pain blossomed hot and furious. Blood ran down his chest and stomach in a scalding sheet.

Oh, God! It got me.

The creature stopped and stood. It grasped the steel rod sticking out of its ruined left leg and pulled. Oscar shuddered at the wet sucking sound the rod made as it slid free of the creature's flesh. He could hear the wet pop and crunch of the shattered joint reassembling itself. Despair, cold and heavy settled over him.

Here is where it ends.

He crouched—weight on the balls of his feet— he held the knife low, the clipped point making small circles.

Here in the dark. Nowhere left to run, nowhere to hide.

He shuffled back keeping his feet in firm contact with the rough floor.

Not gonna make it easy.

"Come and get mahhh—" Oscar squawked.

A forceful hand wrapped around the collar of his ruined shirt and jerked him sideways into the narrow fissure.

"Come on!" Tommy pulled harder, dragging Oscar awkwardly toward him.

The creature howled in frustration. A blood-crusted hand darted into the fissure; black claws tracing a bloody line of fire down Oscar's arm.

Oscar stumbled, fell, and slid to a stop on damp stone. The sound of rushing water filled his ears. Shadows jumped and danced as he looked about. Tommy stood in front of the narrow fissure; covered in mud, prized letterman's jacket a tattered mess, steel drill rod at the ready. Jimmy leaned against the mine wall inches away from the torrent that foamed down the slick stone and vanished into a dark fissure half in the floor, half up the wall.

"You're bleeding," Jimmy shouted over the rushing water.

"Yeah." Oscar pulled the shirt aside to look at the four deep gouges. "Hurts like a bitch."

"Now what?" Jimmy slid over next to Oscar.

"Tommy?" Oscar called. "Think we can hold that thing off 'til help gets here?"

"Shit!" Tommy shook his head jabbing the drill rod into the fissure. The creature's shrieks crescendo. "How the hell is it just forcing its way through like that?"

"Let me see." Oscar scrambled up the damp, slick stone, peering into the narrow gap. The creature was clawing its way toward them, skin, meat, and blood lubricating its way forward. "It regenerates, Tommy." The bedraggled senior stared blankly at Oscar. "Like Wolverine."

"I didn't take biology." Tommy shrugged.

"Not like *a* wolverine." Oscar rolled his eyes. "The Wolverine. You know? X-Men comics?"

"He don't read much." Jimmy said. "Not unless you count nudie mags and Sports Illustrated."

"Hey, that counts." Tommy said.

"Oh, for Pete's sake. It grows back!" Oscar rolled his eyes again. "Nearly anything we do to it, it just grows back. Gimme that drill rod, will ya."

He grabbed the rusted length of steel from Tommy's slack grip.

"What are you doing?" Tommy asked.

"Buying time."

Oscar slid back into the fissure. Drill rod held high, he waited.

It inched closer, clawing its way forward. Blue eyes shone in the darkness; two cold windows into hell.

Grandpa's voice echoed through his head. *Samurai lived as though they had already died. The dead need not fear death.*

Oscar's heartbeat slowed.

The creature came on, shedding skin and meat, roaring.

Oscar waited.

The creature's leg reached toward Oscar.

He struck. Drove the steel rod down through the top of its knee once again, smiling at the crunch of ruined cartilage and its agonized shriek.

Oscar shouted wordless triumph and scooted back out of the fissure. Behind him, came shrieks and the scrabbling of claws on rock.

"Did it work?" Jimmy asked.

"For now." Oscar slumped against the wall, dizzy with exertion and blood loss. He stared at the water, watched it rush down the slope of the wall and into the floor.

Sonuvabitch!

"The pool!"

"What?" Tommy peered through the fissure.

"I'll bet this makes the fish pool have that weird-ass current."

"Did you hit your head Rockwell?" Jimmy asked.

"No, this stream has to feed that pool!"

The creatures' shrieks crescendoed again.

"It just pulled that rod out of its leg!" Tommy called.

"No way." Jimmy shook his head. "No way am I trying to swim out of here."

"Beats being ripped to shreds by that thing." Oscar nodded toward the fissure. "Hell, I can't even swim."

"Shit, Hillbilly Bruce Lee," Jimmy said, grinning. "I was beginning to think there wasn't nothing you couldn't do."

"Come on Tommy," Oscar said. "We're getting out of here."

"How?" Tommy slid down the slope, to stand next to Jimmy.

"Crazy bastard thinks we can swim out." Jimmy nodded at Oscar.

"Not swim, slide. Like Bonzai Pipeline." Oscar shoved the buck knife back in its scabbard, thumbing the keeper-loop over the hilt.

The growling, howling shriek of the creature grew louder, closer. Oscar looked over his shoulder and saw a black-clawed hand grasping the edge of the fissure.

"Besides, we're out of time."

"Okay. Let's do it." Jimmy inched forward, gasping in pain. With a shrug he slid into the rushing water and disappeared.

"Hey," Tommy rested his meaty hand on Oscar's shoulder. "For what it's worth I'm sorry." Turning, the big senior took a deep breath and slid into the roaring stream.

"Yeah, me too." Oscar stepped into the foaming white water.

Dark comes quick in the mountains, quicker in the bottom of mountain canyons. Three bedraggled shapes limped through those early evening shadows. Tommy and Oscar half-carried Jimmy suspended between them. The pale, rutted dust of the road snaked its way through the darkening canyon. A mournful, squalling, shriek echoed through the mountain air. Jimmy's head jerked around, his eyes wide he stared towards the sound.

"We are so screwed." Jimmy sagged against Oscar.

"Wait." Oscar cocked his head, listening.

It came again, accompanied by the growl of a big block V8 and a distinct, clattering clank.

Grandpa's truck.

Hope flashed through Oscar, lending fresh energy to his battered and exhausted muscles. "Grandpa!" They broke into a shambling run, Jimmy all but hanging between Oscar and Tommy.

A growling, shrieking howl split the early evening air.

Oscar hunched his shoulders, tried to pick up the pace. It sounded different out here in the open; it sounded triumphant.

"Faster." Oscar wheezed between burning, agonizing breaths.

Apparently, a near drowning makes running suck even more.

They were nearly there. A faded Forest-service green Dodge pickup hurtled around the corner, pursued by a cloud of dust. It flew past, worn belt squalling, tailgate chains clanking in counterpoint. Grandpa was standing up in the bed of the old Dodge, one hand gripping the steel backrack for support.

Was that Shannon driving?

"Shit!" Tommy and Oscar stumbled up onto the road, dust settling around them. "We'll never catch up to them." Tommy didn't even sound out of breath.

Oscar looked back down the slope, towards the fishing spot. A spindly lanky shadow darted towards them.

It knows we have nowhere to run.

"Tommy," Oscar reached down unfastening the keeper-loop from the Buck knife's hilt. "Take Jimmy and follow the truck."

"No way."

Jimmy's face was pale and pinched. The ride down the waterway hadn't done his broken ankle any favors and had left him looking like he'd been dragged down a gravel road.

"It'll just run us down after it kills you."

The stuttering crunch of tires skidding on dirt came from up the road, followed by the sound of gears grinding and the whine of a manual transmission accelerating in reverse.

"No time for debate." Oscar ducked out from under Jimmy's left arm. "Run Tommy!"

Still on desperate ground.

Oscar drew the hunting knife and forced his weary legs into a run.

Tommy scooped up his friend and ran towards the reversing pickup. An old man stood in the bed, one hand gripping the backrack, the other a rifle. The well-chewed stub of a cigar jutted from his mouth. He was wearing some sort of dark green vest festooned with hardware and an old, curved sword was strapped to one hip. The old man banged one gnarled hand on the roof and the truck skidded to a stop.

"Heard you boys needed a ride!" He had a deep voice, sharp and piercing like river boulders dumped on an iron plate. "Where the hell is Oscar?"

"Trying to fight that thing." Tommy nodded back down the slope.

"Damned fool boy. Gonna get dead trying to be a hero." The old man raised the gun to his shoulder, the muscles in his forearms stood out like gnarled and knotted rope. "Best get your friend loaded in the cab."

The creature raced toward Oscar. The malevolent glow of those winter-blue eyes visible in the failing light. Unconstrained by low ceilings and narrow tunnels the creature was fast and huge like a grizzly bear's and Bigfoot's nightmare love-child.

Oscar crouched as he ran towards the thing, hoping for a chance to wound it or slow it down. He had no delusions; it was going to tear him to pieces.

Hopefully, they get to the truck before it finishes with me.

Time seemed to slow. He could see the blades of grass in sharp relief; the yellow clover and blue larkspur vivid in the fading summer light. Oscar held the knife low, ready to stab or slash. He heard a distant shout, a single word in a parade-ground bark.

"INCOMING!"

Incoming? Shit!

Oscar turned the run into a slide. The creature's head followed Oscar to the ground for a moment before several rounds—placed center-mass— ripped it from its feet.

"Let's go boy!" Grandpa triggered another burst, hammering the creature.

Oscar rolled to his stomach and scrambled back up the slope, bent double in a half-panicked bear-crawl, trying to stay under Grandpa's covering fire. Burst after burst thundered, the rounds cracking above Oscar's head. He fetched up against the faded green door of Grandpa's old Dodge Power Wagon, gasping for breath. The hammering roar of Grandpa's weapon abruptly cut off.

"You getting in or what?" Shannon pointed toward the bed of the truck with her thumb.

"Keep those mags coming!" Grandpa barked, his voice loud in the absence of gunfire. Oscar looked back to see the old marine locking another of the bulky gray magazines into his old Browning.

Oscar ran around the front of the truck, spotted Jimmy in the passenger seat and grinned.

We might just live through this.

Gripping the steel rail of the backrack, he vaulted into the bed of the truck. Grandpa slapped the roof. With a grinding of gears and a lurch that dumped Oscar on his butt, Shannon headed up the road, away from the creature and toward the Turnaround.

"Here." Grandpa shoved the Browning into Oscar's hands. "Controlled bursts. We don't have ammo to burn."

"It's gone!" Oscar cradled the heavy old rifle and squinted into the failing light searching for a target.

"Keep your eyes peeled." Grandpa pulled a rag from his hip pocket and wiped the beaded sweat from his face and buzz-cut gray hair. "That thing ain't gone, it just changed tactics. Gillette, hand me the grenade launcher."

"This?" Tommy held up something that looked like a shotgun with an over-large barrel and an upside-down stock.

"That's the one." Grandpa took the grenade launcher from Tommy. "Look, move this lever to the right, and it breaks open like a shotgun. Then you just drop in the round, close it, aim and pull the trigger. Understand?"

"I think so." Tommy said.

"No." Grandpa shoved the weapon into Tommy's hands. "Can't afford *I think so*'. Do you understand how the weapon works?"

"Y—yeah. I understand." Tommy gripped the grenade launcher tight.

"Good." Grandpa put a hand on Tommy's shoulder. "Show me." Tommy thumbed the lever, broke open the launcher, and mimicked loading it, before snapping the barrel closed again. "Good, now look in that green bag there by your foot. Long and white is illumination, the others are buckshot. When I call for it, you give me illumination, then get buckshot loaded. We'll need it."

The old Dodge truck crunched to a stop. Jimmy's disabled Chevy cast strange and ominous shadows in the pale glow of the headlights. The steel door yawned open, a deeper black in the shadow of the canyon wall. Somewhere between their escape and arrival at the Turnaround, night had arrived, unannounced and unwelcome.

"Now what?" Oscar asked.

"Now we wait." Grandpa rummaged around in the bed of the pickup.

"For what?" Tommy's head turned back and forth, straining to see.

"For that sumbitch to come for us, Gillette." Grandpa fished a tube up from the truck bed, pulled on one end extending it to near double length. "Then we're gonna blow it to hell." He flipped up a rectangular sight and leaned the tube against the cab of the truck.

"Hey," Jimmy called. "Don't I get a gun?"

"Give this to the Hake boy," Grandpa said, passing a pump-action shotgun and leather bandoleer of shells through the driver's window to Shannon. "You still got that 1911 handy, Mutz?"

"Yep." Shannon waggled it out the window for Grandpa to see. "One in the chamber, spare mags on the seat."

"W—where is it?" Tommy stammered. "What's it waiting for?"

"We hurt it back there." Grandpa said. "It's stalking us now, keeping out of sight, keeping quiet. Looking to pick the right moment—so keep your eyes peeled. First sign of movement, you send up one of those illumination rounds. Be ready with the buckshot rounds after. Once it decides to go, it won't stop til we're all dead or it is."

"The long ones, right?" Tommy thumbed the lever, opening the grenade launcher. He dropped a pale, oblong-shape into the tube and snapped it closed.

"Yep." Grandpa picked up another tube, and extended it with a sharp snap, resting it next to the first one. "The short stubby ones are loaded with silver buckshot." He reached down and picked up a sawed-off double-barrel shotgun, snapped it open to check the load then closed it with a practiced flip of his hand. "Silver'll slow it down. Then we'll finish it off with consecrated fire."

An eerie growl split the night. It started low and rumbling, then climbed to an ear-splitting shriek that made Oscar's scrotum shrink up tight and all the hair on the back of his neck stand on end. He swiveled his head back and forth desperately trying to find the creature. The sound came from the shadows near Jimmy's truck.

"Gillette, now would be a good time for that illumination round." Grandpa slipped another bandoleer of shotgun shells over his shoulder. "Oscar, you see that thing, you open up. Don't take too long to aim. It'll be moving and fast." He sounded calm, almost bored.

Tommy aimed the grenade launcher up into the night sky and pulled the trigger. The weapon fired with a muffled *bloop*. An instant later the entire Turnaround was lit-up with stark white light.

The creature was moving—a black blur of racing shadow, the white glare from overhead reflecting off of its bared teeth and narrowed blue eyes.

"Shit—Shit—Shit." Oscar tucked the stock of the BAR into his shoulder, brought the barrel to bear and triggered a burst of fire.

Too late.

The thing leaped into the truck bed shrieking and clawing. The BAR flew from Oscar's hands and fresh agony bloomed across his chest. Blood flowed, hot and wet, soaking his shredded shirt, cascading down his chest and stomach. The sawed-off shotgun boomed, staggering the creature. Another muffled crack sent the creature stumbling back.

"DOWN!" Shannon sat in the driver's window, 1911 in a white-knuckled, two-handed grip resting on the roof. Oscar and Grandpa both dropped to the bed of the truck. Blood and flesh flew in time to the staccato bark of the rapid-fired pistol.

The creature half-fell, half-scrambled over the edge of the truck bed and vanished beneath Jimmy's disabled Chevy. Grandpa grabbed one of the LAW rocket tubes from the truck bed and took aim. "More illumination Gillette!"

"I can't." Tommy stared down at his mangled left hand and arm. Dark blood spurted from torn and ragged flesh.

"Damn." Grandpa turned back to the truck, took careful aim, and triggered the launcher. A moment later Jimmy's truck erupted in flames. Flickering firelight taking over for the fading illumination round.

"My truck!" Jimmy pushed the door to the old Dodge open and slid out onto his good leg.

"Shannon, grab that med-kit and take care of Gillette." Grandpa dropped the empty rocket tube and sagged against the cab of the truck clutching his abdomen.

"On it." Shannon leaned into the old Dodge and came back with a zipper-bag. She crawled the rest of the way out of the driver's window and into the bed of the truck. "Get some pressure on that arm Tommy."

Pale and shaking, Tommy dropped the grenade launcher and squeezed his forearm just above the awful wound.

"Grandpa!" Oscar knelt down next to his grandfather. He pulled a flashlight from the old man's vest and thumbed it on. Grandpa's stomach was a mess of blood and torn fabric. "No—no—no…"

So much blood!

"Oscar—Oscar—Oscar!" Grandpa cuffed Oscar with his unengaged hand. "Focus. You've got to finish this."

"You're hurt." Oscar fished a pack of quik-clot out of the vest.

"Rockwell. Shannon!" Jimmy called, racking the slide on his weapon. "That thing's still moving."

"I'll do that." Grandpa took the quik-clot from Oscar's shaking hand. "You take the sawed-off and my sword and you finish this sumbitch!"

"Guys!" The 12-gauge boomed. "Guys!" Jimmy racked the slide again.

"O—Okay." Oscar pulled Grandpa's old marine sword from its scabbard, picked up the sawed-off from the truck bed, reloaded, and stood. Pain blossomed across his chest and abdomen, fresh blood leaking from wounds old and new. "Shannon, when you're done with Tommy, see to Grandpa; he's hurt."

Oscar vaulted down from the old Dodge and headed towards the burning wreckage of Jimmy's truck. The pallets and old tires had caught fire. Flames leaped high into the night, bathing the Turnaround with a primitive flickering light. The creature stalked towards him, dripping blood and ash, back-lit by the burning truck. Blue flames flickered and danced along one arm and those blue eyes still glowed with an awful vitality.

God, this thing is tough!

It began to pick up speed.

Jimmy's 12-gauge boomed; silvered-buckshot punched a ragged wound in the creature's chest. Oscar planted his feet in the dark earth of the Turnaround and waited, Grandpa's sword clasped in one white-knuckled hand, the sawed-off in the other. He was done running.

The creature leapt at Oscar—still greasy fast— swiping and hooking with those black-tipped claws.

Not as fast as you used to be.

Oscar ducked under the creature's attack and jammed the sawed-off into its gut, yanking both triggers. The blast sent black blood and glistening bone rocketing out of the creature's back.

The creature fell on Oscar in a shrieking avalanche of snapping teeth and flailing claws. Oscar hit the ground hard, driving the air from his lungs with the impact. Wheezing, he tried to get his legs wrapped around the thing's middle—tried to get close and limit the damage from tooth and claw. He felt its claws dig into his back, gouging and ripping. Icy agony shot through him, stealing the strength from his limbs. The old marine sword fell from his numbed hand.

This is it… this is how I die.

The creature rose above Oscar's limp form. One black-clawed hand pinned him to the ground. It raised the other high—the icy promise of death in those glowing blue eyes.

Time slowed.

Hodichin Chaha'oh shrieked in triumph. Oscar stared into those cold blue eyes. The hand started its final downward arc.

I won't flinch, won't give the sumbitch the satisfaction.

A hole blossomed in its chest. Then another. Then two more. Time snapped back to regular speed, the creature tumbling away from Oscar— its shriek replaced by the stuttering roar of a BAR on full-auto.

"Cut that sonofabitch's head off!" Shannon snapped another magazine into the old rifle.

Oscar rolled to his right, picked up the Mameluke blade and staggered to his feet. The BAR roared again, the creature jerked and twitched as bursts of .30-06 rounds tore gobs of flesh from its body. Oscar limped towards the creature, one arm clenched tight against the breath-stealing agony in his chest and side. He stepped on the thing's chest—locked eyes with it—and swung the sword. Once. Twice. Three times. The creature's head rolled free, blue eyes still glowing.

They sat on the tailgate of Grandpa's truck and watched the creature burn. The fire glowed with a white-hot intensity, fueled by consecrated oil and supernatural flesh.

"Hold still Oscar." Shannon pulled another stitch tight, working by firelight to close-up the worst of Oscar's wounds.

"Sorry." Oscar grimaced as the hooked needle pierced the torn flesh of his back once more.

"What do we do now?" Jimmy asked.

"We wait for that to burn down." Grandpa swapped the cigar stub from one corner of his mouth to the other. "Then we'll gather the ashes, and hand 'em over to the boys from Quantico."

"What's in Quantico?" Shannon pulled another stitch closed.

"The One Three." Grandpa let his head fall back against the cab of the old Dodge. "I put in a call before we rolled. They'll be here by sunup."

"What do we do about Brice and the others?" Tommy sat next to Grandpa, cradling his mangled arm.

"The same thing we always do son." Grandpa patted Tommy's leg. "Bury our dead and prepare."

"Prepare for what?" Shannon pulled another stitch tight.

"The next fight. 'Cause another one's always a'comin.'"

Back in the Saddle Again

By: L.A. Behm II

Isle Harve, French Polynesia
30 July 1978

"**M**ajor, there's some idiot from the Company waiting to ambush you in Marvin's," Master Guns Huggins said by way of greeting.

I'd tried to get him to address me by my first name over the years since we'd resigned from the Corps in 1975. It hadn't worked.

I'd left the *Bedstemor Havfrue* in the capable hands of her skipper and crew, down on the beach. I'd even left the 'security detail' to help offload the pigs. When she'd worn Navy gray, she'd been known as *Graham County*, and would have had a surfeit of crew to handle the work. Today, since she was flying Miller Shipping colors here in the south Pacific, we'd cut the crew to a profitable minimum–even if I was living aboard as owner.

I stopped for a minute in the sleepy main street of Harve, reaching into a pocket for a pack of Camel non-filters. I got the smoke lit with my Zippo and took a couple of drags before replying.

"How do you know he's Company?"

"Who the hell else would wear a bespoke suit from Brooks Brothers in French Polynesia, but a damned CIA agent?"

"Good point, Master Guns," I said. "Shall we see what he wants?"

"Sure," Master Guns said, turning up the street towards Marvin's. "He's got a couple of goons with him, and they're definitely overdressed for this little burg."

He touched his right hip as he said it, about where a holster would ride under a suit coat.

Not that Master Guns and I weren't what a more genteel era would have called heeled. We'd just learned less obvious places for the hardware than those promoted by the Boys Finishing School at Langley.

I stepped up to the veranda surrounding Marvin's. Back when Paul Gauguin was painting native girls in and out of their colorful costumes, Marvin's had been built by a French ship captain who'd had enough of France and the sea, but still wanted to smell salt water. The place had gone through several owners in the years since then, until the late 1940s when Marvin had bought the place, rebuilt it, and started renting a few rooms to the tramp captains that wanted to spend the nights while they were offloading at Ilse Harve ashore.

Marvin himself was a mountain of a man. He'd been born the son of a poor black sharecropper in Alabama. World War II had gotten him out of that particular hell and dropped him into another one—he'd joined the Navy on his seventeenth birthday, and they'd trained him as a coxswain just in time for the Battle of Tarawa. From there, he fought his way across the Pacific, seeing all the major tourist attractions—The Marianas, Iwo Jima, and Okinawa with the Fifth Fleet. They were on station off Oki, hauling supplies in early August when the Japanese surrendered. Marvin and his crew started doing the 'we're going home' shuffle—until they learned they'd spend the next three years repatriating the Japanese Army from various locations around Asia.

About the time I'd enlisted in the Corps, Marvin had exited the Navy. He bummed around the Pacific for about a year, and finally ended up on Isle Harve, buying a rather run-down hotel/bawdy house with his mustering out pay. Now, most days, he held court behind the bar. Today he was sitting on the veranda, under a lazily spinning fan.

"Majah," Marvin said.

"Boats."

"Majah, you know, I likes you. I put up with moar shit from you an' that batch of unhung pirates in yoah crew than I'd put up with from any otha' boat plyin' these watahs. Hell, I even let you trade in dat dey cursed red gold y'all come up with in tha bah."

I couldn't really reply. In my defense, we'd gotten the gold in payment for taking care of a small infestation of Deep Ones near Hiva Oa. I'd even paid to have the place blessed by the local priest afterward.

"But I draws the line at visits from 'duly appointed rep-re-sent-tives' of Uncle Sugah," Marvin continued, pausing to take a pull off a bottle of beer.

"He told you he was with the Government?"

"Tried to sell me some line about him bein' with the State Department or som' shit like that," Marvin said, gesturing to the chairs across the table from him.

We sat. Marvin raised a hand over his shoulder, and one of the bar girls brought out a tray with glasses, a bottle of Old Crow, and, most importantly, ice. He waited patiently while Master Guns and I fixed ourselves a drink and lit cigarettes.

"Why the change in attitude?" I asked, once the first third of my glass was down the hatch.

"Look on yoah face said everything when I tol' you he was a duly appointed representative of the governmen'," Marvin replied. "If y'all had known he was comin' yoah face'd shown it."

"He let slip what he wants?" Master Guns asked, lighting a truly vile-smelling cigar.

"Something about a job fo' y'all. Apparently 'State' needs some diplomat's furniture moved from Point A to Point B and can't find space on a Navy Hull to do it, so theys slummin'."

"See Major, simple answer," Master Guns said.

"Simple as the pig shit in the cargo deck on Grandmother," I replied.

I finished my drink and stubbed out my cigarette, then stood.

"I guess I'll go find out what the Cookie Pusher wants."

It took a minute for my eyes to adjust to the light inside Marvin's. Not that it wasn't well lit, but the difference between sunlight and the interior was that much.

Sure enough, there were three . . . individuals, seated at the bar. Two of them screamed 'security detail'—a couple hundred pounds each of muscled-up beef, uncomfortable in off-the-rack suits that weren't designed for the heat of the South Pacific in winter. They were built like middle linebackers and had probably played for some non-Ivy League School before joining the Company to avoid the draft.

The principle? He was a different ball of wax entirely. Tall and lithe, he had the look of a Yale lacrosse player. Moreover, Master Guns was right—he looked comfortable in a bespoke Brooks Brothers suit. Hell, he looked like something just off the rubber plantation in his white linens. I expected him to be drinking gin and tonics, honestly.

Lacrosse looked down at the bar, gathered some papers, and put them in an attaché case that Middle Linebacker #1 held up, and then stepped towards me.

When he did, I could see the grip of a gun hanging under Lacrosse's left armpit. Took me a minute to realize where I'd last seen a grip like that—one of the last missions we'd run for SU-13 in Vietnam had involved going north of the DMZ to a 'special' NVA training site where the officers all carried Skorpion machine pistols. Either this clown was with the CIA, or my bad habits had caught up with me and someone from the Soviet side was after me. Again.

"Ah, Colonel Miller," Lacrosse said, stepping across the bar and offering me his hand.

"You have me at a disadvantage, Mister?"

"Ah, yes, I'm Jonas Smith," he said, reaching under his jacket.

My hand slid back under the Hawaiian print shirt I was wearing. He fished out one of those combination ID/Passport holders and extracted an artistically worn US government ID card.

Sure enough, it showed Jonas Smith was a member in good standing of the Foggy Bottom Social Club. I might have bought it, if I hadn't seen the little Czech party-starter he carried in his armpit.

"What can I do for you, Mister Smith?"

"Would you join me for a drink? I've got a business proposition for you and your ship." He gestured broadly at a table.

"Sure," I replied, a false grin plastered on my face.

I'd hear the asshole out, and then probably get one of the bouncers to toss him and his meat puppets out the door on their asses. I made it fucking clear on the flight deck of *Okinawa* that I was done watching people I cared for get used up and tossed away by Uncle Sugar in 1975. I'd even accepted exile to the South Pacific to prove it. I'd be damned if I got involved with any games the CIA was running out here.

I looked over at Little Billy, standing behind the bar. At six ten and four hundred pounds, Little Billy was 'little' in the same sense as Robin Hood's Little John. The Maori had washed up on Isle Harve and Marvin had put him to work as a half-bartender/half-bouncer.

"The backroom free, Billy?"

"Yeah, it's open," he replied, tossing me the key. "You need anything?"

"My usual and whatever these guys are drinking."

Billy sniffed. "Bottle of Old Crow, two Cokes, and a pitcher of mint juleps."

No wonder Billy was sniffing. Mint juleps weren't that common around here, and the mint would come from Marvin's private crop.

I led the way to the back room. Marvin kept it for 'business meetings' and big parties—ships crews could rent the place for special occasions. I wanted it because it was semi-private.

One of the linebacker twins took the key from me and opened the door, while the other one gave it a quick sweep, one hand under his jacket.

"You know, not pointing out where you're carrying your hardware is a little easier long term," I said to the room around me.

"Sometimes you want the world to know you're packing a gat," Smith replied.

A gat? Did he grow up watching bad gangster movies? Knowing the fucking Company, it was probably a job requirement.

One of Marvin's wives swept past into the room, with two bar girls in tow. They opened the windows and the shutters. A third bar girl brought the drinks and set them up on the table.

"You need anything else, Major?" Marvin's wife asked.

"Not right now, although if you see Master Guns, send him this way."

"I'm here, Major," Huggins said.

"Right," I replied

I walked into the room and took a seat on the left side of the table. Smith and his followers sat on the right. Master Guns leaned up against the wall in a corner.

I poured a measure of Old Crow into a glass and added ice, while Smith pulled folders from his attaché and arranged them neatly on the table in front of him.

Old habits die hard. I'd spent a lot of time gathering intel for SU-13, and more time figuring out what the next trick was going to be by reading things upside down.

The label on one folder read 'Trahn'.

Once he had the papers arranged to his liking, Smith took a deep breath and looked at me.

"As you've probably guessed, Colonel Miller, I'm not with State."

"Let's start there," I said. "Yes, my final rank in the Marine Corps was Colonel. However, as you've probably noticed, most people call me Major."

"Yes, I noticed that."

Score one for the CIA. Not that I was going to let him know he'd impressed me.

"Why?"

"I spent five years as a Major. General Conrad pinned the oak leaves on my shoulders *after* I resigned onboard *Okinawa*, and then rammed through my promotion to full bird just before I finished processing stateside. It's a bump in retirement pay for getting fucked over by the White House and State Department in '75."

"I... I see," Smith replied. "Then, as you've realized, Major, I work for another organization, concerned with national security."

Master Guns coughed. Under the cough, I heard 'bullshit', loud and clear.

"Look, Mr. Smith, let's lay all the cards on the table, face up. You're CIA, and want me to do something very illegal, probably in South East Asia, am I right?" I held up a hand to forestall his protests. "You're not a Cookie-Pusher with State, by your own admission. You also state you work in National Security. That means the Company, DIA, or No Such Agency, and last time I checked, neither DIA nor NSA were as... aggressive about national security interests as the CIA."

The Linebacker Twins looked openly hostile. How dare some broken-down former Marine Colonel doubt their Holy Writ?

Smith grinned wryly.

"You know, I told General Conrad he should do this himself, but he said no, that'd be the wrong touch. Yes, I'm with the CIA. More importantly, I'm seconded to SU-13."

"Not this bullshit again," Master Guns said. "What now? Some Congressman's mistress get eaten by a *bakuwana* while the Congressman was on a fact-finding trip to Po City?"

"Not... not quite, Mister Huggins. As you both know, the US Government decided to... leave behind..."

"Abandon," I said.

"Yes, if that's how you feel about it, abandon, certain elements of the Vietnamese military in place during the fall of Saigon in 1975. The new regime has spent the last three years in efforts to re-educate..."

"Re-create," Huggins said.

"What?"

"The Vietnamese phrase *hoc tap cải tạo* doesn't translate as 're-education'. A better translation is 're-create' as in re-creating the individual in the mold the State prefers," Master Guns said, turning towards me. "You'd think the CIA would have better translators."

"Good point, Master Guns," I said. I judged the ash on my cigar needed tapping, and my glass was suffering from evaporation loss. Smith waited patiently while I took care of business, then continued.

"The... the new regime has spent the last three years in efforts to re-create personnel that were captured during the Fall of Saigon. The CIA has monitored the camps, to ensure that no important intel falls into the hands of the Chinese or Soviets."

"Which has exactly what to do with us, Mr. Smith?" I asked.

"A year and a half ago, we monitored traffic from the North Vietnamese Army about a unit they were hunting in northern Laos. We were able to confirm that there were elements of the RVN

Marines operating in the area with a group of Hmong."

"*And?*" Huggins asked.

"The signals intercept officer had spent some time in the Marine Corps before coming to work for us at Langley. When he heard the phrase Tho san ma in the intercept, he pushed the intercept up the chain, and sent a message to General Conrad," Smith said. "My understanding is that Mr. Fox had lunch with the General and passed the message there."

Fox had been with SU-13–he'd lost an arm in 1970 when we were chasing down a Hmong village god that had gotten a little too powerful for the local shaman to control. He'd know exactly who the Tho san ma–*Ghost Hunters* being a rough translation from Vietnamese to English–were and why the North Vietnamese would be hunting them.

"Fox would know how to get in touch with the General," I said. "I take it you confirmed that the Tho san ma were Colonel Trahn's troops?"

"General Trahn, but yes, we were able to confirm that General Trahn was still alive and leading the remnants of the Tho san ma and a group of Hmong in Laos. They've apparently been conducting guerrilla operations in the area."

"Which still doesn't tell us why you want the Major and me to stick our dicks back in a meat grinder," Huggins said.

"Yes, that. The NVA are looking for the Tho san ma for two reasons—one the aforementioned guerrilla operations and two, the NVA believe the Tho san ma are responsible for a series of attacks on NVA installations in the area by what the NVA describe as a 'white goddess'."

"Her again," I said.

Huggins nodded.

"Her again?" Smith asked.

"Oh come now, Mr. Smith. You're read in, so are your guys here, or we wouldn't be having this discussion. This shit is classified above 'Suicide after reading' levels. You've probably seen the files. We were chasing a 'white goddess of death' all over Southeast Asia before Kissinger got his panties in a twist over the Peace Accords and pulled Military Assistance Command, Vietnam (Special Unit-13) out of country. Hell, even if you hadn't had the intel on the Tho san ma, General Conrad would have sent you out here with that bit of information, just to see if he could lure me back into harness again."

Smith looked down at the briefing papers he'd carefully arranged on the table.

"Major, I'm not going to lie to you. Yes, the General suggested I use *all* the information I had to, as you say, lure you back into harness with SU-13. There is one more piece of information I haven't given you yet, however," he said, holding up a hand to forestall me this time. "General Trahn has asked for your help personally."

"You can take that with a grain of salt," Huggins scoffed.

"Or you can talk to the General in–in three hours," Smith said, checking his watch and the papers on the table. "Confirm the information yourself."

"No need," I said. "Tell General Conrad I want to meet with him."

"He anticipated you," Smith replied, sliding an envelope across the table. "General Conrad will be at those coordinates for the next ten days."

Back in the Saddle Again

I looked at the chart in the envelope. Since retiring from the Corps, I'd learned what my younger brother referred to as the 'real family business', shipping. The position was about one hundred nautical miles south of Tarawa Atoll.

"Four to five days from here, if we sail at the next high tide," I said. "Let the General know we'll be there–and let him know this is costing me money."

"How so?"

"I'm going to have to turn down the load we were supposed to pick up here and run up there in ballast," I replied. "I don't work for Uncle Sugar anymore, and I can't afford to burn fuel for a friendly visit."

"I'm authorized to request the Miller Shipping Company deliver this," Smith pulled out a package about the size of a hardback book from his attaché case, "to the coordinates listed in that envelope. We'll pay standard delivery rates."

Smith also dropped a block of currency on the table.

"Ten thousand dollars should cover the trip, I believe?"

Four days later, we were steaming circles around the position. We'd made a couple of modifications to *Grandmother* when she'd become the property of Miller Shipping that we hadn't felt necessary to inform her former owners of. Bigger engines, better radar, and we'd purchased some things to help with the side jobs I knew would crop up.

I was up on the bridge wing, soaking up coffee and nicotine in almost equal measures when the radar operator reported a contact to the north. I drank more coffee and watched as a ship came over the horizon–a destroyer that blew past us and took up station fifteen miles to the south. A second hull came over the horizon.

"Shit, Major, the General has balls," Master Guns said.

I'd caught the hull number on the gator freighter that was slowly coming into view. USS *Tarawa.*

Back in the Saddle Again

"Yeah, you can say that," I replied, walking onto the bridge. "Mister Grumby, heave to. I'm going to go meet with the General."

It took about ten minutes to lower a boat and cross the distance between the ships. *Tarawa* opened her well deck, and we slid up inside.

General Conrad was waiting in the well deck when we tied up and I stepped aboard.

"Colonel Miller."

"General," I replied, offering him my hand. I was in civilian dress, and I damn sure wasn't going to salute.

Besides, our last interaction off the coast of Vietnam on Oki hadn't been... pleasant.

We shook hands.

"There's two ways we can do this," Conrad said. "I can hand you the briefing packet here, or we can go up to my cabin and discuss things."

I looked around for a minute before answering.

"Sir, the only reason I'm taking this job is Father Trahn. We fucked him over three years ago."

Conrad grinned.

"I seem to remember you telling me that on the Oki's flight deck."

"Nothing's changed."

"How many men do you have?" he asked, leading me to a table set up in the run-up area on the well deck.

"Ten, not counting Master Guns or myself. Call it a short squad. And before you ask, all of them were with SU-13 when we were in-Country."

"How's their Vietnamese?"

"They all took the Combat Viet course the Amazing Nguyen Brothers put together. Why?"

"That's good. The guys you're going to be working with will all speak Viet fluently. You might even know a couple of them."

"Oh?"

The General gestured to one of the marines standing along the inner bulkhead of the well deck. The marine stepped through a hatch and came back with two Viets following him.

The Viets were dressed in tiger stripe camouflage. It took a minute for me to recognize the Amazing Nguyen Brothers. Last time I'd seen them, they'd been wearing USMC issue fatigues and carrying M-16's.

"Major," Mihn Nguyen said, offering me his hand.

We shook, and then I repeated the gesture with Huynh. Both of them were wearing the epaulets of a South Vietnamese captain.

"I take it you gentlemen are part of this?"

"Yes sir," Huynh replied. "We've got a full company of Tho san ma that trained under the General and escaped when the NVA took over."

"Equipment?"

"AK-47's, RPD's, RPG-2's mostly. No sub-machine guns. We've got one platoon carrying US M2 mortars."

I turned to the General.

"Sounds like someone was thinking ahead."

"They might have done some work for the Company along the Thai border," he admitted with a shrug.

"Speaking of the Company..." I left it hanging.

"Yes, Agent Smith," Conrad said, a wry smile on his face. "State actually foisted him off on us."

"State?"

"He was working with them in-Country," Conrad continued. "Seconded from CIA to State's in-house intelligence group there. I asked State for some help in the region, and they 'gifted' him to us."

"That explains the Skorpion," I said. "So, are we being paid by SU-13 or the Company for this trip?"

"CIA's got a bigger budget. Smith has already lost the cost of this little jaunt."

"Probably paid for out of the money Air America made running drugs," I replied.

"Not my problem," Conrad said. "Did you get the full package from Smith?"

"You mean the White Goddess of Death? Yes, sir."

"Your thoughts?"

"Depends," I replied. "We both know Trahn isn't coming out without taking care of her."

"What would you say if I ordered you to drag him out if necessary?"

"First, I'd point out I don't work for Uncle Sugar anymore, and then I'd give you the middle finger, hop back on my boat, and go back to being owner aboard *Grandmother*," I replied.

"That's what I told Kissinger when I briefed him," Conrad said. "He wasn't happy with that answer but accepted it."

"Show me what you've got," I said.

Conrad led me into the ship, up to the cabin he was occupying, where Master Guns Lee waited with the briefing materials on the mission.

It took eleven days to sail from Tarawa to Bangkok. Smith met us on the docks—he'd arranged for us to offload the 'packages' we'd shifted from USS *Tarawa* to *Grandmother*, along with the Amazing Nguyen Brothers and their company of Tho san ma.

I'd convinced the Nguyen brothers not to muster the Tho san ma on the dock—and they'd brought along civi's, so it didn't look like we were staging an invasion of Thailand.

Before leaving *Grandmother*, I looked at her captain, Jonas Grumby.

"Skipper, get *Grandmother* back down south where she belongs. If we survive up north, Master Guns and I'll make our way back down there to you."

"Yes sir," he said, touching two fingers to the bill of his hat in a lazy salute. "Mr. Egan, let's see about taking on fuel for the run back south."

Smith was waiting on the dock, wearing the same linen suit, which he'd topped with a white straw Panama hat. If anything, his goons looked more uncomfortable than they had back on Isle Harve.

"Wool sucks here, doesn't it?" I asked the universe, watching the Tho san ma and my security crew load into Thai Army trucks Smith had arranged.

"We're headed to a rubber plantation outside town," Smith said. "Spend a couple of days there so you can get your land legs back, and then head up to Nakhon Phanom, where a couple of former Air America birds will carry you across the border into Laos."

"Nobody said anything about jumping out of an airplane," Master Guns said.

Back in the Saddle Again

"We aren't," I replied. "Father Trahn is meeting us at a site in Laos. We'll load the Hmong villagers on the birds, and then we'll go monster hunting."

"A site in Laos?"

"Yeah," I grinned, "you might remember it, Master Guns--we Arc-lighted a rundown rubber plantation there a few years ago."

It took a week of travel to cross Thailand. I'll give Smith this--whatever Thai officials he bought stayed bought. We didn't have any issues crop up, even after the third day when we all changed into tiger stripe cammies and started carrying the weapons openly.

Conrad had supplied the hardware--sanitized AK-47's matching the ones the Tho san ma carried. Master Guns had detail stripped them and gone over them with a fine-toothed comb before declaring them acceptable for Soviet made hunks of junk.

Nakhon Phanom was still bustling--even if the USAF wasn't running strike packages and rescue out of there-the Thais were keeping a wary eye on the Lao People's Democratic Republic across the Mekong River.

Smith and his goons were waiting for us again.

"Must be nice, having the money to fly everywhere," Master Guns said when he saw the agent and his minders waiting by the base command building.

"At least they're dressed for the weather," I said.

Smith and his goons were wearing tiger stripes as well. The goons were carrying an AK and an RPK, while Smith had added an SVD sniper rifle to the Skorpion that was still under his left arm.

"I see you made it here," Smith said when I approached.

"We had a decent travel agency. Speaking of which, how long are we going to be here?"

"The planes should be ready tomorrow," Smith said. "Had to give them a new paint job. On the upside, one of them actually used to belong to the Royal Laotian Air Force, so if the new government over there captures it, it technically belongs to them anyway."

"That's a rather... bright way of looking at it," Master Guns said.

"I find that makes some of the things I've had to do for the government easier to do," Smith replied. "Let me show you where we're bunking down for the night."

We spent the night going over weapons, checking loads and, for some of the men, talking to a Vietnamese Catholic Priest.

It never hurts to get things right with God before killing monsters.

The next morning, there were four C-47's painted in the colors of the Lao People's Liberation Army Air Force parked on the ramp, their doors open. The Amazing Nguyen Brothers were directing troop flow into the birds—we'd split the Tho san ma and my former Marines among the birds, just in case something went wrong—we'd still have enough manpower to do the job.

"Major," one of the Marines on my bird, John Holmes, approached. He carried an RPG-2 in addition to his AK.

"Staff Sarn't."

"We went over most of the RPG's last night. They're in better shape than the M67's the Army gave us in 'Nam."

"Yeah, the CIA's got a better budget, Staff Sarn't."

"Doesn't hurt we've been using them for the last year ourselves either."

The South Pacific was awash in weapons—had been since WWII. Modern Soviet gear was cheaper than its US equivalent.

"I couldn't agree more, Staff Sarn't," I replied, starting up the steps into the Gooney Bird.

The flight plan was... tricky. We'd fly south along the Mekong for a while—low and slow down on the deck, and then turn a dogleg into Laotian airspace.

Smith swore he had good codes for the flight. Not that the LPLAAF had a lot in the area—they were concentrated up at Vientiane, with most of the pilots still undergoing 're-education' for their running dog capitalist sins.

I did what I always do on long flights. Took a nap.

Three hours later, we were circling the site of the Baird Rubber Plantation/Monster Factory. From the air, it was still a reddish lunar landscape, with a few patches of green where the jungle was slowly reclaiming the area.

Thank God Gooney Birds are rough-terrain capable. Trahn and his Hmong had hacked out a strip down by the river, but Lord was it rough.

We landed first, while the other three birds circled. It wasn't quite a combat offload, but it was close, and the first group of Hmong women and children started into the bird as soon as we were clear.

General Trahn, dressed in frog pattern camouflage pants and a black shirt and dog collar, was waiting for us under the tree line. With him was a young Vietnamese woman and several Hmong men.

"Colonel," he said when I stepped up and shook his hand.

"General. I see your intel sources are as good as ever, even here in the ass-end of nowhere."

"Yes," he replied. "I might have asked General Conrad about you, after we got back in contact with the US government."

The second bird landed, and the load swap repeated.

"Did you bring the supplies?" Trahn asked.

"Last two birds, General," Mihn Nguyen said, trotting past with a group of troops. "I'll get the command post established in the bunker."

"How do you want to play this, General?" I asked, watching the Gooney Birds dance again.

"It's about a two-day march to the Mountain," he replied.

I could hear the capital letter when he said Mountain.

"Mountain?"

"Yes. The White Goddess of Death lives..." he stepped to a break in the tree coverage and pointed at a mountain to the north, "there."

If this were bad fiction like Master Guns reads, I'd say at this point the Mountain looked ominous. It didn't. It looked like any other jungle-covered mountain I'd seen in the ten years I'd spent in Southeast Asia working for Uncle Sugar. At that, it looked better than a couple of them that Master Guns and I had retreated down during the Frozen Chosin.

Back in the Saddle Again

General Trahn said something in a Viet Dialect to the girl. She replied in the same. Trahn gestured to the Hmong, who picked up the girl and carried her on the plane, which was idling, waiting for something. Two of the Hmong jumped off and helped the crew chief close the hatch on the plane.

"Who's the girl?" I asked.

"My niece," Trahn replied. "She refused to leave Saigon when it fell and has been up here with me since then. She agreed to extraction."

"I take it she changed her mind?"

"Something like that, yes."

"Two days to the Mountain. Is there a rush?" Master Guns asked. He'd overseen getting the supplies offloaded and started moving up towards the remains of the plantation.

"The sooner we get the job done, the sooner you can go back to spending your days fishing off Colonel Miller's yacht in the South Pacific," Trahn replied. "Perhaps you can even ogle a few pug-nosed native girls while you're at it."

The last Gooney Bird clawing its way back into the air covered Master Guns' reply, which was probably a good thing.

"We'll spend the night here and move out in the morning," General Trahn said.

We took three days to hump to the mountain. There was no rush, and we planned to spend a day looking for the White Goddess's lair.

The group of cultists walking up a well-worn trail put an end to that.

"You've got to be fucking kidding me," I said, watching the men and women walk up the side of the mountain.

Five men wearing the uniform of the Lao People's Liberation Army were herding the obvious locals up the mountain. Behind them were two officers—one in the LPLA's uniform, and the other wearing a Soviet Army uniform.

I'll admit, I felt a little sorry for the Russian. The Russians had one uniform design for all climates. The 'tropical' version was supposedly made of cotton. With the way he was sweating, he'd probably been sent to Laos after being told he was going somewhere nice, like Siberia.

"Warrant officer," Master Guns said, looking at the Russian through a pair of binoculars. "Probably here to train the LPLA. And the LPLA LT decided to show his Russian buddy a real good time."

"Or decided the White Goddess might like a white man's blood better than that of some inbred hill savages," Mihn said.

We followed the party up the side of the mountain and watched them enter a cave.

I say cave, for lack of a better term. The stone had been dressed into columns, and the columns were carved into female grotesques.

Two of the LPLA troopers took up positions outside the entrance, while the other three herded the sacrifices inside. The Soviet Warrant Officer and the LT paused outside for a minute, smoking a cigarette or two.

The harsh smoke of the Russian's cigarettes drifted down to where we crouched along the edge of the trail.

"Pass the word for Mr. Smith," I said to Master Guns.

The Russian and the Laotian officer entered the cave before Smith worked his way to the front of the column. I pointed out the targets to Smith. He nodded and took a knee.

He fired twice, shifting aim from one target to the other as the action on the rifle cycled.

Both men were still falling to the ground when four of the Hmong broke cover and dashed forward–grabbing the bodies and dragging them into the jungle.

"They'll bring back any documents after they hide the bodies," General Trahn said. "They trained with the Green Berets during the war."

"Right," I said, looking at the cave. "The Nguyen Brothers and their company will stay out here, keeping watch for any latecomers to the party. Mr. Smith, you and your bodyguards will accompany us into the cave, followed by you General, and a squad of your Hmong along with my security detail."

"We're going with plan two," Master Guns muttered.

Back in the Saddle Again

"Plan two?" Smith asked.

"Plan two is when we don't know what the fuck we're sticking our collective dicks into, so we're going to wing it," Master Guns replied. "For all we know, they've got a necromancer in there turning out daemon-infested zombies."

"No such thing as zombies outside of Haiti, Master Guns, you know that," I said with a grin.

"Fucking policy," Master Guns replied. "I'll pass the word"

I took point. Master Guns followed, and the others fell in.

I'll admit, the two CIA goons with automatic weapons being behind me caused my sphincter to tighten a bit.

On the upside, someone had strung lights along the low ceiling of the cave—the outer portal had a shape reminiscent of certain aspects of the female anatomy.

"Oh great, in addition to being a death goddess, she's an earth mother," Master Guns groused as we entered the cave.

"I have to admit, I've never been with a woman," Trahn said, trying to break the tension.

"I've never been with one *this big*," Master Guns replied.

The passageway was narrow for Americans—Trahn and the Hmong fit fine. As we walked deeper into the mountain, I felt we were being watched. Eyes just over my shoulders were following our movements, and something was tickling at the edges of my mind, trying to get a feel for something.

"You are much better than the local offerings," caressed my mind. *"I see you have served me well without even knowing it."*

Images from my years in the Corps flashed through my mind—starting with the landings at Inchon, rolling through all my years of ground combat, and oddly enough, ending with us putting down the fish men.

"You have even killed for profit—how interesting..."

The voice had become cloying. I struggled to move and then stopped.

"Yesssss... you will be mine..."

I couldn't move. The air was solidifying; light touches caressed my face.

Back in the Saddle Again

I'd always known I'd die doing this job, but I hadn't thought I'd go over to the other side first.

Somewhere in the background, I could hear a sonorous droning.

"You are mine!"

The touches were becoming more serious–the hands were now holding my face. Ahead, I could see a light.

The droning got louder. I caught occasional words in... *Latin?*

"What is this... the words of the middle eastern child have no effect on me..."

It wasn't the words... but they were breaking the concentration of whatever it was. I took a step forward.

"Nooooooooooooooooooooo!!!!!!!!!!"

It felt like the air around me shattered into pieces. I bent at the waist and took a deep breath.

Turned out, the breath was a good thing–a burst of fire from up ahead split the area where my chest had been.

I dropped to the floor and returned fire in the general direction.

Rounds ricocheted in all directions. Somewhere behind me, someone stopped one.

Problem was, there weren't many places to hide in the passageway. We were going to have to force things and do it the hard way.

The upside was we weren't packing Soviet grenades. I could count on the baseball I was about to pitch to have a five second fuse. I pulled a grenade out, pulled the pin, and let the spoon fly.

"Frag out!"

I lobbed the grenade as far forward as I could, then tucked-in tight against the wall.

There was an earth-shattering KABOOM, and I bounced down the passageway. The grenade put a stop to all the fire and ricochets going in both directions. Deafened us for a bit as well.

Master Guns was first on his feet, and he stepped in the middle of my back as he ran down the passageway. We got lucky—the grenade had blown some of the light bulbs out but hadn't cut the wires.

There was a short burst of fire from ahead as I scrabbled to my feet.

"Clear."

"You ok?" Trahn asked, coming up behind me.

"Yeah," I replied, shaking my head. "Although that was weird."

"Attempted possession always is," Trahn replied.

"Thanks for breaking it."

"Oh, it wasn't me," he replied. "It was Paja Thao. He started chanting when you froze up, and that allowed me a certain freedom of action. Although I'll have to write up a report for the Church when we get clear. The archives indicated that a series of prayers might have some effect on the White Goddess of Death."

"Remind me to thank him when this is over."

"Gentlemen? Y'all might want to see this," Master Guns called from ahead.

"First, who got hit?" I asked the men behind me.

"That was me," Master Guns called. "Hit me in the magazines. One good thing about commie magazines being made of steel—they'll stop a low-energy bouncer," he said, pointing to a hole in the front of the magazine vest he was wearing. "Gonna have a beaut of a bruise in the morning, though."

Trahn and I walked to the end of the passageway. It widened out into an oblong room. There were a couple of passageways at the top of the oblong, one left, one right. Down the right one, I could hear the steady thrum of a generator.

Bodies, and parts thereof, were strewn everywhere. The locals that had been herded into the cave were pinned to racks attached to the walls between the two corridors that lead off the top of the room.

They'd been opened like a frog for dissection, without the advantage of being dead first. Fortunately, the grenade had killed most of them. General Trahn said something in Hmong, and two of his followers went and began pulling the... sacrifices from the walls as gently as possible. They probably even eased a couple of them over to the other side, but I'll admit I wasn't watching too closely.

In the center of the room, a single column of quartz rose out of the floor. Halfway to the ceiling, it flared into an egg shape. Something in the egg... moved.

"I've heard of these," Trahn said, approaching the egg. "Don't touch it."

"No, really?"

"Well, don't touch it barehanded, anyway," Trahn said, reaching into a cargo pocket and pulling on a pair of gloves.

"What is it?"

"The Church's literature calls them 'dragon's eggs'," Trahn replied. He'd laid a gloved hand on the egg.

"I thought you said not to touch it," Master Guns said.

"Bare skin contact, according to the literature, leads to possession. The entity inside isn't strong enough to make contact through leather or cloth, however."

"What about what happened out in the corridor?"

"That was different. The entity inside here," he tapped the quartz with a leather clad knuckle, "had already possessed someone. Probably the Lao Lieutenant or the Russian Warrant Officer. From there, it could reach out and touch someone else."

"Someday, having access to everything the Catholic Church has learned about the various entities it's encountered through the centuries might be helpful."

"I'd agree, Colonel," Trahn replied with a grin, "but to quote Master Guns Huggins, fucking policy."

I thought Master Guns was going to choke to death–he'd waited till that precise moment to take a drink from his canteen.

"So, how does the Church recommend putting an end to one of these?" I asked, after slapping Huggins on the back a couple of times.

"Shattering the quartz usually works fine," Trahn replied.

"That won't release whatever is inside, will it?" I asked.

"Church research indicates these are... fossilized gateways to another dimension. The entities trapped within cannot survive in ours, so destroying the egg destroys the entity."

"That explains the C4 you requested," Master Guns said, motioning Holmes down the passageway.

Back in the Saddle Again

Holmes wired the Egg. We hadn't been sure what we'd be destroying, so we'd brought as much C4 as twelve men could carry on top of their normal combat loads.

It was an impressive amount of C4. The Amazing Nguyen Brothers had supplied some more, and General Trahn's Hmong found room in their hearts to donate several pounds of PVV-5A Plastic Explosive to the party.

"Y'all want to hump all the RPG's to the extraction point?" Holmes asked, stepping out into the corridor.

I'd herded most of the troops out of the cavern, and the command group was waiting for Holmes to finish laying charges.

I know it's safe to smoke around C4, but the Soviet shit gives me the willies. Quality control in the land of vodka isn't quite what it should be, even for high explosives.

"Save enough to keep us out of the shit if things drop into the fire," I said, "but yeah, add the rest to the explosion."

It took Holmes three or four hours to rig everything—time drags when you're having fun and killing monsters, after all. We even drug the bodies in–never hurt to dispose of the enemy in a way that no one can figure out.

"It shouldn't even show from the outside," Holmes said, rigging the wire to the blasting key. "You want to set it off, sir?"

"No, go ahead," I replied.

Holmes looked around to make sure the blast area was clear.

"Fire in the hole! Fire in the hole! *Fire in the hole!!*"

He hit the plunger.

The earth moved.

A plume of dirty smoke blew out of the cave mouth, followed by glittering dust. The dust formed the shape of a weeping woman before falling to the ground–when she fell, the cave collapsed.

"Damn, Holmes, you haven't lost your touch," Master Guns said.

"Hell, Master Guns, if I'd have had this much explosive on Hiva Oa I could have destroyed all the caves in one shot, rather than having to keep going back in and checking on what I'd blown up," Holmes said, a reproachful tone in his voice.

"Yeah, well, the Company wasn't paying for that job," I said, pulling a smoke out and lighting it.

"We could have," Smith quipped. "But the local governor didn't put the French Government onto the issue until you'd already taken care of it."

"Oh fuck no," Huggins said. "I'm through working for the Company."

Blood Sacrifice

By: Casey Moores

29 August, 1847

Dearest Virginia,

I hope this letter finds you, little Addy, John Junior, James, Andrew, Rachel, and Dolley in good health. I do hope you're staying strict with the boys and not spoiling them too much. My time on this trip has only reinforced my belief that the world is a hard, harsh place and they need to grow up to be hard men if they're going to be successful in it.

I'll bet the leaves are starting to turn up there and I can only imagine how beautiful it must be. Starting to cool down a little as well, I'd wager. I envy that. Down here, it's hot as hell and so dusty I doubt we'll ever be able to wash it all out of my clothes. I might just have to burn them when I get back and get some new ones.

You'll be glad to know we haven't seen much proper action since we left Texas, at least not in the sense of our true purpose. I had feared we might be catching up to General Scott too late to be of any use, but his pause in Puebla gave us time to catch up and, from what I hear, there have been no open threats to the Army of the sort we're meant to handle. We've been chasing down local myths here and there—such as a Tlahuepuchi or some nonsense. It's a kind of sorceress who feeds on blood, reads minds, and can change her form at will. It's the sort of wives' tale meant to explain the unexplainable and accuse your neighbors of devil worship. However, so far on the whole we've been employed more as scouts for the regular army. The regulars have taken to calling us the Axemen, as you might guess, on account of the collection of large-handled axes and hatchets our men carry.

The war itself is going better than I expected. The engineers are a major advantage to keeping the Army moving, and move we have. From one battle to the next, there hasn't been all that much to slow us down. I'll make sure we Axemen do our part to ensure that continues. At the very least, I resolve to make sure it's not failure on our part that jeopardizes a victory down here.

As I write of that purpose, don't take my words above to make you think we're going slack. Myself and those who were with me in the Aroostook affair know better than to let our guard down just because things have been quiet. We've been using stories of that assignment as a lesson to keep the newer ones vigilant.

The biggest concern of the men in the unit are stories of gods and giants. The men ask how to deal with such things, and I answer in the same manner I plan to answer our boys, someday. I told them nothing will keep fighting if you take their head off.

I know when you read that last part, you'll plan to admonish me as soon as I get home. I'm sure I should be passing down some more appropriate fatherly wisdom like "Learn your scriptures", "Always make sure you're a good man before you try to be a great man", and "Always listen to your mother as if the Lord Almighty speaks through her". I'll get to work on teaching them those sorts of things as soon as I get home. After this one, I mean to stay home for a while. I can only hope to stand by that intent.

I know you're taking good care of yourself and the children, so I won't waste words telling you to do so. I can't wait until I get the chance to see you all again.

Yours with great affection,
John

A Hill in Cholula

Blood Sacrifice

Captain John Greene kicked a loose rock off the edge of the hill out of simple curiosity as to how far it would tumble down. It bounced down the long, perfectly sloped hillside, picking up speed the whole way. A bit further down, Sergeant Levi Miller grumbled when his foot slipped, and it looked as if he might follow the rock down. With a hard pull on the rope, he kept himself from tumbling and regained his footing.

As soon as he was certain his sergeant was stable, he pointed up to the church—the *Iglesia de Nuestra Señora de los Remedios*, or Our Lady of Remedies Church.

"Guide said this is a pyramid," John said. "*Tlachihualtepetl* in old Aztec, but the local villagers call it the *Pirámide de Cholula*."

"Other than that old set of steps down at the bottom, around that stone terrace, it looks like a hill to me, sir."

While Miller strained to work his way up the last few yards to the top, John squatted down to line his eyes up with the slope.

"I don't know, sergeant. This very well might be some ancient construction we're standing on and, if so, it's pretty damn impressive."

"If you say so, sir," Miller replied.

"People built this hundreds of years ago, with nothing but hard labor and maybe some ropes or logs to roll the stones," John said. "What's not impressive about that?"

"Sir," Miller said, "when you say *hard labor*, I hear *slaves*. Poor old souls forced into it, just like in the southern states. More than a few died doing it, I'm sure."

"I hadn't thought about it like that, Sergeant. But that's the way of history, I suppose. God willing, maybe someday we'll break the cycle."

John braced himself into a squat and threw a hand out to Sergeant Miller. The sergeant grabbed his hand and climbed the last step to the top of the hill.

"Impressive up here, either way," John said.

"Which part, sir? The burning-hot sun, the steep slope that's sure to kill me if I slip, or that this might be a big pile of rocks built by slaves, then murdered to appease some heathen god the moment they'd finished building it?"

"Oh, I get it, Sergeant Miller. You're sour there hasn't been any action. Eager to kill something, are you?"

"Now you mention it, sir, my shotgun does feel neglected. The excitement in Texas wasn't much. We haven't done anything really useful since Aroostook."

"Ah yes… the Agropelters, or whatever the natives called them. That was a good scrap… an enemy we could find and kill. Still a damn shame about poor Hiram."

"Like I keep saying, it was his own fault. I told Private Smith to stay in the line, but he kept stepping forward. I still wonder what pulled him into that pond. Wasn't one of those big-footed beasts, I know that much."

"I think it might've been a—"

"Sir, lookout!" Sergeant Miller threw his rifle to his shoulder and fired in a smooth motion, but the kick knocked him backward. He lost his footing and tumbled away with a curse.

John heard a footstep scrape against gravel and felt the slightest rush of wind as he spun on instinct. A knife-wielding attacker stabbed the space he'd just occupied. John snatched the man's wrist with one hand and the collar with the other. He kicked the man's leg out from under him. As his attacker collapsed, John shoved the man's face down and put a foot on his shoulder. With a hard wrench, he cracked the attacker's arm out of the socket. The knife dropped.

Movement caught his attention, and he found a rifle pointed at him. He dropped and rolled as the rifle fired. Kneeling, John drew his Colt Walker pistol, cocked the hammer back, and fired as quickly as he could find a target. The rifleman clutched his stomach and crumpled.

One last man charged out from behind the church doors, a much larger knife in his hand. Before John could bring his pistol to bear, the man slashed his right arm and John drew it back in pain. Strength left his arm, and the pistol fell from his hand. John bowled into the man with his left shoulder to make space and used the gap to draw his own blade—a bone-handled Bowie knife.

The two squared off against each other, throwing a series of feints as each sought to find some sort of advantage. The attacker's gaze flicked to the Bowie knife and John knew it was only a matter of time before the man came at him in earnest.

He saw the lunge coming, ducked back, and tried grabbing his opponent's wrist. At the same time, he swept his blade towards the man's face. The man dodged the swipe and easily wrenched his arm free, as John's right hand was too weak. As another hard stab came in, John tried to dodge back, but stumbled and fell onto his back. The attacker followed him down and John just barely got his own knife in the way.

The man punched him in the ribs several times while trying to drive the knife down into John's chest. Sensing that he was losing the fight, John wriggled in a vain attempt to roll and throw the man off. Nothing worked and the knife's tip slowly pressed against him.

Bang!

The attacker jerked and fell to the side.

"You alright, sir?" Miller asked. The sergeant walked up and offered a hand to help John up.

"I'll live. I think." John took the hand, hopped back to his feet, and looked around. A shot of pain reminded him of the cut on his arm. "Ah, I guess I could use a dressing for this, if you got something."

Sergeant Miller shook his head as he pulled a strip of cloth out of his knapsack.

"I told you we shoulda brought a few more of the fellas up here, sir. At the very least, sir, this is the sort of job you send the Lieutenants to do."

John nodded and shrugged in embarrassment. "Then I'd have a dead lieutenant, Sergeant. Anyway, I didn't want to invade a church with a mess of soldiers. Didn't seem proper."

"Well, there's proper and there's dead, sir. It's your job to be proper, and it's my job to keep you from being dead, sir." Miller finished wrapping the bandage around John's arm and tied it as tight as he dared.

"I'll do what I can. What the hell were they doing up here?" As soon as Miller pulled the knot tight,

John retrieved his pistol and walked to the doors of the church.

"Hold up a second, if you would, sir," Miller said. "Along the lines of making sure you don't get killed and all."

John glanced back to find Miller carefully reloading his rifle. When Miller nodded, they cautiously entered.

Three dead locals—two women and one man—were laid out and bloody across the aisle. At the far end, the padre lay dead at the foot of the altar.

"What the hell were they doing here?" John said.

"I'd say just here to rob them, sir," Miller said. "Though I can't imagine there's all that much of value. Should I wave the rest of the detachment up, sir?"

"I assume they're already on their way up, but if not, by all means."

The padre lay dead face down towards the altar with his arms trapped beneath him, as if he'd been praying when executed.

From everything he'd seen from the local population, it didn't follow that simple bandits would target a church, of all places. Especially since this particular church seemed somewhat meager in its possessions. The crucifix behind the altar was wood, the candlestick-holders made of brass. The only thing of any real value seemed to be the stained glass, and the beautifully painted frescoes—neither of which was worth plundering.

An unfamiliar officer stepped inside—a lieutenant in a well-maintained Regular Army uniform. A double-barreled shotgun hung from a strap. He wore a revolver on each hip, a Bowie knife sheathed on his right, and a saber sheathed on his left. From the weaponry, John formed a favorable impression of the man.

A notion that he dispelled immediately after the man spoke.

"By your very unofficial manner of dress, I presume you are Captain John Greene?" As the lieutenant asked the question, his gaze floated up and down, examining every inch of John with an eye of disapproval. "I wasn't expecting to find a company of volunteers when General Scott sent me on this errand."

The way the young lieutenant spat the word *volunteer* told Greene everything he needed to know.

Miller strolled up behind the lieutenant at a respectable distance, but with a look that said, "If you want me to dispatch him and hide the body, I will." John made eye contact with Miller and gave a slight shake of his head. Miller relaxed but stood by.

"What's a West Pointer doing out here, away from the main Army, Lieutenant?" John walked by the lieutenant and outside without even bothering to give the smug little pumpkin rinds the satisfaction of eye contact.

"General Scott sent me out to determine the location of Special Unit Thirteen, so that I might ensure it would rejoin our efforts. The Army is approaching Mexico City itself, and the general wonders why the Special Unit is not with it."

John turned and inspected the lieutenant up and down. All the weapons and gear looked shiny and new. John would've been surprised if the lieutenant had seen a single action since his graduation which, by his rank, would've been in the most recent class or two.

If the little brat from West Point—and an Engineer, to boot—wanted to play power games with a Captain and veteran of more battles than the kid had years, then John would follow suit. This little shit, puffed up as he was over where he'd gone to school, was nothing compared to any of the demons, creatures, and manifestations of evil—the sorts of things that would've sent this lieutenant pissing himself. John locked eyes and glared.

In less than a handful of seconds, the lieutenant dropped his gaze to the ground.

"As I was saying, Captain, with all due respect, General Scott wishes an audience with you," the lieutenant said.

"Sergeant Miller," John said, "would you please head down and inform the Unit that our reconnoiter of this area is complete and that they are to prepare to move out?"

"Yes, Captain," Miller responded. "Sir, would you like me to leave a detachment of men here to inform us of any change in the situation?"

"No, Sergeant, we'll all move out together," John said. "Whatever happened here is none of our concern, as far as I can tell."

John turned back to regard the lieutenant.

"Lieutenant, I must say that when I joined, I was trained to announce my name and rank to any superior officer at once before delivering any sort of orders or report. Is that no longer the custom in this Army?"

The lieutenant blanched, and his shoulders dropped. Then, he snapped to attention and rendered a salute.

"Apologies, Captain. Lieutenant George McClellan, at your service, sir."

The Ceremony

A while after all sounds of talking and the stomping of boots had faded away, Coyotl watched Sean Murphy ease the stone slab up and peered out. Finding no one, the Irishman worked a corner up until he could slide the whole slab out of the way. He retrieved his revolver and saber before cautiously stepping up into the church. After scanning in a full circle, he went and checked the door.

"All clear, Señor Coyotl," he said in rough Spanish. The Irishman had been in Mexico for a little over a year since deserting from the United States Army, yet his Spanish had improved little. "Though I'm sad to say it looks like the bloody yankees took out your men up here. You should've let me stay with them, would've turned out better."

"They were unimportant," Coyotl said. "Whereas you still serve a purpose. Are you sure we are entirely alone now?"

Brandishing the saber and leading with his pistol, Murphy pushed the door open and stepped into the fading light of the sunset to scout around. Coyotl followed him out and squinted into the west with a hand up to block the last bit of sun.

He smiled when he spotted the dust cloud in the distance. Whatever scouting party that had passed through was well on their way to rejoining the rest of the US Army. When Murphy returned, he pointed to the dust cloud.

"Won't be troubling you anymore, Señor. You're free to do whatever it is you plan to do."

"Excellent," Coyotl said. "Then we must get to work. There is much to do in the following days."

Coyotl knew the time of the ceremony was at hand when the full moon rose, shortly after midnight on the 5th of September. It was the largest moon he'd ever seen, in exact accordance to prophecy.

"Señor Coyotl, there may be trouble brewing in the town," Murphy came to tell him. "I'm seeing a torch here and there, and every now and then I see someone run from one building to another. I think they might be organizing."

"That is why you are here, Sean Murphy. Trouble me no more."

"Yes, Señor Coyotl." The last of the sunstones was put in its proper location and Coyotl spent over an hour to guarantee its alignment was immaculate. With the sacrifices muffled and secured below each altar stone, there was nothing to do but wait.

When the glow of the morning sun grew, he found Murphy standing at the edge of the courtyard, his gaze fixed on the town.

"We approach the crucial hour, Sean Murphy. If, as you say, the townspeople are planning something, they will act soon. I trust you will deal with them."

The Irishman drew and checked his revolver. Then, he swept his saber back and forth in two great slashes. After rolling his shoulders and his neck, he nodded.

"I'll be ready, Señor Coyotl."

"Excellent."

The sacrifices' expressions told him they knew what was coming. Some whimpered, others remained quiet with vacant stares. A couple cried out in resistance, but a single menacing look from Coyotl silenced them.

At the exact moment when the first ray of sun broke over the horizon, with the great moon climbing high into the sky, he began the ceremony.

"Great spirits of the *Nahui-Quiahuitl*, hear me now…"

He recited the call with slow precision, imploring the ancient giants to hear him, to see him, to witness his great sacrifice in their honor. When the introduction was complete, he checked the position of the sun and the moon, called for the ceremonial knife, and moved to the first sacrifice. Knife raised high, he made the first summoning.

"*Xelhua*, son of *Mixcoatl*, architect of the *Tlachihualtepetl* upon which we stand, hear me. I make this sacrifice for you!"

He drove the knife deep into the sacrifice's heart. The man's eyes bulged, and he struggled against his bindings for a few seconds before he relaxed, and his spirit left him. The next sacrifice, a woman, escaped her muzzle and screamed.

"That's done it," Murphy said. "Here they come."

He fired his revolver once and stepped back from the edge.

"That'll slow them down, but I can't keep them back forever."

Though Coyotl heard him, he did not allow himself to be distracted. He moved to the woman and raised the knife. When she cried again, the attendant jammed a cloth into her mouth.

"*Tenoch*, son of *Mixcoatl*, founder of *Tenochtitlan*, hear me. I make this sacrifice for you!"

He plunged the knife deep. All the other sacrifices squirmed and cried. A musket fired from down below.

"*Ulmecatl*, son of *Mixcoatl*, founder of *Cuetlachcoapan*, hear me. I make this sacrifice for you!"

The knife plunged.

"*Mixtecatl*, son of *Mixcoatl*, founder of *Mixteca*, hear me. I make this sacrifice for you!"

The knife plunged. More musket fire sounded from outside the courtyard, growing closer. Every so often, Murphy's revolver barked in response.

"*Xicalancatl*, son of *Mixcoatl*, founder of *Xicallancatl*, hear me. I make this sacrifice for you!"

The knife plunged. From deep below the *Tlachihualtepetl*, he heard and felt a great rumbling. The sacrifices and attendants alike began to glance around in fear and confusion.

"*Otomitl*, son of *Mixcoatl*, founder of *Xilotepec*, hear me. I make this sacrifice for you!"

The knife plunged. The rumbling grew.

"*Cuauhtemoc*, who supported the sky at the dawning of the Fifth Sun, hear me. I make this sacrifice for you!"

The knife plunged. By now, it was soaked with the blood of seven sacrifices, but still it demanded more.

"*Izcoalt*, who supported the sky at the dawning of the Fifth Sun, hear me. I make this sacrifice for you!"

The knife plunged. Shouting increased and the reports of Murphy's revolver came with more regularity.

"*Izcaqlli*, who supported the sky at the dawning of the Fifth Sun, hear me. I make this sacrifice for you!"

The knife plunged. The ground shook as if from a great earthquake. The musket fire let up and screams grew up from the direction of Cholula.

"*Tenexuche*, who supported the sky at the dawning of the Fifth Sun, hear me. I make this sacrifice for you!"

For the last time, he drove the knife into the sacrifice. Coyotl stared into the man's eyes as the spirit left.

Movement caught Coyotl's eye, and he found one of the villagers had reached them. With a grim face, the man raised an old musket to his shoulder.

"Blasphemer! This is God's ground you desecrate!" the man shouted. Then, a neat, black hole bloomed in his forehead and his head bucked back.

As he tumbled from sight, another villager stepped up into view, carrying a pitchfork. Murphy, his pistol still smoking, charged the man with his saber. The villager blocked two swings before Murphy twisted and stabbed the man in the stomach.

"Whatever is supposed to happen, I hope it happens soon!" Murphy said.

Two more villagers stepped into view. Both aimed muskets at Murphy. Before either fired, the ground shook so violently that the two men fell.

Smiling, Coyotl stepped away from the altars.

From the middle of the courtyard, two enormous arms stretched out from the earth and clawed at the ground. Within seconds, a giant head emerged, followed by the body of the massive being. When the giant pulled his legs free, he rose to his full height, some six times larger than a mortal man. Murphy froze with his jaw hanging wide open. Coyotl prostrated himself as low as he could.

"Mighty *Xelhua*," Coyotl shouted, "I, your humble servant Coyotl, have returned you to this world. The pathetic gods who banished you are no more and the god who replaced them has proven his weakness. The time for you to reclaim this land has come."

In an ancient tongue that few outside of Coyotl understood, *Xelhua* spoke. Coyotl cringed at the giant's great, booming voice.

"Tiny mortal, you have proven yourself useful. Tell me how my brothers and I can conquer this land once again."

The ground continued to rumble as other giants crawled through the veil into the world of men.

"Mighty *Xelhua*, a great enemy has invaded our country. Defeat them, and the people of this land will worship you once more."

Casey Moores

Ghost Stories and Fairy Tales

A fly landed on John's nose as he stood at parade rest outside General Scott's headquarters tent. With a quick flash of his hand, he swatted it away and returned his hand to the small of his back. At that very moment, a major had rushed out of the tent and eyed John's shoulder, indicating he'd seen the maneuver. The major stomped away, shaking his head and muttering something about "Volunteers".

Having stood outside the tent, burning up under the early September sun for the better part of an hour, John's legs were getting impatient with him. He wriggled them as slightly as he could to keep the blood flowing without giving onlookers cause to criticize his bearing. The weight of his many weapons grew heavy, and he began to reconsider having kept all of them on his person when he reported in. On his next visit, he wouldn't make the same mistake. He'd also make sure to drink more water the next time. Of course, that was a double-edged sword. If he drank too much and was left waiting like this, he might find the need to leave to relieve himself. That could be devastating, as the general would surely pick that very moment to finally call him in.

Another fly flew into his ear canal. A glance to his left revealed a handful of regular army officers who'd taken to staring at him—likely to take turns insulting him on the assumption he couldn't hear it. Of course, with the fly in his ear buzzing so loudly that it overcame all thought, he couldn't hear it.

The tent flap rustled and out stepped the illustrious young Lieutenant McClellan. When the baby-faced officer opened his mouth to speak, John gave up and swatted the fly out of his ear, so he'd be able to hear.

"—requests your presence at this time," McClellan finished saying while pointing his hand inward.

John nodded and went in.

Inside, several other high-ranking regular officers and two volunteer colonels stood around a long table covered with maps. Following McClellan around the table, John spotted General Winfield Scott just before they reached him. John snapped a tight salute, which McClellan repeated. Scott casually waved his hand somewhere near his head in reply.

"General Scott, sir, I am prepared to make a full report on my activities, sir," John said

Scott made no sign of hearing him and instead reached out to move a marker across the table.

"Well, gentlemen, if you're certain there's a foundry there, and that we might deprive Santa Anna of artillery production, then I've made my decision. General Worth, you will organize your division to assault Molino del Rey on the morning of 8 September."

Salutes and acknowledgements followed. Then, the collection of colonels and generals cleared the tent. When things settled, the general looked at John.

"Yes, the lieutenant has given me the full report on your activities," Scott said in a dry, disinterested tone. "I'm told you were taking in the sights when the good lieutenant here found you."

"Yes, General, sir," John said. "Sir, I took the unit out to follow up on a few good leads."

General Scott put a hand up in annoyance. "I didn't think marines were meant to travel this far from a large body of water."

The pause grew long enough that John suspected the general might be awaiting a response. As he opened his mouth to give one, the general continued.

"When I was first informed of the existence of your unit, I believed it a joke. Then, I learned it was real and was told to give you unlimited freedom to operate. Well, after hearing that your *Axemen* have been doing nothing but chasing ghost stories and fairy tales, I've decided it's time to put some limits on that freedom. As I understand it, as useless as your unit has been to safeguarding this army's movements, it has been wildly successful fighting bandits and whatnot throughout the countryside. Your problem, it seems, is not fighting ability, but direction."

A dozen responses flooded through John's mind, but it was clear the general was not looking for any.

"Therefore, I have decided to give you some direction," General Scott continued. "You are to assist the good lieutenant here, in reconnoitering passable roads north of Lake Xochimilco. I was told your unit's contribution would be immeasurable, if I were to give you free rein. I have found that to be incorrect, at best, and a great lie at worst." Scott stretched his arm out to point at Lieutenant McClellan. "It is my engineers whose contributions are immeasurable. They've cut roads, surveyed artillery emplacements, mapped out the enemy's supply lines, and performed dozens of other similar miracles. If you can protect one of my engineers as he performs his duties, I will not count your presence to have been a complete waste."

John swallowed and glanced at Lieutenant McClellan, who seemed mighty pleased with himself.

"Sir, you're putting my company under the command of *Lieutenant* McClellan?"

Scott shot a sharp glare at John. "Of course not, Captain. Your company is still yours, for now at least. I'm simply giving you an assignment to support Lieutenant McClellan in any way he might see fit. That is all. You are dismissed."

Repressing the urge to fight the matter further, John snapped another salute and received another half-hearted wave in reply. He left the tent as calmly as he could.

Outside, McClellan turned to face him.

"Prepare your men to depart before dawn tomorrow morning. We head east, past Piedad, then southeast towards Mexicaltzingo." McClellan grew a proud smile and put a hand on his hip. "We engineers found the roads that flanked Santa Anna to the south, and now we're going to find the roads that'll flank him to the east. You do your job, and we'll help this Army march right into Mexico City."

Hard to Miss

As ordered, all of Special Unit Thirteen marched east the next morning before the break of dawn. Atop his horse, the lieutenant kept up a grueling pace, as if daring the unit to fall behind, but they didn't. Quite the opposite—Captain Greene and his men took the pace as a challenge. He remained dutifully next to the mounted lieutenant throughout the march and made a point to stride ahead whenever McClellan slowed for any reason.

After a short hour, they paused north of Piedad, where the engineer inspected the Gate of Belen from less than a mile away. John dispersed the men to make a strong, deterrent showing in the event on-looking Mexican forces attempted a sortie from the defenses.

The process repeated as they moved further east towards the Gate of San Antonio. Once they moved south of that position, McClellan picked up the pace once again as they wound their way down the roads to Mexicaltzingo. There, it was clear the Mexican Army had constructed a series of earthworks with a line of artillery batteries, but they'd been abandoned sometime prior.

The lieutenant ordered the unit to camp for the evening just to the west of Mexicaltzingo. With John, he discussed plans to continue northward to determine the suitability and defenses of the road to Mexico City.

As John settled onto the ground by a small campfire, his own Lieutenant Andrew Walker strode quickly into John's clearing, with a local man close behind. John jumped to his feet and Sergeant Miller strode up to join them.

"Captain Greene," the lieutenant said, in a low tone that hinted he brought some sort of secret. "This man is one of your paid observers from Ayotla. He's clearly exhausted, and I think he rode hard to get here. He asked for you by name, so I presume he has a report to pass."

Walker stepped aside and waved the man forward.

"Yes, of course, I remember him," John said, in a similar low voice. Switching to Spanish, he addressed the man. "José Morales, it's good to see you again. Is your family well?"

José's eyes bulged and darted all about as he leapt forward to unleash a string of speech that John could barely follow. He caught that the man had come at a full gallop and feared he might have killed his horse, but the news was just as important to the people of Mexico as to the American Army. Something was scouring Mexico and *eating* people as it went, but John didn't catch exactly what. At length, John grabbed the man gently and tried to settle him.

"José, please, you must calm down," he said. José took in a deep breath and seemed to collect himself. John asked, "Now, *what* is eating people? What's coming?"

While he took another long breath, José closed his eyes. When he opened them, he said one word. "*Quinametzin.*"

John blanched and gasped.

"What's that mean, Captain?" Sergeant Miller asked.

"Giants," John replied, in English. He tightened his grip on José's shoulders and peered deep into the man's eyes. "Where?"

José turned, pointed east, and said, "Ayotla. They filled their bellies with everything and *everyone* they could find and lay down to sleep. They kept muttering a single word amongst themselves—*Americans.*"

Sergeant Miller chuckled. "Well, that just figures. I suppose we found ourselves something to do."

"Well, sure," Lieutenant Walker said, "but what are we supposed to do with our esteemed *engineer*?"

"Nothing," John said. "Or near about. Lieutenant Walker, keep an eye on his tent. If he stirs, you pass me a signal. If he steps out of the tent, you get in his way and distract him however you can."

"Distract him, sir? How?"

"I don't care. Plant a big kiss on him if you want, but you must keep him from seeing what we're doing."

"Which is what, exactly, sir?" Walker asked.

"We're going to move up into that mountain there, the, uh, *Cerro de L'Estrella*, if memory serves. It'll be the best place to see them coming and figure out a plan. Sergeant, you get everyone moving, as quiet as you can."

Cerro de L'Estrella

Perched atop the peak of the hill, John stretched his telescope out to observe a growing cloud of dust on the horizon.

"Anything, sir?" Miller asked.

"No," John answered, "Just another dust devil."

"I sure hope that report was true," Miller said. "I'd hate to think you just disobeyed the general for a rumor."

"I don't think it was," John said while continuing to scan the ground to the east. "José seemed awfully convincing. Even if this was some sort of setup, I can't guess the game. It's not like José could know our orders. I can't imagine the Mexican Army gives a lick about this unit, so I can't figure why he'd lie about this."

"It's because they've worked out the importance of my mission," said a familiar, annoying voice. "They're distracting you to leave me vulnerable."

John bowed his head and cursed to himself. Then, he turned to greet the man.

McClellan waved a quick salute, which John returned. As the engineer spoke, his gaze drifted up to the flag that fluttered overhead. It was a field of deep scarlet, into which was stitched a lithe golden dragon. Below the dragon was a simple "13" stitched in white.

"The general made it clear that you were to serve as my escort, *Captain*," McClellan said. "So imagine my surprise when I awoke to find you'd all absquatulated."

"Thought I'd take the men out for a bit of scouting," John said. "Apologies. Didn't mean to stay out so long. You did a fine job tracking us down."

"Well, I'm good at my job, Captain. Besides, it's not hard to follow the boot prints of over a hundred men."

John nodded. While he searched for his next words, the lieutenant scanned down the hill in front of them.

"Since you're clearly lying to me, which I'll put in my report, can you clarify for me what your men are doing? Do I see them digging holes? Is this some form of punishment? Are you so angry you're taking it out on them? I have to say, that's even lower than—"

John followed the lieutenant's gaze down to his men below when the lieutenant abruptly stopped talking. He turned to find McClellan stretching his own telescope out. John looked out and found a new, larger dust cloud, half a mile down the road.

"What in the name of the almighty lord are those?" McClellan asked.

John snapped his telescope back up to take a look. Rising out of the dust cloud were ten enormous men. They had obsidian black hair, skin of dark orange as if made of clay, and thick, squat bodies even though they towered above the ground. If he estimated the trees beside them to be about ten feet tall, it put these giants at over thirty feet tall.

"*Quinametzin*," he muttered to himself.

"Sir?" Miller said, expectantly. John passed the telescope to Miller, who took a look.

"Here they come!" John shouted at the top of his lungs. "Unit Thirteen, make ready!"

The order echoed down the hillside as it was relayed from one group to the next.

"Here *what* come?" McClellan asked.

"Fee, fi, fo, fum," Miller said grimly.

John discovered the lieutenant had frozen and gone pale.

"*Quinametzin*, giants of Aztec legend. They're what I was trying to track down on that pyramid in Cholula."

Something about the words returned the engineer to himself, and he shook his head. "*Pyramid?* That old hill with the church on top?"

"Again, in old Aztec it was called *Tlachihualtepetl*, which means 'made by hand'. That was a pyramid, I'm sure of it. A local legend told me it was the burial site of the *Quinametzin*, when they were exiled by the Aztec gods."

"Lesson aside, Captain, those creatures out there can't exist. It's a trick of the air or something, a refraction of the light."

"You see what you see, Lieutenant," John said. "And we're going to fight them."

McClellan's breath picked up as he put the telescope back up to his eye, dropped it, looked at the hill below, and then back to Captain Greene.

"It can't be," he said low. "And if it is, we can't—we can't fight them. I should… we *should* head back. Report this to General Scott."

"After what General Scott told me, you think he's gonna believe a story about giants?"

"Well, shouldn't we at least get back to the Army lines? These things can't take on the whole US Army, can they?"

"*Regular* soldiers can't deal with this, *Lieutenant!*" John was sure to lace the words with the same disdain McClellan had used to say *Captain* and *Volunteer*. "These giants march up on our army, today in particular while they're locked into battle with the Mexicans at Molino del Rey, and they're going to crack like an egg. God knows who's steering these things, but in case you hadn't noticed, they're heading straight for *Tacubaya*, where your General Scott has his headquarters, and less than a mile from the assault he's just ordered. If Worth's division folds, and Scott's forced to flee his headquarters, all the other divisions will follow. Then, Santa Anna will flood out of Mexico City and the entire US Army will crumble in an instant. If we're lucky, they'll be ransomed—for say Texas or so, and maybe a few more territories to boot. No, *Lieutenant McClellan, Engineer*, we will fight them here, because that's what this unit does."

McClellan stared, with his jaw open for a long moment before John continued.

"Lieutenant George McClellan, this is not your fight," John said in the soft tone he used when he told his son Addison hard truths about the world. "You're an engineer… and a good one, if General Scott knows you by name. You need to go back and find a way into Mexico City. You go do your job, understand me? We'll do ours."

Tears formed in McClellan's eyes. "I never ran from a fight before."

"And you aren't now. You got a job, and we got a job. Simple as that."

McClellan looked west, back towards Mexicaltzingo. Then, he looked back towards the growing cloud of dust. The giants had gotten so close that John could now see them with the naked eye.

"You've definitely chosen decent ground. I don't have to be an engineer to see that."

John smiled. "Do you know the Aztec name for this mountain? *Huizachtepetl.* It means 'Mountain of Thorns'. Those beasts'll have a hell of a time getting up here. The men have littered the climb with deep holes that'll catch their legs. I got a few more surprises beyond that."

"How do you mean to bring them this way, Captain? They seem pretty intent on *Tacubaya.*"

"Leave that to us, Lieutenant. Like I said, we got plenty of tricks. You remember all those rockets we fired at Vera Cruz?"

"The Hale rockets? I'd heard they went missing after Vera Cruz, when General Scott told Major Talcott to get rid of the useless things." He chuckled and shook his head. "Anyway, I guess you'll want to call your boys up for a speech about now."

"I don't have boys in this unit… and I don't give speeches. Men know their jobs, know what's at stake, and I know they'll fight like the devil to the last. Ain't a man among us who'll run when it gets bad. This unit's never failed the Army, much as most don't know it, and we're not going to start now. We've dealt with worse than this, believe me."

After a smile and a nod, McClellan straightened with resolve and stuck his hand out.

"Captain John Greene, sir, I was wrong about you and Special Unit Thirteen."

"Most officers are, Lieutenant," John said. He locked eyes with McClellan, grabbed his hand, and gave it a good, firm shake. "Now go."

After a final salute, Lieutenant George McClellan spun and marched away.

When he was outside of earshot, Sergeant Miller leaned in close to John and whispered, "Captain, maybe my memory isn't as good as yours, but I swear we've never dealt with anything worse than this."

"We haven't, Sergeant, but he doesn't need to know that. Better to let the legend grow when he tells the others. Get those rockets ready."

Mountain of Thorns

Chapped as his lips were, John had to actively fight the urge to lick them. He took a sip of water from his canteen as he waited for the *Quinametzin* to get closer. They were following the road from Santa Maria to Iztapalapa, which meant they'd pass within a hundred yards of his men. From the way they stalked along the road in a single file line, heads bowed like predators and not bothering to scan around for threats, he judged they had supreme confidence in their position at the top of the pecking order.

John took one more swig, stowed his canteen, and prepared his fipple flute. When the leader reached the spot John had chosen, John blew the highest pitch note he could. The note was repeated down the hill as his lieutenants blew into their own flutes.

The base of the mountain was nearly a mile away, but he still heard a series of screams in reply as streams of smoke erupted from the tree line. The rockets tore into the line of giants, who stopped and raised defensive arms. Through his telescope, John judged them to be angered, but not greatly injured. Lieutenant Christopher Stewart, commander of the rocket men, had been instructed to fire again until they got the giants' attention.

Instead of charging the lines, the *Quinametzin* stood on the road for a spell and seemed to bicker back and forth with each other. Some pointed towards Iztapalapa, while others pointed at the mountain. John wondered if they might stand there arguing forever when a second round of rockets shot out at them.

Good work, Stewart. That'll seal it.

A few still stood their ground, but one giant had taken a rocket to the face. Face blackened and squinting one eye, the giant roared and charged at the hill. Two others, sporting their own minor injuries, joined him. The others stopped their chatter and looked towards the front of the line where the largest one stood. That one looked at the mountain, back to his fellows, and bellowed something. The whole line of giants surged forward.

"That seals it, Sergeant," John said. "Let's head down."

Miller hefted his axe into one hand and cradled his double-barreled shotgun into the other. "Thought you'd never ask, sir."

The pair headed down the hill as fast as their knees would allow. John attempted to see what was happening as they headed down, but as soon as they were among the pine, cedars, and thorn bushes, it became impossible. He could hear distant gunfire and loud noises that reminded him of falling trees.

The rocket men below had been instructed to fall behind the first line as soon as the giants advanced. The first line would be lying concealed beside their holes, ready to strike the moment a giant stepped into them. If one did, the men would hack away at their Achilles' heels as hard as they could. If the giants missed their hole, they would remain concealed until the whole line had passed by. Then, they'd run to assist any nearby who had caught a giant.

Blood Sacrifice

The rockets and sharpshooters would hold above the next line—sharpshooters targeting eyes and rockets targeting groins. The irregular shrieks of rockets and *pops* of long rifles, followed by bellows of anger, told him they were already doing so.

In a few minutes, John got to the clearing with the tall boulder where he could better see the developing battle. Nine heads rose above the canopy, all glaring down with murderous intent. A few struggled in place, hopefully trapped in some of the holes. Several swung ripped-up pines at unseen targets. He noted two of the giants had an eye squeezed shut, while one had a hand across both eyes, as he flailed blindly about. John had hoped one of the giants had been slain altogether—until the tenth rose up with one of his soldiers in its hand. Before he could raise his M1841 Mississippi rifle to try and take a shot, the giant shoved the soldier into his mouth, and crunched down hard. The soldier—too far away for him to identify—went limp as the giant chewed.

John raised the rifle, aimed for the left eye, and fired. The giant spit pieces of his trooper out as he recoiled and squinted the eye. The smoke of an explosion billowed up from below and the giant howled in pain while hunching forward. To the left, a different giant's left shoulder shifted sharply down, and as its foot dropped into a hole. It thrashed about in place with gritted teeth. The surrounding trees cracked and groaned as he crashed into them.

"Captain!" someone shouted from below. John looked down to find Lieutenant Walker looking up at him.

"Walker! Report!"

"Well, Captain, as you can see, they're well past the first two lines and up into the third. Rockets sure are pissing them off, but that's about it. Those eyes are as soft as we thought, but god awful hard to hit. Takes a whole lot to get through that thick skin of theirs with the axes, but the boys—sorry, the *men*, sir—are giving them hell. We've lost quite a few and haven't taken any down, but a few of the big bastards are about to drop, I just know it."

"Thank you, Lieutenant Walker. You organize the men to cluster on the ones you think are ready to go down. Tell the rocketeers to knock it off, and close in with the other men."

"As you say, sir!"

At that moment, another giant disappeared downward and re-emerged a few seconds later with a soldier in his mouth. After reloading, John fired at another of the giants. It squinted, raised a defensive hand against gunfire to its eyes, stepped back, and collapsed backwards, followed by a tumultuous cracking of splintering wood. A chorus of cheers went up near it, followed by dozens of *thunks*, as axes chopped deep into flesh and bone.

John reloaded, watched the spot to see if the giant would stand back up, and smiled when it didn't. The smile went away when a soldier flew high into the air over the area, so high up there was no way he'd survive the landing. As he slid the ramrod back into its place, he scanned to see how everything else was progressing.

"Captain, down!" Sergeant Miller shouted. John felt the sergeant grab onto his collar, just as he saw a pine tree swinging in towards him from the left. John pulled the axe from his belt as he was jerked back. The branches swept over him as he and Sergeant Miller tumbled off the boulder and toppled into a heap behind it.

An enormous hand grabbed the boulder he'd been on, and the head rose over it to look at him. When the pine raised up again, Sergeant Miller kicked John hard, sending him into a roll down the hill during which he lost hold of his rifle. As John collected himself and glanced back up, he witnessed the great club as it crashed straight down onto Sergeant Miller. Miller's arms and legs flew up around the sides and then dropped.

"Levi!" John screamed, but he knew it was too late. He clenched his eyes and fists to push away the pain of watching his oldest friend being crushed to death.

Miller's shotgun had slid down the hill. John reached it in a couple quick steps. Shotgun in one hand, axe in the other, he jumped around the base of the boulder to find the giant kneeling in a most vulnerable way. He jammed the barrel of the shotgun into the back of the giant's bent knee and jerked the trigger. Anticipating the spasm, he dropped the gun as the leg jerked back. Grabbing the axe with both hands, he swung it into the side of the knee with every ounce of strength he could muster. The axe-head went deep through flesh and muscle, before cracking hard into the bone. When John wrenched the axe loose, the knee fell back to the ground, and the earth shuddered.

The enormous hand slapped horizontally against the boulder, presumably to help the giant leverage himself to get a look at his assailant. John didn't hesitate before chopping at the wrist with a strong, overhead swing. The axe hit hard and went deep, but John didn't even have the chance to work it free before the hand reared back towards him. The captain threw himself backward and rolled until he was free. He scrambled up the hill, snatching up his discarded rifle and pulling the axe from his friend's cold, dead fingers. He climbed back atop the boulder and took a knee to aim his rifle at the giant's only open eye. He fired, dropped the rifle, and rolled to the side as the tree crashed down where he'd just been.

A chorus of *whoops* resounded from nearby. John sat up and saw a group of his soldiers, led by Lieutenant Stewart, piling onto the giant's legs with axes and shotgun blasts. The great beast fell under the onslaught and, when he fell onto his back, they swarmed him.

Climbing atop the boulder, John counted four giants who still rooted about through the hillside forest. All four clustered together a hundred yards down, sweeping up the hill in a more organized manner than before. The largest of them hid behind the other three and seemed to be scouring the ground for any surviving soldiers. Now and then, it'd reach down and stuff another soldier into his mouth, crunch a few times, and spit them out.

"Coward's using them to screen," he muttered to himself. He leaned over and looked at the group in front of him, who'd finished dispatching the giant below. "Stewart! Rally up what you can and set a new line here. I'm gonna give the fall back order, you and yours disregard it!"

"Yes, sir! Sergeant Johnston, you heard him! Set a line off me!"

John retrieved his fipple flute from his pocket and played the fallback signal. Then, he set to collecting and re-loading every weapon he could find—his M1841 Mississippi rifle, Miller's shotgun, and his Colt Walker pistol. With the shotgun hanging from a sling, the axe stuffed into his belt, and the pistol re-holstered, he fired the rifle into the lead giant's eyes. It shifted just as he squeezed the trigger, and he was certain he missed. However, a moment later the giant buckled, assaulted from below. He crumpled and didn't get back up.

"Stewart!" he shouted as he re-loaded. "How many men we got left?"

"Just under a couple dozen, sir," Stewart replied as he stepped up on the boulder. Screams and cries poured up from below. The three surviving giants tore into the men who'd just killed the other. "And I don't think many more are coming, Captain."

"Walker?" John asked.

Stewart simply pointed at the giant on the left, who rose up with poor Lieutenant Walker in his jaws. As the giant bit down, John saw the young officer stab his saber up into the giant's gums. For a brief moment, John hoped Walker might escape, but the giant reacted by snatching the lieutenant out of his mouth and crushing Walker in its hand. The giant tossed the corpse and continued climbing the hill.

Cursing, John finished another reload and aimed a shot for that giant's left eye, as its right was squeezed shut. The shot struck true, and the giant alternated blinking both eyes as it staggered forward. The larger one put a hand on the back of the nearly blinded one's neck and guided him forward.

"They're finally working together. Lieutenant, get me a few good shooters up here to blind the other two. The rest of you are going to swarm the one on the left, while I distract the big one."

"Are you sure, sir?"

John glared and chewed his lip in response.

"Yes, sir," Stewart said after a moment. "White! Hinson! Clark! Up here!"

Three men responded, "Yes, sir!"

"The rest of you," Stewart continued, "On me! We're taking down the big bastard on the left!"

"Once you take him down, you shift to that blinded one," John said. "Then, we take the last one down together."

"Yes, sir," Stewart said. "I'd tell you to be careful until we're with you, but truth be told I've always thought I'd do a good job leading this unit. So, be as reckless as you want, sir."

Stewart held a hand out and smiled. John shook it and laughed.

"You'd lead them straight to hell, Chris, but I guess that wouldn't be any worse than what I've done. Get to it. Harrow him until you hear me *whoop*. Then, go at him with everything you got."

The three sharpshooters moved up to the boulder and lined up their shots. The lieutenant ran back to join the remaining men. John went the other way to work his way down the hill as stealthily as he could. He rushed from the cover of one tree to the next, heading down the slope until he was about level with the blind giant. Then, he advanced laterally as the three giants stepped up the hill.

The blinded one swung a ripped up tree back and forth to clear its path. His legs were scratched up and bloodied from the thorns and some axe strikes, so much they looked like raw, ground-up meat in spots. John felt confident that one'd go down easy if they could handle the other one. However, John's target lagged half a dozen yards back.

The big one didn't look to be all that hurt. It squinted both eyes, but John guessed that to be more of a defensive measure to keep them from getting shot up. It occasionally put a hand back up, to keep the blind one moving forward.

As the blind one moved past, John steeled himself. His back ached, his knees ached, a few of his blisters felt like they'd torn open, and the knife wound on his arm had split back open as well. He crouched and tensed his muscles up to push all the pain out. He brought the image of his fiery wife Virginia, his brave young sons Addison, John junior, and Andrew… his pretty young daughters Rachel and Dolley.

I'm going to beat this Goliath and I'm going to make it home to them. I have to.

"Whoooop!" he screamed at the top of his lungs as he charged forward. At a sprint, he chopped the axe at the big one's ankle. Rewarded with a roar of pain, John yanked the axe free, and kept moving for the next tree to hide behind. He spun around and crouched to catch his breath.

The forest above exploded in gunfire and war cries, as the last men of Unit Thirteen swept down the hill at their target. Their target squatted down and smashed one of the soldiers into a bloody pulp. The rest took advantage, unloading rifles and shotguns into the giant just before they leapt right at him, swinging axes, stabbing with sabers and knives, and bowling him over with their collective weight.

John poked his head around the other side of the tree to see if the big one was coming for him. As he looked, the big one ripped a pine out of the way to look down. It grinned and reached forward. John stood and tried to run past the big one's legs again, but the other giant slammed down right between them. The last dozen of his men leapt atop the felled giant and hacked away like woodcutters all over. He smiled, but then remembered he'd failed to do his part.

To John's horror, the big one snatched Lieutenant Stewart up and smashed him against a thick white cedar. Yelling with rage, John scooted down and braced the shotgun in both hands. A few quick steps took him to the prone giant's head. He cocked both barrels, placed the shotgun deep into its ear, and jerked the trigger. Knowing he'd never be able to reload it, he dropped it and drew his pistol.

The giant stopped thrashing and went still. The men cheered, but their celebration was cut off when the big one brought a fist down on Private Thomas with a resounding *thud*.

"Go get the blind one, men!" he shouted. "I'll get this one."

The soldiers scrambled up the hill toward the blind one, who appeared to be reaching the boulder. The big one grabbed a soldier in each hand and slammed them hard together. Looking up the hill, John didn't see many of his men left.

John had to hop down the hill to get below the dead one's head before he could stagger his way back up to the big one. By now, the big one was fully engaged with the last few soldiers. Sparing no time, John pumped his legs up the hill, barely making any ground for the amount of effort, but getting closer to the big one bit by bit. When he was close enough, he hacked the axe into an ankle again. This time, the axe stuck true.

The giant roared and swatted a hand down, which John narrowly dodged. He fired a round into the giant's palm as it shifted to try again. With a quick stamp of its foot, a massive heel caught John, and knocked him onto his back. He tumbled head over tail down a couple yards but kept hold of his pistol.

The big one twisted to focus its attention on John. As much as it was exactly what he'd been going for, he did his best to push the growing doubts away. Scattered reports of rifles told him that at least a few of his men were still in the fight. Moreover, by the distance, he knew they were far enough up that they must be harrowing the blinded one. If he could maintain the big one's attention, they'd have a chance.

When the big one reached down for him, he danced to the other side of a white cedar and fired his pistol at one of the enormous toes. He was close enough to see the bullet bounce off with no effect. He holstered the pistol, drew his saber, and thrust it into the gap next to the big toe. The massive foot flew away, and the giant howled.

The cedar was ripped out of the ground in an explosion of roots, dirt, and rocks. John fell back again and scrambled to back away towards another tree. He made eye contact with the giant just before it jabbed the roots of the cedar toward him. He leapt at the last moment and felt the ground shake as the tree crashed down.

Exhausted and legs on fire, he ran straight away as fast as he could—which wasn't much. He heard wood splinter and pines falling behind him as he ran. After a minute or so, the thunder of cracking trees ceased. John spun about, to see if he was still being chased.

He wasn't. The big one, getting bored with hunting down just one man, had gone back after the others. Through the bramble, he could just make out the blind one hunched over the boulder John had used for observation. It didn't appear to be moving.

Though his strength was fading, he climbed his way up the hill on all fours. Another tree crashed off to his right, and a soldier screamed. A rifle fired, followed by another thundering *whomp*.

John worked his way back to the boulder and confirmed the blinded one was dead. Only one gargantuan head still moved about above the trees. The largest of the *Quinametzin* was the last one. However, he knew that it alone might be enough to scatter Scott's forces.

It sported nicks and cuts all over and it had one bloody eye squeezed shut. As John spotted it, it reached down to crush another of his soldiers. John couldn't see nor hear any more of them, but he could only hope he wasn't alone.

"Unit Thirteen! On me! Let's finish the bastard!"

No one responded. Worse, the shout had gotten the big one's attention. It twisted and launched a pine towards John, who flattened to the boulder. It passed over his head, but as John stood up, he found the giant had already stomped its way to him. With his saber tight in his right hand, he pulled his hatchet out with his left as the giant reached for him. He tried to jump back, but he was too weak and the giant too quick. The mighty hand closed around his waist and lifted him up.

The hand crushed his stomach, and his ribs cracked. He coughed and sprayed blood. As he was drawn towards the giant's mouth, he braced himself. When the jaws opened, he hacked the hatchet into the giant's thumb. The grip loosened, allowing John to drive his saber into the giant's neck. With the last of his strength, he drove the blade in up to the hilt. Using his body weight as leverage, he jerked the saber sideways to lengthen the cut. A torrent of blood sprayed out.

He tried to scream in rage and triumph, but gurgled blood instead.

Captain John Greene and the giant fell together as consciousness slipped away.

George McClellan's Unpublished Letter

10 September, 1847
To Mrs. Virginia Greene,

Blood Sacrifice

By now, you will have heard of your husband's passing, and you have my greatest condolences. You would not have known this, but I found him in his last moments and heard his last words. I do not know what you were told, but I am writing to tell you the truth of his sacrifice. I must confess, when I first met Captain John Greene I thought him just another simple-minded Mustang, but I could not have been more wrong.

I am forbidden from giving you the finer details of his final battle in this letter, but I have the impression you know what it was your husband did. When I return to our nation's shores, I promise to make a visit to pass the story directly to you and your children. The official statement from the War Department is that your husband was killed during the Battle of Molino del Rey because the events happened on the same day, but the truth is your husband and his exemplary band of soldiers fought a Much Greater enemy to the east.

His sacrifice saved the entire Army and, by extension, the entire war down here in Mexico. Through the newly formed Aztec Club, an organization of the officers who served down here, I have made it my duty to make it known just what Captain John Greene and Special Unit Thirteen accomplished. I knew my tale would not be believed, but a simple trek to the site of his last battle silenced all doubt.

The truth of the matter will never be made public and all who know of it are sworn to secrecy, but I wanted you to know that his legend will live on as a tale passed down among the officers and soldiers of our nation's military. His glory, and the glory of his men, will live forever.

Your Devoted Servant,
George B. McClellan
Lt. of Engineers

Historical Note

Any of you who are familiar will know that General Winfield Scott was the commander of the expedition to capture Mexico City, which was successful in ending the Mexican American War. It was the engineers who received a great deal of the credit for finding and developing ways for the US Army to travel so deep into an enemy country while maintaining its logistics train and freedom of movement. Captain (later brevet Major) Robert E. Lee was one of the chief engineers, but I only had so much room in my story.

Lieutenant George B. McClellan was a freshly commissioned second lieutenant, having graduated second in his class at West Point on 1 July 1846. It was the same class in which George Pickett graduated dead last. The officers of that class as a whole became some of the most prominent in the US Civil War. At the time, entry into the engineers was an exalted position awarded only to those, like McClellan, who were at the top of their class.

McClellan's diary and letters from this period were collected and published in 2009 as The Mexican War Diary and Correspondence of George B. McClellan, edited by Thomas W. Cutrer. McClellan's entries paint a picture of a young lieutenant who was eager to get to the war his country had recently entered, disdainful for those who had not been educated at West Point, and highly proud of the capabilities and accomplishments of the engineers.

After the Battle of Molino del Rey, McClellan was offered a medal, which he declined as he was not present at that battle. His diary entries and letters are also absent from this time frame. This is easily explained by his being as busy as everyone else in the final days leading to the capture of Mexico City, but the dearth of writings and the odd occurrence of his being offered an award for a battle he did not attend beg the question—what was he doing at the time? As you just read, I took the liberty of filling in the blanks.

The Aztec Club was a real thing, and I chose it as my venue by which the rest of the Army learned the truth of Special Unit Thirteen's sacrifice. Thus, officers on both sides of the Civil War will be familiar with the exploits of Captain John Greene and his *Axemen*.

As a final note, any Civil War aficionados will know that General Winfield Scott held overall command over the Union forces at the outset of the war and developed the Anaconda Plan, which included blockading actions that Lieutenant Addison Greene and his unit joined in my novel Witch Hunt.

After the debacle at Bull Run, Scott resigned, and General George B. McClellan was named the Union Army's senior officer. I expect we'll be seeing him again.

To find more titles in the Joint Task Force 13 universe, go to our information page about the series on the Three Ravens Publishing website at:

https://threeravenspublishing.com/joint-task-force-13-jtf-13/

Or on the Amazon Series page at:

https://www.amazon.com/gp/product/B08QJK1KQL

If you are an author interested in writing in the universe, please contact us at threeravenspublishing@gmail.com.